Praise for

The Last Library

'I'm totally in love. A wonderfully warm and uplifting story of kindness, community, love and libraries. *The Last Library* made me laugh, cry, cheer and want to champion all of our fabulous libraries'
Clare Pooley

'A powerful reminder about the importance of community, kindness and friendship. Beautifully nostalgic, with a gorgeous cast of characters you are set to fall in love with, this is a truly stunning debut'
Hannah Tovey

'Such an uplifting story with a cast of characters I fell head over heels in love with. A heartwarming portrayal of the vital role libraries have in our communities. I adored every page'
Jessica Ryn

'*The Last Library* is sheer joy from the first page – a story of love, loss, self-discovery and courage. Funny, poignant and a celebration of books, libraries, stories and everything that makes us human. Unmissable'
Katie Marsh

Sampson
(LAST NAME OF AUTHOR)
The Last Library
(BOOK TITLE)

DATE DUE	ISSUED TO
2/12/11	June Jones
6/6/13	ALEX CHEN
6/9/14	Marjorie Spencer
15/10/15	Stanley Phelps
1/2/19	Mrs B
2/7/21	Chantal Williams

About the Author

Freya Sampson works in TV and was the executive producer of Channel 4's *Four in a Bed* and *Gogglesprogs*. She studied History at Cambridge University and is a graduate of the Faber Academy. She lives in London with her husband, two young children and an antisocial cat. *The Last Library* is her debut novel.

https://freya-sampson.com/

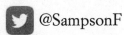 @SampsonF

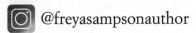 /FreyaSampsonAuthor

@freyasampsonauthor

The Last Library

The Last Library

Freya Sampson

ZAFFRE

First published in the UK in 2021 by
ZAFFRE
An imprint of Bonnier Books UK
4th Floor, Victoria House, Bloomsbury Square, London, England, WC1B 4DA
Owned by Bonnier Books
Sveavägen 56, Stockholm, Sweden

This is a work of fiction. Names, places, events and
incidents are either the products of the author's
imagination or used fictitiously. Any resemblance to
actual persons, living or dead, or actual
events is purely coincidental.

A CIP catalogue record for this book is
available from the British Library.

Hardback ISBN: 978–1–83877–369–4
Export ISBN: 978–1–83877–465–3

Also available as an ebook and an audiobook

1 3 5 7 9 10 8 6 4 2

For Andy, Olive and Sid

Chapter One

YOU CAN TELL A lot about a person from the library books they borrow.

June liked to play a game when things were quiet at work. She'd pick a patron and make up their life story based on the books they read. Today, she'd chosen a middle-aged lady who took out two Danielle Steel novels and *The Rough Guide to Iceland*. After some consideration, June decided that the woman was trapped in a loveless marriage, perhaps with a boorish, aggressive husband. She was planning to run away to Reykjavik, where she'd fall in love with a rugged, bearded local. But just as she thought she'd found true happiness, her husband would track her down and announce—

'Well, that was a pile of shit.'

June was snapped out of her daydream by Mrs Bransworth, who was standing in front of the desk waving a book in her face. It was Kazuo Ishiguro's *The Remains of the Day*.

'What a pointless load of rubbish. Masters and servants? Capitalist propaganda, more like. I could write better than this.'

Mrs B came into the library several times a week, wearing an ancient Afghan coat and fingerless gloves, even in the height of summer. She chose her books seemingly at random; one day, it would be a manual on plumbing, the next, a Nobel prize-winning author. But whatever she borrowed, it always had the same outcome.

'I'm thinking of handing my library card back in protest.'

'I'm sorry, Mrs Bransworth. You can have first pick of the new stock if you like?'

'Probably all crap,' Mrs B said, and she stormed off towards the Sports shelf, leaving a faint smell of wet goat lingering at the desk.

June finished loading up the ancient returns trolley and began to navigate it around the room. Chalcot Library occupied what had once been the village school, a draughty, red-brick building erected in the 1870s. It had been converted into a library eighty years later, but had retained many of its original features, including a slate roof that leaked in heavy rain, floorboards that creaked underfoot and a family of persistent mice who were eating their way through the boxes of archives stored in the loft. The council had last redecorated the library sometime in the nineties, with strip lighting and institutional green carpets. But June still liked to imagine what it must have been like in its earliest incarnation, when grubby-faced children sat in rows of desks where the shelves now stood, learning to write their letters on dusty slates like a scene from *Jane Eyre*.

As she pushed the trolley towards the front of the room, June saw her boss marching towards her, a copy of *Mrs Dalloway* poking out of her handbag.

'I need to see you in my office. Now.'

Marjorie Spencer was the library manager, a title she wore pinned to her blouse like a war medal. She claimed to only read highbrow literary novels, but June knew she'd renewed *Fifty Shades of Grey* at least three times.

June followed her boss into the office. It was actually a stock cupboard-cum-staffroom, but Marjorie had put in a desk years ago and had even hung a name plaque on the door. There was no space for any other chairs, so June perched on a stack of printer paper.

'This is strictly *entre nous*, but I've just had a call from the council,' Marjorie said, fiddling with the string of pearls around her neck. 'They want me to go in on Monday for an urgent meeting. In the boardroom.' She paused to check that June was suitably impressed with this inform- ation. 'You'll have to manage on your own while I'm gone.'

'OK, that's fine.'

'It's too short notice to cancel Rhyme Time, so I'll need you to take it for me too.'

June felt her chest tightening. 'Actually, I'm sorry, I forgot but Alan has a—'

'No buts. Besides, it will be good practice for you – once I retire at Christmas, my replacement may want you to take over the sessions anyway.'

June's stomach dropped at the thought. 'Marjorie, you know I can't—'

'For goodness' sake, June, it's children's nursery rhymes, not *Songs of Praise*.'

June opened her mouth to argue, but Marjorie had turned to her computer in a manner that said 'Do Not Disturb'.

June left the office, trying to ignore the tightening in her chest. It was almost five o'clock, so she began the closing-down routine. As she tidied up the abandoned books and newspapers, she pictured all the expectant faces at Rhyme Time, the children and parents watching her impatiently, waiting for her to speak. June let out an involuntary shudder and dropped a pile of newspapers on the floor.

'Do you need a hand, my dear?' Stanley Phelps was sitting in his chair, watching her.

'Thanks, but I'm fine,' she said, picking up the scattered pages. 'It's five o'clock now, I'm afraid it's time to go home.'

'May I request your assistance first? *Organise liaison to prevent this*. Nine letters, first letter I.'

June thought for a moment, breaking the clue down in her mind like he'd taught her. 'Could it be isolation?'

'Brava!'

Stanley Phelps, who enjoyed historical fiction set in the Second World War, had come to the library almost every day since June started working there ten years ago. He wore a tweed jacket and spoke like a character from a P.G. Wodehouse novel, and she pictured him living in faded grandeur, sleeping in silk pyjamas and eating kippers for breakfast. The *Telegraph* crossword was one of his daily rituals.

'Now, before I leave, I have a little something for you.' Stanley reached into a crumpled old Bag for Life and pulled out a small bunch of wilting flowers, held together by a piece of string. 'Happy birthday, June.'

'Oh, Stanley, you didn't have to,' June said, feeling herself blush. She never discussed her private life with anyone at the library, but years ago, Stanley had somehow discovered her birthday, and he'd never once forgotten it since.

'Are you doing anything special tonight?' he said.

'I'm just seeing some old friends.'

'Well, I hope you have fun. You deserve a grand celebration.'

'Thank you,' June said, staring down at the flowers so she didn't have to look him in the eye.

At five thirty, June stepped outside into the warm, early-summer evening. She locked up the heavy library door and made her way down The Parade, past the village shop, the pub with Union Jack bunting fluttering over the door, the old bakery where she and her mum had bought jam doughnuts every Saturday. A couple of library patrons were standing outside the post office, and June nodded a silent hello as she turned down the hill, past the village green and the Golden Dragon takeaway, and left into the Willowmead estate. Built in the 1960s, it was a rabbit warren of identical semi-detached houses, with boxy gardens and wheelie bins sitting in front driveways. It was here that June had lived since she was four years old, in a house with a green front door and faded red curtains.

'I'm home!'

June took off her cardigan, left her shoes on the rack ready for Monday morning and went through into the lounge. One of the picture frames was crooked and June straightened it, frowning at the frizzy-haired, brace-wearing teenager staring back at her. Thankfully the braces were long gone, although she was still stuck with that crazy mass of brown curls, now tamed every day in a tight bun. With the picture back as it should be, June crossed the living room to the large bookcase which filled the left-hand wall, crammed with neat rows of spines. Adichie, C.; Alcott, L.M.; Angelou, M. She found the one she wanted and carried it through to the kitchen, where she put a lasagne ready-meal in the microwave and poured herself a glass of wine.

There was no sign of life, the house still apart from the faint noise of a TV from next door. June picked up this morning's post: a flyer about bin collections and a copy of the *Dunningshire Gazette*. She checked inside the paper in case any birthday cards had got caught up in there, but there was nothing. A small sigh escaped June's mouth and she took a gulp of wine.

The microwave pinged, making her jump. She fetched the lasagne and spooned it onto a plate, adding a few slices of cucumber as a garnish. Sitting down, she picked up her book. It was battered and worn from years of reading, the words *Pride and Prejudice* on the front cover barely legible now. Carefully, she opened it to read the inscription. *18th June 2005. To my darling Junebug. Happiest of twelfth birthdays. You are never alone when you have a good book. All my love, Mum xx*

June ate a mouthful of food, turned to the first page and began to read.

Chapter Two

'ALAN BENNETT, WHERE THE HELL ARE YOU?'

It was Saturday morning and June couldn't find him anywhere. She'd searched the house and the shed and had even checked in the loft in case he'd gone up there looking for something, but to no avail.

'Come on, Alan, the joke's over,' she called, but the house answered with wilful silence.

June put a piece of bread in the toaster and switched on the kettle. She listened to the slow hiss of water boiling and tried to ignore the simmering sensation in her stomach. The weekend stretched ahead of her, long and gloriously empty. But while the prospect of all those hours of solitary reading time usually filled her with joy, this morning June felt jumpy. In her decade working at the library, she'd always managed to avoid taking Rhyme Time, or indeed any activity where she had to speak in front of a group of people. And now, on Monday, she'd have to stand up in front of dozens of children and their carers, talking and singing songs and entertaining them like . . .

June took a mouthful of toast but it felt like cardboard in her mouth, and she pushed her plate aside.

Five minutes later, she sat down on the sofa with a thick, dog-eared copy of *War and Peace*. It was a novel that June had tried and failed to read several times before, but at more than one thousand pages it was the perfect project to distract her this weekend. Besides, it was a book that her mum loved, and for that reason June had always felt guilty that she'd never managed to finish it. She lifted up the paperback and held it to her nose, inhaling the reassuring aroma of aged paper and dust. But there was another scent there too, a base note of soap and the faintest hint of smoke. June closed her eyes and allowed herself to imagine her mum sitting next to her, legs tucked under her body in the way she'd always liked to curl up, the book on her lap and an ashtray balanced on the arm of the sofa. The two of them had spent hundreds of weekends like this, side by side in contented silence, interrupted occasionally by her mother's throaty laugh at something within the pages. The memory of it made June's chest ache in longing, and she opened the book and started to read.

She was about thirty pages in when the doorbell rang. For a brief moment June wondered if it was the postman, delivering a pile of birthday cards that had been forgotten yesterday, but she told herself off for even entertaining such a ridiculous thought.

As June opened the front door, she was confronted by the sight of her next-door neighbour, Linda, wearing a fuchsia dress and a huge pair of gold earrings. Linda was obsessed with Jilly Cooper novels and always dressed as if Rupert Campbell-Black was about to turn up in Chalcot and whisk her off to the hunt ball, even at nine in the morning. In her arms was an indignant-looking Alan Bennett.

'Look who I found hiding in my airing cupboard, the sneaky little bugger.'

Alan let out a hiss of rage and sprang from Linda's grip.

'I'm so sorry, Linda. I've been looking everywhere for him.'

'No bother. You're not busy, are you?' Before June could reply, Linda had bustled in through the door and made her way into the living room, calling back, 'No milk for me, I'm doing Slimming World.'

June made tea in two chipped mugs and carried them through, where she found Linda sprawled on the sofa, leafing through *War and Peace*.

'Jesus, love, why do you put yourself through this?' Linda said, casting the book onto the floor in disgust.

'It was one of Mum's favourites.'

'She always did have terrible taste in books. You know I bought her all of Jilly's and she never read one?' Linda's heavily pencilled eyebrows shot up in horror and June laughed.

'I have to admit, this one's a bit tough, even for me.'

'It's a good thing your mum also loved gin and a gossip, otherwise we'd never have been friends.' Linda took a swig from her mug. 'I was thinking yesterday, do you remember your seventh birthday when we made you that *Charlie and the Chocolate Factory* cake? We tried to make a great glass elevator, only we ended up getting a bit tipsy and the whole thing was skew-whiff like the Leaning Tower of Pisa.' She let out a loud guffaw, splashing hot tea on the sofa.

'You guys always made me the best birthday cakes,' June said, smiling. For her sixth birthday, her mum and Linda had baked her the giant spider and luminous pink pig from *Charlotte's Web*, and for her tenth birthday, they'd tried to make Hermione and Hagrid from *Harry Potter* out of sugar fondant, although it had ended up looking like something out of a horror movie.

'Why you couldn't have just had a princess cake like other girls your age?' Linda said, rolling her eyes in mock irritation. 'Anyway, how was your birthday? Did you see friends?'

'It was good, thanks,' June said.

'Hmm ...' Something in Linda's tone suggested she knew all too well that the only friends June had spent it with were Elizabeth Bennet and Mr Darcy. 'Well, I got you a little something.'

Linda produced a rectangular parcel from her handbag, which June opened with some trepidation. Linda's birthday presents always stuck to a certain theme: last year it had been a book called *How to Make Anyone Fall in Love with You* and the year before that it was *How to Stop*

Worrying and Start Living. Now, June pulled the wrapping paper off to reveal *Now What? 90 Days to a New Life Direction.*

'I saw it in the charity shop and thought of you,' Linda said, with obvious pride.

'Great. Thank you.' June scanned the blurb on the back cover and tried to look enthusiastic.

'Do you like it? I just thought . . .' Linda paused, and June waited for the words she knew were coming. 'It's been almost eight years, love. And I know you still miss your mum – we both do – but maybe it's time to shake things up a bit?'

June took a sip of tea. This was a conversation Linda brought up every year around her birthday, and June had learnt from experience it was best to keep quiet until she got it out of her system.

'I mean, this is hardly what you dreamt of when you were younger, is it?' Linda continued. 'Before your mum got sick, you had big plans to go away to university and become a writer. Don't you think it's time you gave that a shot?'

'All kids have silly dreams, Linda. Besides, I love working in the library.'

'Well, OK, but you don't have to do it in a tiny village like Chalcot. You always wanted to go to Cambridge; I'm sure they have libraries there too.'

'But why would I want to leave? This is my home.' June's eyes scanned the living room: the bookcase full of her and her mum's books, the mantlepiece covered in a menagerie of china ornaments they'd collected over the years, the walls busy with pictures and photos in mismatched frames. 'And what about Alan Bennett? I'm not sure he'd cope moving somewhere new.'

At the sound of his name, Alan gave a half-hearted snarl.

'Look, I'm not putting pressure on you, love. If you're happy here, that's wonderful. I was just wondering if you might want a bit more from your life. That's all.'

June put the book down and gave Linda her most reassuring smile. 'I really appreciate your concern. But I love my life. I wouldn't change a thing.'

'Well, in that case I assume you'll be coming to the summer fete this afternoon?'

The smile disappeared from June's face. 'Ah, well I'm a bit busy today.'

'Come on, you said yourself that *War and Peace* is crap. And you used to love the fete.' Linda pulled herself up off the sofa and handed June her empty mug.

'Really, Linda, I've got lots on this—'

'I'll knock for you later,' Linda said. 'And I know what you're like, young lady, so don't you dare try and pretend you're not here.'

Chapter Three

AT THREE O'CLOCK, June made her way up the hill towards the village green, trailing behind Linda. It was a boiling hot day, the sun blazing down in a cloudless sky, and she could already feel herself getting red. June had never been a fan of the summer, and not just because of the sunburn that tormented her pale, freckly skin. Even at primary school, while most of her classmates had spent the long summer holidays playing down by the river, June had preferred to stay in the cool of the library, with her best friend, Gayle, and a pile of good books.

Chalcot Summer Fete had been the one exception to that rule. The smell was the first thing that used to hit her as she walked up the hill: the intoxicating mix of fresh popcorn and candyfloss that sent all the kids wild with excitement. As soon as she'd smelt it, June would grab Gayle's hand and they'd run away from their mums towards the village green, squealing in delight as they spotted the bunting-topped stalls holding hook-a-duck and splat-the-rat, the sweet stand with its lurid array of Panda Pop bottles, and the competition tent where the local WI would battle it out over marrows and cakes.

'Right, I'll meet you in the bar tent in half an hour,' Linda said, once they'd arrived. 'If you see my Jackson, tell him I've got some pocket money for him.'

Linda bounded off and June began to make her way through the fete, trying to stay calm as the crowd of people surged around her. Everything was exactly as she remembered it: children charging around playing tag between the stalls, the smell of burnt sausages and the buzz of the old Tannoy system. There was the raffle, run as it always was by the local Brownie troop, and a table of novelty animals made by the Knit and Natter group who met at the library every Wednesday. June turned her face away as she walked past them; she always found it uncomfortable talking to patrons outside of the library, without her professional armour of a 'LIBRARY ASSISTANT' badge and a date stamp. She reached the end of the aisle and turned right towards the competition tent, and then stopped in her tracks. Up ahead, next to the bouncy castle, was the white elephant stall.

June's first instinct was to turn and run in the opposite direction, but the crowd behind her was too thick and she found herself being swept towards it. As she got nearer, she saw the table was covered with the usual strange assortment of goods: she spotted a garden gnome, a salad spinner and a pile of Barbie dolls in various states of undress. All objects that were no longer needed by their owners and had been given away to be sold for charity.

'Do you know why the white elephant stall is my favourite?' June's mum used to say. 'It's a place for the unloved, the outcasts that nobody wants. And I've always loved an underdog.'

June's mum had run the stall for fifteen years, making it one of the most successful at the fete. June used to join her every year, eating sweets and listening to her mum chatting to customers. As the librarian, everyone in the village knew Beverley Jones, and there was always a stream of people stopping at the stall to say hi or have a gossip.

'You're like a celebrity,' June once said to her mum, having watched in awe as she'd talked to an elderly lady for five minutes, remembering the names of every one of her grandchildren.

'Don't be daft,' Beverley had said. 'Although some days my job is more like a social worker than a librarian.'

Even when Beverley was sick with cancer, nauseous and vomiting from another round of chemo racking her body, she'd still insisted on running the stall.

'Who'll find all those sad things a new life if I don't?' she'd declared, as June pushed her wheelchair across the bumpy playing field. Beverley had been too weak to do much more than sit behind the table that year, but almost every person at the fete had come over to say hello, to give her a hug and wish her well.

Three months later, her mum had passed away.

June hadn't been back to the fete since.

Tears started to blur her vision, and she turned and pushed her way back against the flow of people towards the exit, panic rising in her chest. She should never have come. June pictured the familiar comforts of home – her mum's possessions, Alan Bennett and her books – and increased her pace.

As she was passing the face-painting table, she heard a voice behind her.

'June!'

For a split second she wondered if she could pretend she hadn't heard and make a run for it, but then June felt a hand on her shoulder and turned around to see Stanley Phelps, dressed in his tweed suit and tie.

'How lovely to see you, my dear.' He was smiling at her, but his expression turned to concern when he saw her tear-stained cheeks. 'Are you all right?'

'I'm fine, thanks,' June said, wiping her face. The last thing she wanted was a library visitor taking pity on her.

'Well, I'm very glad to have bumped into you. Did you catch the Morris Dancers? And have you been into the Competition Tent yet?'

'No, sorry.'

'Oh, you must go in, the standard is particularly high this year. There's a miniature version of the Hanging Gardens of Babylon made entirely from root vegetables. Why don't I show you now?'

'I was actually just heading home.'

'But the Victoria sponge judging is in fifteen minutes and you don't want to miss that. Last year the woman in second place was so angry she threw her cake at Marjorie Spencer's head.'

'Thanks, but I—'

June was interrupted by a commotion to her right, and she and Stanley turned to see Mrs Bransworth, wearing a homemade sandwich board daubed with the words 'Protect Chalcot High Street' and 'Local Businesses, Not Big Chains'.

'Our village is being destroyed,' Mrs B bellowed, causing a nearby child to drop her ice cream in surprise. 'We've lost our butchers, our greengrocers, and now the bakery is being threatened too.'

'She's been marching round like this for the past hour, yelling at anyone who'll listen,' Stanley whispered to June. 'And anyone who *won't* listen, for that matter.'

'The council are putting up rents and selling off our Green Belt land to those bloody property developers. We need to tell them we don't want bookies and estate agents in our village – we want local businesses that serve the community.'

'Keep it down, love, some of us are trying to have fun,' shouted a man.

Mrs B stopped and unleashed a torrent of abuse at him.

Stanley moved towards them. 'Come on, June, we'd better step in before she starts a fight.'

June froze, feeling trapped. There was no way she could help; she was far too shy to make either of them listen to her, and the one time she'd tried to break up a fight at the library, she'd ended up making the situation worse. She glanced at Stanley, standing between the gesticulating man and a red-faced Mrs B, and then turned and hurried towards home.

Chapter Four

ON MONDAY MORNING, June unlocked the door a little before nine o'clock and stepped into the welcoming silence of the library. This was one of her favourite parts of the day, before Marjorie and the patrons turned up, when it was just her and seven thousand books for company. She liked to walk around the room, breathing in the heavy, still air, and sometimes, when she closed her eyes, June imagined she could hear the books whispering their stories to each other.

One of her earliest memories was of visiting Chalcot Library when she was four, shortly after her mum started working there. The building had felt huge and imposing as June walked in under the clock tower, books everywhere she looked, the lending desk so tall she could barely see over it. Her mum had given her a library card, and June could still remember her delight as she was told that she could take home twelve books and swap them whenever she wanted new ones. Once she started school, June and Gayle would spend most afternoons together in the Children's Room, playing and reading. And later, as a teenager, June would come alone to do her homework and chat to her mum, the library a haven of calm after the crowded, noisy classrooms of high school.

Now, more than two decades after her first visit, June knew that Chalcot Library was actually pretty small, even by provincial village library standards. Visitors regularly complained about the poor lighting, unreliable heating and terrible acoustics. But for June, the building always retained some of the magic she'd felt coming here for the first time. Even after ten years of working here herself, ten years of underfunding and depleted resources, the library was still a place of wonder, especially early in the morning with no one else around.

June began her setting-up routine: turning on the computers, stamping and putting out today's newspapers, restocking paper in the printer. She normally enjoyed the quiet, meditative nature of these jobs, but this morning she couldn't relax. It was going to be another scorching day and June was hoping that families would decide to go to the park or the river rather than come here for Rhyme Time. Yet when she unlocked the front door at ten o'clock, there were already several parents with small children waiting to come in, along with Stanley.

'Good morning, my dear. Isn't it a beautiful day?' Stanley didn't wear a hat, but if he did, June imagined he'd tip it to her. 'I'm sorry I lost you in all the commotion on Saturday. Did you hear that Mrs Bransworth nearly got arrested for disturbing the peace?'

'Is she OK?'

'Of course – you know how she loves a fight. Would you be so kind as to clock on for me?'

'Sure,' June said, following him over to the computers. Stanley had recently opened an email account to communicate with his son in America, although he'd not managed to log in once without June's help. She typed in his password.

'Thank you,' Stanley said. 'Are you on your own this morning?'

'Yes. Marjorie has a meeting so I'm covering Rhyme Time.'

He must have heard the tremor in June's voice because he gave her an encouraging smile. 'I'm sure you'll be marvellous. I'll save the crossword until you're done.'

By ten thirty, the library was full of buggies and the noise levels had risen by ten decibels. When she couldn't put it off any longer, June made her way to the Children's Room and peeked in through the door. Most of the floor space was filled with children and adults, all facing towards the front, where a single empty chair stood. An unbidden image flashed into June's mind of her mum sitting in that very spot, dressed in a pair of dungarees, at complete ease as she strummed a guitar and sang to the delighted children.

Gripping the door handle, June exhaled slowly and walked into the room, her mouth dry as she picked her way to the front.

'Hey, you're not Marjorie,' said a small boy, who she recognised as a serial book-destroyer.

'Hello everyone, I'm June.' Her voice came out as a weak croak.

'Speak up, love. We can't hear you at the back,' called one of the mums, who borrowed psychological thrillers.

'Where's Marjorie?' said her friend, who secretly took out Mills & Boon romances.

'She's busy, I'm afraid,' June said.

There were 'Awwws' from several of the children.

'I want "A Big Red Truck",' shouted the book-destroyer.

'We can get the toy box out after the session,' June said.

'Noooo, the song.'

'Ah, sorry, I'm not sure I know that one.' She heard a tut and felt her cheeks growing hot. 'How about "Old MacDonald"? One, two, three . . .'

All eyes were on her. When no one started singing, it dawned on June that she was going to have to go first. All she could hear was the pounding of blood in her ears.

'Old MacDonald had a farm . . .' June hadn't sung in public for years and her voice was a small, tuneless squeak. She saw an unfamiliar woman raise her eyebrows and there were a few titters from the children.

'E-i-e-i-o.'

Still no one joined in and June wiped the sweat from her top lip. Her heart was hammering and when she closed her eyes she was back at school, standing in front of the class and hearing the whispers and sniggers of her teenage peers.

'And on that farm there was a . . .'

There was an agonising pause before a boy shouted, 'Cow!'

June saw that it was Jackson and gave him a grateful, 'E-i-e-i-o.'

A few people joined in now. By the time they got to the second verse most of the room was singing and June lowered her voice.

They sang a few more nursery rhymes: 'Wheels on the Bus', 'Incy Wincy Spider', 'Twinkle Twinkle Little Star'. But the children kept asking for songs she'd never heard of, songs about spacemen and sleeping bunnies, and when June apologised for the sixth time, she could see some of the parents exchanging looks.

'Do you know any actual nursery rhymes?' said the Mills & Boon mum.

'I am sorry, but I don't usually do this.'

'What's the point of Rhyme Time if you can't sing the songs?'

'I really am sorry.' Tears pricked at June's eyes. *Please, please don't start crying in front of all these people.*

'For god's sake,' said the psychological thriller mum, and she stood up and pulled her grumbling daughter out of the room.

The other children were starting to fidget, and the parents were talking amongst themselves. June looked around for something, anything she could do to reclaim the room. On one of the low boxes was a discarded copy of *The Very Hungry Caterpillar*, one of June's favourite stories when she was little. She grabbed the book and started to read, even though no one was listening.

When she got to the last page, June looked up and realised the whole room was silent, entranced by the story. There was a wonderful, peaceful pause.

'I want another one,' a little girl said, breaking the spell. 'I want *The Gruffalo*.'

'I'm sorry but that's all we have time for today.' June stood up and started tidying before anyone else could complain.

Most of the families drifted off home and June made her way towards the office to get a glass of water, her heart still racing. Behind her, she could hear a couple of the parents giggling as they walked out, and June's heart sank at the thought they were laughing at her. She was just relieved that Marjorie hadn't been there to witness what a disaster it had been, although no doubt someone would take great pleasure in telling her soon. And they'd be right, of course. What kind of library assistant couldn't take a simple children's session without almost crying?

It was twelve o'clock and the start of the lunchtime lull. The only other people in the library were Stanley, snoozing behind a newspaper in his chair, and Mrs Bransworth, skulking around the shelves muttering to herself. June sat down at the desk and took a few deep breaths, filling her nostrils with the comforting scent of the library. As a child, she used to believe that each book had its own smell, specific to its story, and the smell of a library was the combined scent of thousands of different tales. She once explained this theory to her mum, telling her that the Children's Room smelt best because everyone knew that kids' books had more exciting stories than grown-up ones. For months after that they'd played a game whenever they read a book together, deciding what particular aroma the story had. *The Secret Garden*, for example, smelt of mud and roses, while *Charlie and the Chocolate Factory* smelt of both sugar and cabbage soup.

'Excuse me, can I take these out, please?'

June looked up to see a tall pile of books in front of the desk, with a pair of eyes blinking at her over the top. 'Of course you can, Jackson.'

Linda's eight-year-old grandson was one of June's favourite visitors to the library. He was homeschooled, and from a young age he'd come on his own, clutching his library card as if it was his most prized possession. He was a voracious reader and was already breezing through books intended for children twice his age.

'Ah, *Lord of the Flies* is a great choice,' June said, taking his books. 'If you enjoy this, you might like *Watership Down* too.'

'I read that when I was seven.' Jackson wiped his nose on the sleeve of his bright purple jumper, no doubt knitted for him by Linda. 'Do you have a copy of *Oliver Twist*?

I'm doing a project on the Victorians and Stanley said I'd enjoy it.'

'Let me check for you.' June typed it into the computer. 'Did you know this library was once a Victorian school? I can help you do some research about it, I'm sure we have some old photos in the archive.'

'Yes please,' Jackson said. 'Did you know that the Victorians used to make orphaned children live in work-houses, and they weren't even taught to read and write? I read about it in the encyclopaedia here.'

Linda often complained that Jackson should be outside playing with children his own age, rather than spending so much time in the library. But for June, the boy was a kindred spirit. She recognised the look in his eyes every time he walked in, that mixture of anticipation and excitement at the promises held within the shelves. And she understood implicitly what it felt like to be more at home with books than people, to prefer the adventures and travels within their pages to those in real life.

There was a crash at the front door, and a young man wearing an ill-fitting suit came rushing into the library, his face a dot-to-dot of angry red pimples. 'Have you heard the news?'

'Sorry, what news?' June said. 'Who are you?'

'My name's Ryan Mitchell, I'm from the *Dunningshire Gazette*. Haven't you heard the council's announcement?'

'What's that about the council?' Mrs Bransworth was striding towards them from the Science and Technology shelf.

'They've issued a press release saying they're looking at closing six libraries in the county. Chalcot is one of them.'

June's breath caught in her throat. 'What?'

'They've been threatening it for years, but they've just made it official,' Ryan said. 'They're doing some sort of consultation and then they'll make their decision.'

'Those bastards!' Mrs B shouted, with such force that Stanley leapt up from his chair.

'I was hoping to get a comment from a librarian,' Ryan said to June, pulling his phone from his bag.

'I'm sorry . . . I'm just a library assistant,' June stuttered. She felt dizzy and grabbed hold of the desk to steady herself. Close the library?

'Can they really shut it, just like that?' Stanley said. 'So many of us rely on the facilities here.'

'The council are Tory scum,' Mrs B said, with a growl. 'This is all part of their damn austerity plan; libraries are being closed all over the country.'

'But where will I go without the library?' Stanley said.

'The council says there are bigger libraries in Winton and New Cowley,' the journalist said.

'But they're miles away.'

'Did you know about this?' Mrs B was glaring at June.

'No, I'm sorry . . . this is the first I've heard of it.'

'We can't let this happen,' Stanley said.

'We'll form a campaign group.' Mrs B slammed her fist on the table, making June jump. 'I've been protesting my whole life, I won't go down without a fight.'

'Can I use that in the paper?' Ryan said, scribbling on his notepad.

'What the hell is going on here?'

They all turned to see Marjorie standing in the doorway, clutching her handbag to her chest like a shield. 'This is a library, not a cattle market. I can hear you all from outside.'

'Marjorie Spencer? I was wondering if I could get a quote for the *Dunningshire Gazette*?' Ryan said.

'Unless you're here for a legitimate library activity then you need to leave.'

'Can I—'

'I said, get out!'

Ryan looked like he was about to say something but lowered his head and walked out. The room was silent for a moment and June could hear her own ragged breathing.

'Right, let's all calm down, shall we?' Marjorie said. 'I've just had a meeting with the council and been told the news. I know this is a shock, but we mustn't panic.'

'Easy for you to say, you're retiring soon,' Mrs Bransworth said with a snort. She and Marjorie had fallen out years

29

ago when Marjorie accused Mrs B of defacing a biography of Margaret Thatcher.

'As you know, my husband is the chair of our parish council and a great supporter of the library,' Marjorie said. 'He's going to arrange a public meeting with the county council on Thursday so all our questions can be addressed.'

'That doesn't give us much time to prepare,' Stanley said.

'Of course not,' Mrs B spat. 'The council want to do this as quickly as they can, slip it under the radar.'

'I'm sure the council will listen to all your concerns at the meeting,' Marjorie said. 'Now, could you please quieten down and get back to what you were doing?'

Marjorie stood at the desk until Stanley and Mrs B had dispersed, then turned and walked towards her office. As she did, June saw that her face was white as a sheet.

'Excuse me, June?'

She looked round to see where the small voice had come from and was surprised to see Jackson still standing at the desk. In all the commotion she'd forgotten he was there.

'What is it?'

The boy's brow was creased. 'They're not going to close the library, are they?'

June bit her lip to try and contain her emotion. 'I'm sorry, Jackson. I really don't know.'

Chapter Five

'YOUR USUAL?' GEORGE ASKED, as June walked into the Golden Dragon that evening.

'Yes please, George.'

He headed into the kitchen and June collapsed down on one of the Chinese takeaway's plastic chairs, her head pounding. Word had spread through the village about the council's announcement and everyone who came into the library had quizzed her about it. June had tried to stay positive, reassuring people that nothing was certain yet, but inside she was crumbling. What would she do if the library closed? She'd have to find a new job, which might mean having to sell her mum's house and leave Chalcot and . . .

June reached into her bag and pulled out a book, desperate to divert her brain.

'June Jones?'

She looked up, but didn't recognise the man with messy hair standing behind the counter. Did he come into the library? She tried to picture what books he borrowed but couldn't place him.

'It's me, Alex.'

June hadn't seen Alex Chen since he was a short, plump teenager, reading *Game of Thrones* books on the school bus. They'd been in the same year at secondary school and had occasionally been partnered up on projects. Now, he was tall with broad shoulders and a warm smile.

'Oh . . . er, hi Alex. How are you?'

'I'm great, thanks. I'm just back for a few months to help out while Dad has his hip op.'

'An operation? When is it?' June had no idea that George was going into hospital, but then their weekly conversation only ever consisted of 'Your usual' and 'Seven pounds forty, please.'

'Next Thursday. It's so funny seeing you again. Do you still live here?'

'Yes, I'm the assistant at the library.' June glanced at Alex, expecting him to look unimpressed, but his face lit up.

'That's brilliant. I remember you always having your nose in a book at school; didn't you win the reading prize every year?'

'Not every year, only three times,' June said, feeling her cheeks flush.

'I always tried to beat you but I never could.' Alex laughed. 'So, can you recommend any good books I might like?'

People often asked this when they found out what June did for a living, and she was secretly proud of her ability to guess what books a person might like. 'I can try. Are you still into George R.R. Martin?'

'Oh god, I was such a loser at school, wasn't I?' Alex winced. 'I'm afraid I'm not much cooler these days; I mainly read sci-fi and horror now.'

'I don't know that much about those genres, but I can have a look for you.'

'Actually, I always mean to read more widely but I never know where to start.' Alex pointed at the book on June's lap, which she'd grabbed off the kitchen table on her way out this morning. 'What are you reading?'

'Oh, I don't think it would be your cup of tea,' she said, trying to stuff it back in her bag.

'I'm sure it would. Go on, try me.'

June reluctantly lifted the book for Alex to see the battered front cover. She was sure she saw a look of disappointment flicker across his face, but he hid it quickly.

'*Pride and Prejudice*? Cool, I've never read that. Although I have read *Pride and Prejudice and Zombies*.'

'What?' June was so surprised she couldn't help but laugh. 'How have I never heard of that?'

'It's amazing. I think the plot is basically the same as the original, only in an apocalyptic world where the Bennet sisters are zombie fighters trained in Chinese martial arts. And it turns out that Wickham, who is actually undead and survives on eating pigs' brains, is planning a zombie army to take over England and Elizabeth and Darcy have to stop him.' Alex paused when he saw the look on June's face.

'That is the most extraordinary plot I've ever heard. Are you winding me up?'

'No, I swear. I tell you what, how about I read *Pride and Prejudice* and you read *Pride and Prejudice and Zombies*, and we can compare notes?'

'Thanks, but I've not read a horror book since we did *Frankenstein* at school and I had to sleep with the lights on for a week.'

Alex chuckled. 'God, I remember reading that. What was the name of that boring English teacher? Her lessons were awful.'

Miss Townsend had actually been June's favourite teacher, always recommending books and staying behind after class to discuss them with her, but June didn't want to admit that.

George emerged from the kitchen carrying a bag. 'Seven pounds forty, please.'

'Thanks, George. And good luck with . . .' June started to say, but he'd already walked back into the kitchen.

'Well, good seeing you again,' Alex said, as she picked up the bag and made her way towards the door. 'Let me know if you change your mind about *Pride and Prejudice and Zombies*. You never know, you might love it.'

Back at home, June sat down to eat her takeaway. Chicken in black bean sauce had always been her mum's favourite, and now June ordered it for herself every Monday night. She filled her fork and took a mouthful as the events of today spun through her mind: Rhyme Time, the council's news about the library, Marjorie's ashen face. Was it really possible that the library would close? Of course, June knew that libraries were being shut all over the country, but somehow, she'd always imagined that a place as small as Chalcot would be safe, and that she'd have a job there for as long as she wanted it. June shivered, despite the warm evening, and then jumped when she heard a knock at the front door.

'I just heard the news,' Linda said, as soon as June let her in. She threw her arms wide and wrapped them round June. 'You poor thing, you must be in shock.'

'They want to close it, Linda,' June mumbled into her shoulder. 'Mum's library.'

'Well, we won't let them, will we?' Linda released her and headed into the kitchen. 'Have you thought what you're going to do yet?'

June followed her and slumped back down at the table. 'I don't know. I'm not sure there's anything I can do.'

'If your mum were alive, I can imagine her marching down to the council offices and haranguing them until they changed their mind,' Linda said.

'Apparently there's a meeting with the council on Thursday.'

'You must have loads you want to ask them. Make sure you write all your questions down now, so you don't forget them at the meeting.'

June played with some rice on her plate and didn't answer. There were so many questions she wanted to ask, but there was no way she could stand up in front of a room full of people and say them. Just the thought of all those eyes watching her made June feel sick, and she put her fork down. 'I wish Mum was here,' she said, in a quiet voice.

'I know, love, me too.' Linda gave her a sympathetic smile. 'But your mum isn't here, so you'll just have to fight this for her.'

Chapter Six

JUNE WAS WATCHING A WOMAN sitting with an open copy of *Spanish for Dummies* in front of her. She was a mild-mannered patron, who'd started coming into the library a few months ago; at first, she'd read *The Beginner's Guide to Russian* and next it was *Teach Yourself Complete German*. June had concluded that the woman was married with two young kids but led a secret double life as a spy. After she dropped the children at school each day, she'd go on assignments to follow the mafia in Winton or assassinate a Russian spy posing as a tourist in Favering. And when she told her husband she was going to stay with her sister for the weekend, she was actually having a torrid affair with another MI5 agent who had—

'Massive bollocks!' Mrs B was peering at June over the top of the magazine rack. 'I've never read such complete and utter nonsense.'

'What was it this time?' June said, and a moment later had a copy of *One Hundred Years of Solitude* thrust in her face. 'I'm sorry you didn't enjoy it, Mrs Bransworth. I loved that book.'

'So, I've been thinking – we should band together with the other threatened libraries and form one large campaign. We could call ourselves The Dunningshire Six.'

'That's a great idea.'

'All you library workers should go on strike and we'll form a picket line,' Mrs B continued, her face pressed closer to June's over the rack. 'You know, I spent six months in Wales supporting the miners in eighty-four. That was brutal, but there was no way we were going to let that fucking Thatcher crush all those communities. I won't let the same thing happen here.'

'Maybe we should see what the council say at the meeting first?' June said. 'They might see reason and keep the library open.'

'Are you really that naive?' Mrs B shook her head in disgust. 'When I was your age, I'd already been arrested three times for civil disobedience. But we weren't like you bloody millennials, with your avocado on toast and soya lattes; we actually believed in things and were willing to fight for them.'

Mrs Bransworth paused, an unfamiliar expression clouding her face. June imagined the memories flooding through the woman's mind, all the protests she'd been to and the people she'd known, many of whom must now be gone.

'We have to fight,' Mrs B said, snapping out of her reverie. 'If we don't, then one day your children are going to wake up and there'll be no libraries left.'

June shuddered at the thought.

'Ah, just the two I was looking for.' Stanley was walking towards them, and June saw he had a small plaster on his head.

'Are you OK, Stanley?'

He touched the plaster with his hand. 'Oh, it's nothing serious, I just had a little fall last night. The doctor said she'd never seen an eighty-two-year-old in such good shape.' He raised his arms like a body builder, a pose that looked incongruous for a rake-thin old man wearing a bow tie. 'Now, what news on the council's dastardly plans for this sacred place?'

'I was telling June here, it's our democratic duty to fight for the library,' Mrs B said. 'We have to all speak up on Thursday and make our voices heard.'

'I couldn't agree more. I've been thinking I'd say . . .'

June turned and crept away. The library's potential closure was all anyone had talked about all day and, like Linda, they all seemed to expect that June would be leading the charge at the council meeting. She'd not slept at all last night worrying about it, and now her head was throbbing, so she walked towards the back to get a drink of water. As she did, she saw the office door open and Marjorie stepped out, followed by a young woman in an expensive-looking suit, carrying a clipboard. She had sleek black hair and bright lipstick that made her look a bit like Mrs Coulter from *His Dark Materials*. June half-expected a golden monkey to jump onto her shoulder.

'One more thing,' the woman said. 'Is there any outside space?'

'There's a small staff car park out the back where we keep our bins,' Marjorie said, and the woman scribbled something down. June noticed she had perfectly mani-cured nails, painted a shiny red colour that matched the swirling red logo on her clipboard.

Marjorie spotted June watching them. 'Have you finished doing the periodicals?'

'Not yet, sorry.' June shrank back as they both stared at her.

Marjorie turned to the woman and let out an exagger-ated sigh. 'Honestly, if I need anything done in this place, I have to do it myself.'

'I think I have everything I need for now; I'll be in touch if I have any further questions.'

They shook hands and the woman strode towards the door, not even bothering to acknowledge June.

As soon as the woman had gone, Marjorie hurried up to June. 'I need to talk to you about something, urgently.'

June followed her into the office and watched as Marjorie fiddled with the World's Best Librarian mug on her desk. She seemed even more tightly wound-up than usual.

'Are you OK, Marjorie?'

'I have something top secret to discuss with you, but you must swear you won't tell a soul.'

Had Mrs Coulter told Marjorie something about the future of the library? June braced herself for the bad news.

'It's about Gayle's hen do.'

June's heart sank at the mention of her childhood best friend. Gayle was Marjorie and Brian's daughter, and her upcoming wedding was all Marjorie had talked about for months. June had been bored with every little detail, from the grand proposal in the Maldives to the choice for the wedding favours and the drama with the caterers. Now, she tried to contain a sigh.

'What's the problem with the hen do, Marjorie?'

'So, I told you that they're having it up the road at Oakford Park, didn't I? Well, last night I was talking to my friend Pru, whose daughter works at the hotel, and she said that she'd been hearing all about the plans for Gayle's hen do and how did I feel about the fact there was going to be a' – at this point Marjorie paused, her cheeks colouring, and lowered her voice – 'a stripper. A naked man!'

'I'm sure it will be quite innocent,' June said, trying to sound as diplomatic as possible. A hysterical Marjorie was the last thing she needed on top of everything else.

'You don't seem to appreciate the significance of this. As you know, my husband is the chair of the parish council, and, strictly *entre nous*, when his tenure is up next year, he's being considered for the position of Lord Lieutenant.

Do you know what that is, June? The Queen's representative in the county. The Queen!'

June couldn't work out how this was all connected, but she thought it best not to say. 'I'm sure it will all be harmless fun.'

'Imagine if word got out that there had been a stripper at Gayle's hen do. It could destroy Brian's reputation; I can't risk anything like that happening.'

'Maybe you should try speaking to the bridesmaids about it?' June said, glancing at her watch. They'd left the library floor unsupervised for far too long.

'There's no point. Tara and Becky have never liked me – they're probably doing this just to spite me.'

June didn't say anything, but for once she suspected Marjorie might be right. She and Gayle had been inseparable at primary school, having bonded at the age of six over a shared love of Mildred Hubble. But when they reached secondary school, Gayle had become friends with Tara and Becky, who thought boys were more interesting than books, and who dressed as if they'd stepped off the pages of a *Sweet Valley High* novel. Overnight, Gayle had abandoned June for her new, cool friends, ignoring her in the corridors and turning a blind eye when Tara and Becky laughed at June in class.

'You have no idea of the headache this is giving me,' Marjorie said, oblivious to June's discomfort. 'I know you're single, so you'll probably never have to go through what I'm experiencing. But believe me, organising a wedding is the most stressful thing that can ever happen to you.'

June returned to the magazines she'd abandoned earlier, her face still burning at the painful memories of school. Marjorie was infuriating; she'd always reminded June of Mrs Bennet in *Pride and Prejudice*, but this had confirmed her suspicions beyond all doubt. Here they were, the future of the library and their jobs under threat, and all Marjorie could worry about was her daughter's stupid hen do. June slammed a copy of *Country Living* onto the rack with force. As she did, she caught sight of Alex walking towards her.

'Whatever that magazine has done to you, it can't have been that bad?'

June smiled, despite herself. 'Sorry, my boss is driving me mad.' She lowered her voice and glanced over her shoulder to check that Marjorie was still safely in her office.

'Try working for your dad. Mine's behaving as if I'm taking over the running of a small country, not a village takeaway.'

'How is he?'

'All right, although I'm not sure I'll ever get him out of the kitchen and into the hospital.' Alex stood back and surveyed the library. 'God, I haven't been in here in years. I swear it was bigger when we were kids. And less, you know, run-down.'

'We've been having funding issues,' June said, as she saw Alex take in the ancient, dusty blinds, the peeling walls and chipped tables.

'It's sad to see it like this. I have so many happy memories here. I used to love those games sessions your mum ran.'

June's breath caught in her throat, as it did whenever someone mentioned her mum out of the blue.

'She introduced me to science fiction as well,' Alex said. 'She must have spent hours recommending books to me.'

'We still have a small Sci-Fi section, if you want to take a look?'

'Actually, I was hoping you'd have a copy of *Pride and Prejudice* I could borrow?'

'Are you sure?' June looked at Alex to see if he was winding her up. 'There might be other books you'd prefer.'

'No, I'd like to read *Pride and Prejudice*, please. I've heard it's excellent.'

She found a copy on the shelf and brought it back to the desk. Alex handed her an old, bent library card.

'I've got a book for you, too,' he said, as he reached into his rucksack and pulled out a well-thumbed paperback. 'I know you said you weren't sure about horror books, but this is something special. She's one of my favourite authors.'

June was so taken aback she didn't know what to say. She looked at the front cover and saw it was *The Graveyard Apartment* by Mariko Koike. 'Thanks, Alex, that's really kind.'

'No worries. And thanks for this,' he said, waving his copy of *Pride and Prejudice* as he strolled towards the door. 'I hope you enjoy the book. Just don't read it on your own at night.'

'If I have to sleep with the lights on again then I'll know who to blame,' June called after him, and then felt stupid when several people turned to look at her.

She studied the book in her hands. It must have been at least ten years old, and when she opened it, she saw the name 'Alex Chen' scribbled on the first page. June had a sudden urge to lift it to her nose and smell it, but she put the book down on the desk. She glanced towards the door to see if Alex was still there, but instead she saw a hunched figure limping towards the desk.

'I want to make a complaint.'

With her small piggy eyes, sour expression and substantial girth, Vera Cox had always reminded June of Aunt Sponge from *James and the Giant Peach*. She came into the library several times a week to borrow thrillers and moan at June.

'What's the problem, Vera?'

'The children are being too noisy again. I can't hear myself think.'

'I'm sorry, but as I've explained before, we can't expect the little ones to be silent. They're just enjoying the Children's Room.'

Vera frowned, lines creased deep in her face. 'It's the mothers I blame; they just bring them here and leave them to run wild.'

'I'm not sure that's true.'

'And another thing. Have you heard there's an immigrant family moved into Lower Lane? I saw them myself this morning.'

June took a deep breath. 'Can I help you with anything else, Vera?'

The old woman sniffed. 'I think the toilet's broken again, I can't get in.'

June got up from the desk and went over to the toilet, relieved to get away from Vera. The door was locked when she pushed against it. 'Hello, is anyone in there?'

There was no answer.

'Are you OK? This is June.'

She heard a shuffle on the other side and the sound of the bolt being drawn back. The door edged open to reveal Chantal, a sixteen-year-old who came into the library to do her homework. She was hoping to get a scholarship to university, and June sometimes helped her study. But today Chantal's eyes were red, mascara smudged around the edges.

'Chantal, are you OK?'

'It's nothing,' she said, wiping her face on her jumper sleeve.

'Are you sure? Has something happened at home?'

'No.'

'What's wrong then?'

'You're gonna think I'm stupid.'

'Of course I won't,' June said, as she steered Chantal behind the privacy of a shelf.

The teenager fiddled with one of her long braids. 'It's just . . . I've got an English exam next week and I know I'm going to screw it up.'

'Oh, I'm sure you won't. And I can help with your revision, if you like?'

'Stanley's been helping me but it's the exam I'm worried about. I'm so nervous, I know I'll stare at the questions and not remember any of it. I'm so stressed I can't sleep.'

'Oh, I understand, I really do,' June said, recognising the anxiety in the girl's eyes. 'Perhaps you could try some relaxation techniques? Or find something else to take your mind off the exam.'

'Like what?'

'Well, I usually read a favourite book, but that might be the last thing you want to do right now.' June thought for a moment. 'I know, why don't you come to the library meeting on Thursday? It would be great to have a younger person there and it will be a good distraction for you.'

'What library meeting?'

'The one with the council about the proposed closure.' June watched the teenager's eyes go wide. 'Oh god, I'm sorry, Chantal, I assumed you knew.'

'The council want to close the library?'

'Well maybe. It's not confirmed yet.'

'But they can't do that, I need this place,' Chantal said, her voice rising. 'I can't revise at home, there's no space.'

'It's not definite yet, we'll find out more at the meeting.' June felt a wave of guilt; Chantal was stressed enough already. 'I'm sure it will all be fine.'

'What about my university application? You promised you'd help. And Mum needs the computers for her benefits.'

'Why don't you come to the meeting on Thursday so you can tell the council all of this?'

'I can't, I've got to babysit the twins for Mum,' Chantal said, her head dropping. Then she looked up at June. 'Will you speak to the council for me?'

June felt a familiar tightening in her chest. 'Oh, I'm not sure I'm the best person.'

'But they'll listen to you. Me and Mum need this place, June. Please, you have to tell them.'

Chapter Seven

WHEN JUNE ARRIVED AT the church hall on Thursday evening, it was already crowded. Rows of chairs had been set up facing a makeshift stage, and June could see Stanley sitting in the front row. Next to him was Mrs Bransworth, wearing what looked like a homemade T-shirt with 'Save Our Libraries' written on it in black felt-tip pen, and Linda and Jackson were sitting a few rows behind. June looked around in the hope Chantal might be there, but there was no sign of the teenager.

Stanley spotted her and gave a wave, signalling to an empty seat nearby, but June pretended she hadn't seen him and made her way towards the back of the room. This whole set-up reminded her too much of school, and she took a seat in the far corner, where she hoped no one would notice her tonight.

As June sat down, she saw a woman and two men enter the room. One of them was Marjorie's husband, Brian, a man who only ever read biographies of world leaders.

'Right, ladies and gentlemen,' he said, waiting a moment for the room to quieten. 'You all know the reason we're here tonight. Last week, Dunningshire Council announced that they want to restructure the library service in the county. As I'm sure you're aware, our library is very close to my heart . . .' At this, Brian gestured towards the middle of the room, and June saw Marjorie beaming like the Cheshire Cat. 'So, I asked some representatives from the council to come along and talk to us this evening. There will be an opportunity for you to ask questions at the end, but first, may I introduce Richard Donnelly, one of the councillors, and Sarah Thwaite, the council's head of libraries and information services.'

June watched the younger man on the stage stand up. He was in his mid-thirties, dressed in a pair of chinos and a crisp pink shirt, with a tan that suggested he'd either been on holiday or a sunbed. He looked like he'd probably not read a book in years, let alone been into a library. Next to him the woman, Sarah, sat with a smile that didn't quite meet her eyes. June guessed that she read self-help books.

'Thank you for the introduction, Brian,' Richard said. 'It's great to see so many of you here to talk about the future of Little Whitham Library.'

Sarah let out a small cough and glared at him, but Richard carried on, oblivious to his mistake.

'Now, I won't beat around the bush. Due to reduced funding from central government and increased financial pressures on the council, we need to cut our libraries budget by thirty per cent over the next three years. As

such, the council are launching a programme of modern-
isation and rationalisation of the library service.'

'What's all that gobbledygook mean?' someone muttered
near June.

'We have identified six libraries in the county that we
believe are most suitable for restructure. These are
Favering, Mawley, Dedham, Little Whitham, Chalcot and
Lave-End. Over the next three months, we'll be carrying
out in-depth analysis of the performance of these libraries
in order to ascertain which are providing the council with
good value for money.'

'Value for money? It's a library, not a tin of beans,' said
one of the Knit and Natter ladies, and there was a ripple
of muted laughter.

'Quiet, please,' Brian said.

Richard continued, unperturbed. 'To assist the council
in our decision, we've contracted a firm of management
consultants who will be carrying out this performance
analysis on our behalf. They'll be looking at things like the
number of customer visits and the number of books issued.
We'll then be able to work out the cost-effectiveness of
each library.'

'How can you put a cost value on all the things the
library provides?' June didn't need to look to know this
was Mrs B speaking. 'Literacy, social inclusion, encouraging a love of reading in the young. Do these things have
a price, Mr Donnelly?'

'I said comments at the end,' said Brian. 'Now sit down, Mrs Bransworth, or I'll have to ask you to leave.'

Mrs B let out a loud snort.

'Thank you, Brian,' said Richard. 'At the end of the consultation, the council will look at the findings and make our decision about the future of each library. There are three options we'll be considering. The first is to keep a library open in its current form with no changes. The second is that a library remains open but under community management.'

'What does that mean?' a woman called out.

'It means a local community would take over all respons-ibility for running the library, including leasing the building, the books and equipment, at no cost to the council.'

'What, like a volunteer library?' Stanley said, and there was a low rumble of muttering round the room. 'What would happen to our librarians?'

'Community libraries are staffed by unpaid volunteers,' Richard said.

'Then it's not a library, is it? It's just a room full of books.' Mrs B was standing up again. 'A library requires a librarian, with specialist degrees and years of experience. Are you suggesting that someone like me could provide the same service as a trained professional?'

Richard was looking paler under his tan. 'Community management isn't suitable for every library, and so as part of the consultation we'll be deciding which of the libraries might benefit from this opportunity.'

'What's the third option?' Vera said.

'The third option is that the library will be closed and replaced by a mobile library service.'

At this there was a clamour of voices.

'Quiet. Quiet!' Brian called, but no one could hear him above the noise.

'If I may?' Sarah stood up with a bright smile and waited for everyone to quieten down, while Richard took his chair again. 'Please believe me when I say that we don't relish having to restructure our libraries. But with the cuts imposed on us by the government, we have to be pragmatic. Library visits are down year-on-year across the county.'

'Bloody Tories,' Mrs B said. 'We know what you're up to here, destroying public services with a hundred little cuts so you can bring in privatisation and voluntarisation.'

Sarah pretended she hadn't heard this. 'Of course, we value feedback from local communities, and we want to listen to what residents have to say. So, we'll be circulating a questionnaire where you can tell us what you want from your library service. Along with the findings of the consult-ants, the questionnaires will help us to make a decision about the future of each of the six libraries.'

With that she sat down and whispered something to Richard, who nodded.

'Thank you, Richard and Sarah,' Brian said. 'Now, everyone, this is your chance to ask questions. But I warn you, keep this civilised or you're all out.'

A number of hands shot into the air, but before Brian could pick someone, Vera was standing up.

'How will I renew my bus pass?'

'I believe you can do that online these days,' Richard said.

'But I don't know how to use a computer.'

'Well, I'm sure you can do it over the phone.'

'But it's one of those automated systems and I always press the wrong buttons. That's why I get June to do it for me at the library.'

June cringed at the mention of her name, but no one even glanced at her.

'Well, perhaps you can get a friend to help you?' Richard said.

Vera sat down with a scowl, and June felt a pang of sympathy for her. She was pretty sure the old woman didn't have any friends she could ask for help.

'Next question,' Brian said, nodding towards Jackson.

'I'm Jackson Fletcher. I'm homeschooled and I go to the library every day. Where can I go if it closes?'

Sarah composed her face into an understanding expression. 'Hello, Jackson. We take the welfare of all children in the county very seriously, so as part of our consultation we'll be looking at availability of facilities for families. I believe there's a children's centre in Winton, attached to the library there?'

'But that's miles away and my parents don't have a car. They're bad for the environment.'

'You could always take the bus?'

'But Dad says they're too expensive.'

'Well, maybe your parents should consider enrolling you in a local school, like other children your age?'

Beside him, Linda was rising. 'Now hang on a second—'

'Time for the next question,' Brian interrupted. 'Yes you, Mr Phelps.'

'Good evening, madam, sirs,' Stanley said, standing up. 'I just wanted to say that I think what you're doing is absolutely criminal.'

June saw the smile on Sarah's face flicker.

'You have been running this library down for years. I'm in there every day and I've seen it with my own eyes: you've cut the opening hours, reduced the number of books on the shelves, let the building fall into a state of disrepair. So yes, the library might be struggling but that's entirely your fault.'

'We've been dealing with budgetary issues and—'

'Madam, I have not finished speaking,' Stanley said, and Sarah went quiet. 'The council are destroying this village. You're reducing bus services, selling off Green Belt land to those awful property developers who harass local residents, and now you're going after our library. What will be left of Chalcot when you're done?'

'I assure you we have the best interests of all local communities at heart,' Sarah said. 'But we have to be realistic. The council need to save money.'

'Right, time to move on,' Brian said.

The Mills & Boon mum from the Children's Room got up, consulting a notepad. 'Is this even legal? I've been doing some research, and don't the council have a duty to provide library services under the 1964 Public Libraries and Museums Act?'

'You're right, the council does have a statutory duty to provide library services,' Sarah said, picking her words with obvious care. 'But the law doesn't define the exact requirements of this duty. Many communities find a mobile library service a valuable resource.'

Mrs Bransworth was straining in her seat, looking like she was about to explode. Brian sighed and nodded towards her.

'Well, I think this is a load of fucking bollocks.'

'Language, please!' Brian said.

'I've been fighting injustice my whole life. I was at Greenham Common in the eighties, I went to support the miners in Wales, and I know a set-up when I see one. This whole consultation is a sham. You've made it clear that the council don't want to fund the library, so why are you pretending that we have any say in the matter?'

'I can promise you that we've not made any decisions yet on the future of these libraries,' Richard said. 'That's why we're employing management consultants, and it's why we're keen to hear what you all think. We'll only make a decision once the consultation period is over, at the full council meeting on the twenty-fourth of September.'

'Right, I think it's time to wrap this up,' Brian said. 'Anyone have a final question?'

June glanced around the room; there was a look of sad resignation on most people's faces. She remembered Chantal's tears and thought of her mum, who would have been standing up right now and berating the council, listing all the reasons why the library mattered. What had Linda said the other day? *Your mum isn't here, so you'll just have to fight this for her.*

Inhaling slowly, June raised her hand halfway into the air.

Brian sighed. 'Yes?'

Every eye in the room swung to look at June. Her heart was hammering in her chest, and when she opened her mouth to speak, no words came out.

'Come on, we don't have all night,' Brian said.

'I . . . we . . .' June started to say.

There wasn't a sound in the room, everyone straining to hear her. A few rows in front, Ryan from the newspaper had his phone pointed at her. Behind him she saw Marjorie, a grim expression on her face. June felt a tightness in her ribs, as if someone was pushing against her, and she slumped back in the chair and closed her eyes.

'Right, if that's everything, I call this meeting to a close,' she heard Brian say, followed by the scraping sound of chairs being pulled back, the sudden clamour of voices. June stayed sitting, her eyes closed, wishing the ground would open up and swallow her.

Chapter Eight

THE FOLLOWING AFTERNOON, June arrived for her shift at the library with her head held low. She knew she'd made a fool of herself last night. What happened was exactly why she should never try to speak in public; now everyone at the library would think she was a complete idiot. But as June walked through the front door, the room was buzzing with activity, and no one gave her a second glance.

'What's going on?' she asked Stanley, who was sitting in his usual seat and watching the commotion with delight.

'Haven't you heard? We're forming a protest group. It's called Fuck All.'

'What?'

'We're having our first meeting this evening at The Plough, I'm taking sausage rolls. What will you bring?'

'Fuck All, Stanley?'

'That's not the spirit, my dear – protests are about sharing. I was thinking I could be the group treasurer. And I'll nominate you for secretary, naturally.'

'Oh, I'm not sure I could do that.'

'Nonsense, you're perfect for the job,' he said. 'Isn't this exciting? We're going to fight the council together. We'll show them this library is alive and kicking.'

June sat down at the desk and began to sort through a pile of expired reservations. She was delighted people were forming a group to fight for the library, however strange its name; but there was no way she could be the secretary, as that would mean having to speak in front of everyone, which she'd never been able to handle. No, she'd go to the meeting but hide at the back and keep quiet.

Mrs Bransworth was striding towards the desk, brandishing a piece of paper. 'I've made signs to put up around the library about tonight's meeting,' she said, thrusting one at June. 'That way everyone who comes in can find out about the Fock-el.'

'About that name . . .'

'What's wrong with F-O-C-L? It stands for the Friends of Chalcot Library.'

June blinked. 'Oh, I see.'

'Stanley says you'll be secretary, and he's going to nominate me as chairperson. I ran the Chalcot Supports the Miners group, so none of this is new to me.'

'The thing is, I'm not sure I'm really suited to being secretary, Mrs B. Maybe I could make us a reading list of books about protests instead?'

'You can do that *and* be the secretary. I'll be running the whole thing, so all you'll have to do is take notes and do the dull admin stuff.'

'But I—'

'June!' Marjorie bellowed from the back. 'I need a word with you, now.'

June headed to her office, feeling like a naughty school-child being summoned to see the headmistress.

'What were you talking to Mrs Bransworth about?' Marjorie asked, when they were behind closed doors.

'Nothing.'

'Was it about this group they're setting up? Because if it was, I'm telling you now, you can't have anything to do with it.'

'What? Why not?'

'I just had that awful Sarah Thwaite from the council on the phone – she recognised you at the meeting last night. She told me, in no uncertain terms, that library staff are not allowed to speak out against the council or the planned closures in any way.'

'Why not? She can't do that!'

'You should have heard the way she talked to me, ghastly woman. She said she was reminding all library staff that the council pay our wages, and if we're involved in any kind of action against library closures then, and I quote, "our contracts would be under review".'

'But surely that's illegal?'

'Call it what you like, but the last thing this library needs is you getting sacked for embarrassing the council. I'm sorry but we need to keep our heads down and our issue numbers up.'

June hesitated. 'Are you really saying we can't fight for our jobs?'

'That's exactly what I'm saying. And don't you dare tell anyone about this conversation, either. If people ask you to be involved, you have to tell them you don't want to. Do you understand?'

'I still think this is—'

'I said, do you understand?'

'Yes, Marjorie.'

'Good. And I want you to take down those posters about the meeting. We can't be seen to encourage them in any way.'

June spent the rest of the afternoon trying to avoid the conversations around her about tonight's meeting. Part of her was furious. How dare the council tell her she couldn't join FOCL or fight for her own job? But another part of her, the part that she hated, was secretly a bit relieved. This meant that she wouldn't have to socialise with people outside of work, wouldn't have to speak up or risk embarrassing herself again in public. All she wanted was to go home, put on her pyjamas and hide in the pages of a book.

At four forty-five, June was starting to tidy up when Chantal came rushing in through the door.

'I heard about last night.'

'I'm sorry, Chantal. I wanted to speak up for you but—'

'Stanley told me you're setting up a group to save the library. I don't mind helping with social media.'

'The thing is, I—'

'The meeting starts at eight, yeah? I'll see you there.'

June opened her mouth to tell Chantal she wasn't going, but the teenager had already run off.

At seven fifty-five, June was sitting at her kitchen table, biting her nails and staring at the clock. There was no way she could go to the meeting. If she went, she risked getting fired, and the consequences of that were too terrifying to even consider. June ate a mouthful of lukewarm jacket potato. This was out of her hands; she couldn't go even if she wanted to.

At eight fourteen, having bitten one nail so much that it was bleeding, June went through to the living room. *Matilda* was waiting for her on the sofa where she'd left it last night. In times of stress, June found she always returned to the same books from her childhood: Roald Dahl, Malorie Blackman, Philip Pullman. There was something comforting about getting lost in stories she knew so well, novels that she and her mother had shared together on this very sofa. But now, as she tried to concentrate on the page in front of her, June found her mind wandering back to Chalcot Library. The FOCL meeting would have started by now. Who would be there? Mrs Bransworth and Chantal, and some of the parents from the Children's Room. Stanley would be there too, of course. What would he think when he realised June wasn't coming?

She threw the book down and went upstairs to run a bath. June had never understood it when people said they found baths relaxing; she always got hot too quickly, and the more she told herself it was meant to be relaxing, the sweatier and more uncomfortable she became. But tonight she needed to do something, so she ran water into the tub, added some ancient bubble bath and started to get undressed.

Alan Bennett came up to the bathroom, curious about this unprecedented change in her evening routine, and tangled himself in her feet.

'Bog off, Alan,' she said, nudging him towards the door. He snarled and jumped onto the pink fluffy toilet seat, where he sat glaring at her.

June climbed into the bath and tried to immerse herself in the synthetic strawberry bubbles. As a child this bath had seemed gigantic, but now part of June's anatomy was always exposed. She tried lying on her side but that gave her an unappealing view of the brown carpet. What had her mum been thinking when she chose a faecal-coloured carpet for a bathroom floor, let alone one that had pink walls and an avocado-green bath?

June knew exactly what her mum had been thinking. Beverley Jones had never given the slightest damn about things like interior design or fashion. She had adorned both her house and her daughter in whatever she could pick up from charity shops and jumble sales, an eccentric mishmash of colours, patterns and eras. Every surface in the house was still covered with the random items Beverley had brought home from the white elephant stall, and while all the girls at June's school had worn low-slung jeans and cropped T-shirts, she'd worn a strange assortment of clothes that belonged to recently deceased pensioners.

'Who cares what clothes you have on?' her mum would say, if June ever asked for more fashionable items. 'It's not what you wear that matters, Junebug. It's what you do.'

And Beverley had been true to her word. June remembered one particular instance, when her school had tried to make all the girls wear gym knickers instead of PE shorts, and her mum had declared the policy sexist and formed a one-woman picket line at the school gate.

'I'm a librarian,' Beverley had shouted. 'I know every parent here. I've helped most of them at some point over the years. So, believe me when I say, if I ask them all to boycott this school, they will.'

Her mum had kept it up for three days until the head-teacher changed the policy. June had been mortified by all the unwanted attention it brought her at school, but also ridiculously proud of her mum.

June looked at Alan Bennett, who was still curled up on the toilet seat. 'Mum would have expected me to go to the meeting, wouldn't she?'

The cat stared back at her, unblinking.

'I do want to go and support them, but Marjorie's banned me. It's not my fault.'

Alan narrowed his eyes and yawned.

'Even if I did go, I'd probably just freeze and embarrass myself again. There's no point, right?'

In response, Alan jumped off the toilet seat, with surprising agility for an elderly cat, and sauntered out of the bathroom with his tail in the air. June watched him go with a sigh, then got out of the bath and returned to Matilda and Miss Honey.

Chapter Nine

WHEN JUNE OPENED THE library front door at ten o'clock on Monday morning, Stanley was already waiting on the doorstep.

'My goodness, that was quite the meeting you missed on Friday,' he said as he breezed in. 'Where were you, my dear?'

June had spent the weekend trying to think of a convincing cover story. 'Sorry, my cat got a chicken bone stuck in his throat.'

'Oh dear, I hope he's OK?'

June started tidying some books so Stanley couldn't see her face. 'He's fine now, thanks.'

'Well, allow me to fill you in on the meeting. Mrs Bransworth went head-to-head with another woman for the position of chair; Mrs B won by one vote, but they very nearly came to blows. I wish you'd been there – it was quite the drama. I was unanimously voted treasurer.' Stanley pulled on his jacket lapels with pride. 'You were nominated group secretary in your absence; Mrs B has the paperwork for you.'

'I'm not sure I can do it, Stanley.'

'Nonsense, it's very straightforward. Just a bit of minute-taking and the like, I can help with that.'

'It's not that. I don't think I can be involved with the campaign at all.'

'What do you mean?'

June shrunk back under his gaze. 'I'm sorry, I'm too busy to be part of FOCL.'

Stanley's face fell and for a moment he didn't speak. 'I have to say, this surprises me, June. I thought . . . Well, never mind. You must do whatever you feel is best.'

'I am sorry, Stanley. I—'

'No need to explain.' He gave her a tight smile and June felt a stab of guilt as he walked away.

Ten minutes later, Mrs Bransworth came in and headed straight for her.

'Where were you on Friday?'

'I'm sorry, my cat—'

'Never mind. I've got all the notes for you here.'

June hesitated. 'I'm afraid I've got too much on. I can't join FOCL.'

Mrs B glared at her. 'For fuck's sake, June. Women threw themselves under racehorses so that you could have the same rights as men, and you're telling me you're too scared to fight for your own job?'

'I don't think I'd have much to offer,' June muttered.

'You have plenty to offer, don't use that as an excuse. You're just a bloody coward.' She turned and stormed away, leaving June red-faced at the desk.

It carried on like this all morning. Every time someone who'd been at the meeting came into the library, they tried to talk to June about FOCL. And every time, she saw the same look of disappointment in their eyes when she told them she wasn't joining. By lunchtime, most of the FOCL members had given up on trying to convince her to get involved. Instead, when June fought the returns trolley round the library, she was greeted with unusual silence from the regulars. She tried to carry on as normal, but she could feel Mrs B's angry glare wherever she went, and every time June walked into the Children's Room, the parents all pointedly stopped talking. Even Jackson refused to catch her eye when he came in to return some books. The only one who would talk to her was Vera, and she was the last person June wanted to hear from right now.

'I don't blame you for not getting involved,' Vera said, showering June with shortbread crumbs. 'This place is going to the dogs – there's no point trying to save it.'

June dearly wanted to ask Vera why, if she hated the library so much, she insisted on coming in so often. But she bit her tongue and pushed the trolley past.

At half past three, the doors swung open and Chantal came charging in.

'Why didn't you come on Friday?'

'I'm sorry, Chantal.'

'Has everyone told you what happened? I'm in charge of social media and you've been voted the secretary. Maybe at the next meeting you can see if—'

'I won't be at the next meeting.'

'What, why not?'

'I can't. I'm sorry, but I'm too busy.'

June saw the teenager's face crumple and she had to look away.

'How can you not care about the library? You're just like those council bastards.'

'It's not like that; it's complicated.'

'It's not complicated. If you're not bothered, that's fine. I don't care, I don't even like this place anyway.'

At five o'clock, June rushed out of the library. Never had she been so relieved that a working day was over. She kept her eyes fixed on the pavement as she made her way down The Parade, but she could still feel people staring at her as she walked past. At one point she thought she heard someone mutter, 'Traitor,' but when she glanced round there was just a young mum pushing a buggy. Even so, June increased her pace towards the Golden Dragon.

As she reached the takeaway, June sighed with relief; she could always rely on George not to engage her in conversation or pass judgement. But today she found Alex standing behind the counter, singing tunelessly to himself.

'Hey, I was hoping you'd come in,' he said when he saw her. 'I've finished *Pride and Prejudice.*'

'Great.' June gave a weak smile, hoping Alex could sense that she wasn't in the mood to chat.

'It was better than I expected. Some parts were a bit slow, but Elizabeth was cool, even without the martial arts.'

'I'm glad you enjoyed it. Please can I have chicken in black bean sauce and plain rice?'

'So, what are you reading at the moment? I'm looking forward to another recommendation.'

'I'm really sorry, Alex, but please could you put my order through? I'm in a bit of a hurry.'

A hurt look crossed his face. 'Of course.'

He typed the order into the till and began wiping down the counter. June sat down and took a deep breath, inhaling the smell of frying garlic. On the wall opposite was a portrait of a severe-looking Chinese woman, who had scowled down at June since she'd first started coming to the takeaway as a child with her mum. Today, the woman looked particularly displeased.

'I'm sorry,' June said to Alex after a moment. 'I didn't mean to be rude.'

'Hey, it's fine. I'm sorry I'm too chatty; I'm just going a bit crazy here on my own.'

'Right now, I'd kill for a job where I was on my own.'

'Things bad at the library?'

'Haven't you heard?' June said, and Alex shook his head. 'The council are threatening to close us down.'

'No! I had no idea.' Alex looked at her, aghast. 'Why would they do that?'

'Budget cuts, they say. It's not just Chalcot.'

'It's the same in London. I'm sorry, it's so shit. Are you fighting it?'

'There's a campaign group been formed called FOCL.'

'Fock what?'

'I know,' June said, raising an eyebrow. 'It stands for Friends of Chalcot Library.'

'When's the next meeting? I'm happy to help out while I'm here.'

June stared at the disappointed woman in the painting. 'Actually, I'm not really involved with it.'

'Why not?'

She opened her mouth to say the stock answer she'd given so many times today but stopped herself. Would it be so bad if she told Alex the truth? He'd said he was only back in Chalcot for a few months, so he was unlikely to tell anyone. And there was something about Alex that made June feel like she could trust him.

'What is it?' he said.

'If I tell you something, do you promise you won't tell a soul?'

'Scout's honour.' He held three fingers in the air.

June swallowed. 'The council have banned all library workers from speaking out against library closures. If I get involved with FOCL, or if I'm even seen to be helping them, I risk losing my job.'

'Oh shit.'

'I'm also banned from telling anyone why I'm not getting involved, so everyone assumes I don't care about the library and now hates me. Today has been so, so difficult.' The words came flowing out of June like water from a burst pipe. 'I've worked in the library for ten years and my mum worked there before me. I can't let it close.' She slumped forwards and put her head in her hands.

'There must be something you can do to help?'

'I can't do anything without getting sacked. And even if I could, it's not like I'd be any help, anyway,' she said, through her hands.

'That's not true,' Alex said, gently.

'It is. Do you remember how shy I was at school? Well, I'm even worse now: a complete coward.'

There was a pause before Alex spoke. 'I remember a girl who was the smartest in our class. Who would help anyone who was stuck or didn't understand something. Someone who everybody liked and respected.'

June looked at Alex in surprise, but at that moment a bell rang, and he disappeared into the kitchen. He reappeared a moment later, carrying a plastic bag.

'Thank you,' June said, trying not to look flustered as she took her food from him. 'You won't tell anyone what I said about being banned, will you? If word gets out, Marjorie would kill me.'

'I promise your secret's safe with me. And if you ever want to chat, you know where I am.'

'Thanks, Alex,' June said, and she felt tears well up at the first kind words she'd heard all day. She turned and headed towards the door before Alex saw, and then stopped. 'By the way, I'm reading *Matilda*.'

'The Roald Dahl book?'

'Yeah, she's my all-time favourite heroine. I'll reserve you a copy at the library.'

Back at home, June sat down to eat her takeaway. It felt good to have told someone about her situation at the library; she couldn't remember the last time she'd had a person to confide in. Although she quickly reminded herself that Alex would be going back to London soon.

June was finishing her food when she heard a knock on the door. When she opened it, she found Linda standing on the other side, holding a disgruntled Alan Bennett.

'Look who was in the airing cupboard again. I think he pissed on my good towels.'

'Oh god, I'm so sorry. I'll buy you new ones.'

Linda released Alan and he darted into the house. 'While I'm here, I don't suppose you still have your mum's old copy of *Riders*? The time has come for Jackson to read his first Jilly.'

'I'm sure I've got it somewhere; I still have all her books.' June led Linda through into the living room.

She considered telling her that eight might be a bit young for Jilly Cooper but suspected that Linda would just ignore her.

'Have you really kept all your mum's books?' Linda said, as June searched the C shelf.

'Of course. I haven't thrown any of her stuff away.'

'What, nothing?'

June found the book and handed it to Linda. 'I took some of her old clothes to the charity shop, but I kept everything else.' She saw a look cross Linda's face. 'What?'

'Well, don't you think you could get rid of some of her stuff now? Not the books, maybe, but what about some of her old knick-knacks?' Linda picked up a china figurine of a girl reading a book and waved it around. 'What about this one?'

June winced. 'I like that,' she said, grabbing the figurine from Linda and returning it to its correct place on the mantlepiece.

'Really? It's not like it's antique or anything. I remember Beverley bringing it back from the white elephant stall – I think she got it for free.'

'That's not the point, Linda.'

'I know, but your mum wasn't sentimental about this stuff.' Linda indicated around the room at the jumble of china animals, Toby jugs and snow globes that covered every surface. 'I don't mean to be rude, love. I just don't think your mum would have expected you to keep it all, like some kind of mausoleum. She'd have wanted you to have a fresh start and make this place your own.'

'But I don't want to make it my own.' The words came out of June's mouth with more force than she'd intended, and she saw Linda startle. 'I mean, I like having Mum's stuff around. It makes me feel . . . safe.'

Linda studied her for a moment. 'Well, I'd best be getting back then.'

'Thanks for bringing Alan over,' June said, following her to the door. She felt bad for snapping at Linda.

'No worries.' Linda stepped outside and then turned back to June. 'Please just remember that your mum never really cared about possessions, love. She liked all this stuff, but she was much more interested in getting out there and living her life. And I think she'd have wanted that for you, too.'

Chapter Ten

JUNE OBSERVED THE MAN as he loaded items into a string bag. He came into the library every few weeks, dressed in a beige mac and brown cords, and was always shy but courteous as he borrowed thrillers by Lee Child and John Grisham. But today, he'd quietly asked June where he might be able to find the Dating and Relationship section. When she showed him to the relevant shelf, he'd spent ages browsing before choosing a title called *The Five Love Languages: The Secret to Love that Lasts*, which he was now putting in his bag alongside a Fray Bentos pie and a single banana. June decided that the man worked as a cashier in a supermarket and had lived alone since his elderly parents died. He'd always been too shy to talk to women, but he'd fallen in love with a divorcee who worked at the checkout opposite his. Having never even said hello to her, he'd spent months plucking up the courage to ask her out. Finally, one day he walked over to her and said—

'I'm sorry to interrupt you, but I was wondering if you could help me with a small technical issue?' Stanley was standing by the desk, looking at June. 'I need to print something, but I can't make the damn thing work.'

'Of course,' she said, following him to the computer. Stanley was the only FOCL member who was talking to June, although he'd stopped asking her for help with the crossword. 'How many copies do you want?'

'Twenty, please. It's a petition about the library.'

June kept her face neutral, but she felt a rush of relief. They were four weeks into the council's consultation and, so far, FOCL didn't seem to have done anything except have endless meetings. June had been trying to eavesdrop on what they were planning, but they always stopped talking whenever she was around.

'It was Mrs Bransworth's idea,' Stanley said, when June handed him the printed sheets. 'We're going to leave copies in the pub and Naresh's shop, so everyone in the village should see them.'

June glanced over her shoulder to check Marjorie wasn't nearby to hear them, then lowered her voice. 'You can have this printing for free.'

'Thank you,' Stanley said, smiling at her. 'We're having another FOCL meeting tonight; it's not too late to join us, you know?'

Oh god. 'I'm afraid I have plans tonight.'

'I know you get anxious in group situations, but you don't have to say anything. We would really value your input.'

'I'm sorry, Stanley, I'm busy.'

He let out a sigh. 'Very well, my dear.'

June returned to the desk. She hated lying to Stanley when he'd always been kind to her, but if he knew she'd been banned then there was a risk he'd tell Mrs B, and then word might get back to the council that June had talked and then she'd be—

'June!'

She winced as her boss's voice bellowed across the library. Had Marjorie heard her talking to Stanley about FOCL? 'Yes, Marjorie?'

'I need to talk to you.'

June headed to the office, her mouth dry. But when she walked in, she found Marjorie sitting behind her desk with an odd expression on her face.

'Hello, June. Would you please take a seat?'

In her ten years working at the library, June had never known Marjorie to use such a gentle voice with her. Something must be wrong.

'Please,' Marjorie said again, and she gave another rictus smile.

June sat down, feeling even more nervous.

'I've called you in here because I need your assistance on a . . . personal matter,' Marjorie said. 'One on which I'd appreciate your utmost discretion. It concerns Gayle.'

June stifled a groan; not another job for the wedding. Just yesterday, Marjorie had made June give up her lunch break to research local companies who could provide a dozen live doves to be released during the vows.

'What do you need me to do?' June asked through gritted teeth.

'As you are aware, Gayle's hen do is in two weeks' time. And as you're also aware, the planned stripper has caused my stomach ulcer to return.'

'Would you like me to pop out and get you some more antacids?'

'No.' Marjorie paused. 'I want you to go to Gayle's hen do and stop the stripper.'

June gave a snort of surprise. 'What?'

'Hear me out. You and Gayle used to be close friends, yes?'

'Only at primary school.'

'Well, last night she was telling me on the phone that several of her friends have dropped out of the hen do, and now she doesn't have enough guests for the planned activities.'

'Yes, but—'

'So, I told Gayle that I know you'd love to go, and she's agreed that you can make up the numbers.'

June looked at her boss in disbelief. 'Marjorie, Gayle and I haven't been friends since we were eleven, and I've not seen her for years. Why would I go to her hen do?'

'Come on, you and I both know you don't have a social life. This would be fun for you.'

'No, it wouldn't—' June started, but Marjorie held up a hand to silence her. All pretence of niceness had disappeared.

'June, as your boss, I'm telling you that you have to go to the hen do. I can't risk some sleazy stripper performing and word getting out to the Lord Lieutenancy committee, ruining Brian's and my reputation. You need to stop it from happening.'

'But how am I supposed to do that?'

'You'll think of something.' Marjorie stood up and walked to the office door. 'I appreciate you doing this for me; it won't be forgotten.'

She stood by the door like a sentry until June left.

At the end of her shift, June hurried out of the library, her head spinning. Over the years, she'd trained herself not to think about school or Gayle Spencer, but now all the unwanted memories came flooding back.

June had been devastated when Gayle rejected her in the first term of secondary school. Her response had been to bury herself deeper in her books, withdrawing from everyone around her. People could hurt her, June had realised, in a way that a character in a novel never would. Her mum had implored her to put the books aside and make new friends, but June had made a friend once before, and look how that had ended. Instead, she vowed to keep her head down until she left this school and Gayle behind. Things would be different when she got to university, June told herself time and again; there would be more people there, and she would find like-minded friends. Until then, she had Lizzy Bennet and Jo March to keep her company.

But now, after all these years, Marjorie expected June to go to Gayle's hen do and pretend they were still friends, while Tara and Becky and all those other women sniggered behind her back, just like the old days. And not just that, but June was also somehow supposed to stop a stripper from performing. She grimaced at the thought; whatever happened, she needed to get out of this.

June increased her pace towards home and *Cold Comfort Farm*. But as she passed the bakery, she heard her name being called. When she turned around, she saw Stanley coming out of the library, waving his arm in the air. June waited for him to catch up, praying this wouldn't be another of his attempts to get her to join FOCL.

'Hello, my dear,' he said when he reached her. 'I'm glad I caught you, I'm stuck on today's last clue and I thought you might be able to help.' He produced a newspaper from his carrier bag.

'Stanley, is that stolen library property?' June said in mock indignation.

'It's borrowed, not stolen. I'll return it first thing tomorrow.'

She smiled and took the paper from him, pleased to be asked for help again.

'Seven down,' he said. *'Start angry confused victims protesting*, eight letters.'

June looked at the space in the crossword; several of the letters were already filled in. 'I think it's activism, Stanley.'

'Is it?' He looked at the paper, frowning. 'So it is, silly me. Are you headed this way too?'

They set off side by side, neither of them speaking as they made their way along The Parade. The Chalcot in Bloom committee had been busy in recent weeks, and colourful baskets of flowers had been suspended from every lamp post and shop awning, but June couldn't enjoy them today. She felt the awkward silence hang between her and Stanley, and reminded herself once again that this was why she shouldn't try and talk to patrons outside of work.

'Do you know, I can remember your first day working at the library,' Stanley said, as they turned left at the post office to go down the hill.

'I'm not sure I can, it was all a blur.'

'You were quiet as a mouse, I don't think I heard you speak all day. You looked terrified.'

'I *was* terrified.'

'How old were you?'

'Eighteen.'

'Goodness,' Stanley said. 'May I ask, what made you decide to become a library assistant?'

June took a moment before she answered. 'My mum got sick during my A-Levels, so instead of going away to university I became her carer. We needed money, so Marjorie employed me as a part-time library assistant until Mum was well enough to return to work in the library. But that never happened . . .'

She trailed off, and when Stanley spoke again it was in a voice so quiet, she almost didn't hear him.

'And here you still are, ten years later.'

'I know.'

They walked on in silence, past the village green, where June could see a dad and child feeding ducks on the small pond. When they reached the Golden Dragon, June glanced in the window to see if Alex was there; he often popped out to say hello to her and chat about books, but there was no sign of him today. Stanley didn't speak until they had almost reached the church.

'You know, I've met many librarians in my time, and I think your mum was one of the finest I've ever known.'

'Wasn't she amazing?' June said, smiling. 'She seemed to find it all so easy; it was like she was born to do the job.'

'And weren't you born to do it as well? You certainly have it in your blood.'

'God, no. I love working at the library, but I'm not a natural like she was. I'm too shy and I hate talking in front of people, so I can't run any of the activities like Mum did. I'm pretty useless, really.'

Stanley raised his eyebrows but didn't say anything, so June continued.

'Sometimes I think that the only reason Marjorie hasn't sacked me is out of loyalty to my mum. And she's retiring at Christmas, so god knows what will happen to me after that.'

'Do you really think that?' Stanley said, and June nodded. 'My dear, Marjorie hasn't sacked you because she knows that if you went, the whole place would fall apart. You are the glue that holds Chalcot Library together.'

June couldn't help but laugh. 'That's rubbish, Marjorie is the one who does all the hard work.'

'Can you really not see it?' Stanley stopped walking and turned to face her. 'Tell me, if you weren't there, who would encourage young Jackson with all his projects? Who would humour a lonely old lady's moaning, or assist people with their benefits? And who would do the crossword with a silly old man like me? Every single day, you go above and beyond for people in the library.'

'But Mum always said that being a librarian was like being a social worker, so anyone in my job would do the same. Plus, they'd be able to do loads of other things that I'm too scared to even try.'

Stanley let out an audible sigh. 'What about Jim Tucker?'

June hadn't thought of Mr Tucker in years, and the mention of his name made her throat thicken.

She'd met Jim not long after she started working at the library. Back then it was still open on a Saturday morning and he would bring his grandchildren in most weeks. June had never paid him much attention, apart from noting that he seemed a bit grumpy, dismissing the two kids whenever they brought him a book. Then one day, about six months after she'd started working there, June was coming home one evening when she spotted Jim sitting on a bench, staring into space.

'Jim's grave is over there, you know,' Stanley said, interrupting June's thoughts. He was pointing across the road to the churchyard, and June could see the same bench that she and Jim had sat on all those years ago.

She couldn't remember how their conversation had started that day. But she did remember Jim telling her that he'd had some bad news from the doctor, and he wasn't very well. June had offered some platitude, at which point he'd stopped her in her tracks. *Do you know my biggest regret?* June had looked at him, wondering what on earth he was about to confess. *I've never read a story to my grandchildren.*

June had told him it was OK, he could read them one on Saturday, she'd help him choose a book. Jim had shaken his head and told June his deepest secret: that he couldn't read. He said his wife knew but that all his life he'd managed to hide it from everyone else: his employers, his friends, even his own children. He'd been too stubborn and embarrassed, he said, and now it was too late, and he'd never get to read to them.

'You know, I used to see you with Jim down by the river,' Stanley said.

'He was proud and didn't want anyone to know I was helping him, so we used to meet in secret after I finished work.'

The lessons had gone on for nine months. Jim had been severely dyslexic and even the simplest words confounded him. But eventually, very slowly, it had started to come together.

'I remember coming into the library one day before Christmas and seeing Jim there,' Stanley said. 'He had his grandkids with him, and they were messing around a bit. Suddenly old Jim pulled a book off the shelf and started to read to them. I won't forget the look on those children's faces for as long as I live.'

June could remember it too and smiled. 'The book was *Peter Rabbit.* His granddaughter loved rabbits, so Jim had spent weeks practising it.'

'I've been thinking a lot about Jim lately,' Stanley said. 'Everything that's been going on has made me think about all the people I've known in this village, and how the library has helped them. How *you* have helped them.'

He hesitated for a moment, staring across at the church-yard. 'This is what annoys me most about this bloody council business. What these management consultants with their calculators and spreadsheets will never work out is that the library is about so much more than simply books. Libraries are like a net, there to catch those of us in danger of falling through the cracks. That's what we're really fighting to protect.'

He stopped and June waited for the next line, the 'This is why you need to join FOCL' chat. But when she looked at Stanley, she could see that his eyes were wet. He hurried to wipe them, and June looked away to allow him some dignity. When she looked back, he had composed himself again.

'Well, I've taken up enough of your time, my dear. You have somewhere you need to be.'

'I do?'

Stanley reached out and put a hand on her shoulder. 'You're busy, remember? That's why you can't come to the FOCL meeting tonight.' He turned to walk back up the hill, the way they'd just come. As he did, she could hear him muttering to himself. 'Activism. I should have got that one.'

Chapter Eleven

ON FRIDAY MORNING, June was setting up the library when
she heard a faint knock at the door. When she pulled it
open, she found a woman standing outside, wearing a long
dress and a headscarf.

'Morning. I'm afraid we're not open for another ten
minutes,' June said.

The woman looked at her in confusion.

'Ten more minutes,' June said, holding up ten fingers.

'Cookbooks?'

June was about to say ten minutes again but stopped
herself. Marjorie was a stickler for not allowing patrons
in before the official opening time, but perhaps June could
bend the rules just this once.

'Sure, come on in,' she said, stepping aside. 'I'm June,
the library assistant.'

'Leila,' the woman said, in a low voice.

'Hi Leila. Cookery books are over here.'

'Cake . . . please,' Leila said.

'We have lots of baking books. How about this one?'
June picked up a Paul Hollywood book and showed it to

Leila, but the woman shook her head. They both studied the shelf.

'This?' Leila pointed at Mary Berry's face smiling down at them.

'I'm not much of a baker myself but Mary Berry is very popular. She's on the TV.' June started to mime out the charades action for TV programme. 'You just need a library card and you can take it home.'

Leila frowned again.

'It's fine, I can help you with that. Do you have proof of address? Your home?'

Leila nodded and June led her to the desk.

Fifteen minutes later, Leila walked out carrying *Mary Berry's Baking Bible* and a library card, and June felt a thrill of satisfaction. It lasted approximately ten seconds until Vera appeared at the desk.

'What did she want?'

'Good morning, Vera.'

'That's the immigrant I was telling you about. Is she allowed to use the library?'

'Of course, the library's open for everyone,' June said, in her firmest voice.

'Was that a recipe book she was borrowing?'

'We've got the new Stephen King coming in this week – shall I reserve it for you?'

Vera just gave a grunt and turned to walk out of the library, leaning heavily on her walking stick.

June watched her go. Vera had always been a difficult customer but recently her behaviour seemed to be getting even more hostile, and June made a mental note to say something to Marjorie about it.

She felt a buzz in her pocket and pulled her phone out. There was an email icon on the screen, and when June clicked on it her stomach dropped. It was from Gayle:

Hi stranger, long time no see! Mum's told me you want to come to my hen do – that's so sweet!! It's at Oakford Park, two weeks on Saturday, starting at midday. Come in fancy dress, the theme is film heroines, and we're going clubbing in the evening. I know the girls have got some wild stuff planned, so leave your inhibitions at home!!! See you then, Gx

June read the email twice with a growing sense of dread. This was even worse than she'd feared: fancy dress . . . clubbing . . . wild stuff. She had to find an excuse not to go, even if it meant incurring the wrath of Marjorie. She went to put her phone back in her pocket, and as she did it slipped through her fingers and fell on the floor. Cursing under her breath, June got down on her hands and knees to retrieve it from under the desk.

'Hi. I'd like to take out the librarian.'

June jumped at the sound of Alex's voice, banging her head on the bottom of the desk. 'Ouch!' She sat up, rubbing her head. 'Sorry . . . what did you just say?'

'I said, I'd like to take out the librarian, please?'

June felt her face getting hot. She opened her mouth to speak, but as she did, Alex lifted up a copy of *The Librarian* by Salley Vickers.

'It's for my auntie, she's come to stay.'

'Oh right, of course,' June said, standing up and snatching the book off him.

'I've finished *The Great Gatsby*. You were right, it's amazing,' he said, oblivious to her embarrassment. 'Although what a terrible bunch they were. Gatsby may have known how to throw a good party, but I wouldn't want to be mates with him.'

June and Alex had been swapping book recommendations over the past month. June had shared some of her favourite classics, from *Alice's Adventures in Wonderland* to *Tess of the D'Urbervilles*, and after a few false starts with horror books, Alex was now lending her some of the fantasy and science fiction that he'd loved as a teenager.

'How are you getting on with *The Hobbit*?'

'Good,' June said, relieved to be back on the safe subject of books. 'I never thought I'd enjoy Tolkien, but it's great.'

'Isn't he an amazing storyteller?'

'I can now see why people love fantasy novels: they're the perfect escape from real life.'

'Things still bad here?'

June lowered her voice. 'Yes, but I can't talk about it now.'

'Well, how about we go for a drink tonight and you can tell me then?' June waited to see if she'd misunderstood again, but Alex went on. 'My aunt's helping in the takeaway today so I've finally got a night off. I was thinking of going into Mawley for a change of scene; I'd love some company if you're free?'

June busied herself stamping his book so she didn't have to reply straightaway. It was Friday night, which meant the pub would be crowded and noisy, and once they'd talked about books then what would they say to each other? June imagined the strained silence between them, Alex necking his pint quickly so he could escape from her.

'I can't tonight,' she said, handing him back the copy of *The Librarian*.

'Oh, that's a shame.'

'I'm sorry, I've just got lots on. I have to—'

'Well, well, what do we have here?' Linda was standing behind Alex, grinning at them both. 'Are you George's boy? Look at you all grown up! Your dad tells me you're a solicitor now.'

'Er, yes. Hi . . .' Alex looked to June for help.

'This is my next-door neighbour, Linda,' she said.

'Next-door neighbour? Is that how you describe me to people?' Linda arched an eyebrow. 'I've known June since

93

she was four; I was best friends with her mum. When she was little, she used to run round my back garden completely naked and—'

'Do you need to return those?' June said, pointing at the books in Linda's hand.

'Oh, yes please, love. They may be a little overdue.' She turned to Alex. 'June always cancels my fines for me.'

'It's useful to have friends in powerful places,' he said, with a smile.

June was aware of Linda winking at her madly over Alex's shoulder, and she prayed her face wasn't still as red as it felt.

'I'm afraid I've got to dash now,' Alex said. 'I'm sorry you can't come tonight; maybe we can grab a drink some other time?'

'What's that?' Linda said. 'You're not busy tonight, are you, June?'

'Actually, I am,' she said, glaring at Linda and hoping she'd get the message.

'Doing what, reading boring old Russian books? Surely you can give that a miss for one night.' June opened her mouth to respond, but Linda was talking to Alex. 'June's a shy one, as you might have noticed, so she takes a bit of coaxing to let her hair down. But I'm sure she'd love to go out for a drink tonight, wouldn't you, love?'

June wanted to resist, but she knew that Linda was not going to let this one go without a fight. 'Sure, that would be great.'

'Cool,' Alex said, although he looked bemused by the exchange he'd just witnessed. 'Meet at seven outside the takeaway?'

As soon as he'd left the library, Linda looked at June with satisfaction. 'He seems like a charming young man. And so handsome . . .'

'Linda, why did you just do that?' June said with a groan.

'Do what? I know you wanted to go on a date with him really, you were just being coy.'

'It's not a date! He only asked me for a drink because he feels sorry for me and all his real friends are in London.'

'All right, love, keep your knickers on. Even if that's true, when was the last time you had a night out?'

June didn't want to answer that question, so she started scanning the books. 'Linda, this one is four weeks overdue,' she said, holding up a copy of Marie Kondo's *The Life-Changing Magic of Tidying*. 'You can't keep them that long; Marjorie would be furious if she found out I wipe your fines.'

'Oh, never mind that old battleaxe. It was a good book, you should read it.'

June laughed. 'I know I have many faults, but I don't think untidiness is one of them.'

'But this book isn't just about tidying, it's about how decluttering can improve your life. Here . . .' Linda grabbed the book and began flicking through it. June tried to ignore the rough manner with which she turned the pages. 'Marie says that when you tidy your home, it makes you confront issues you might be ignoring. She thinks that a good tidy can help a person restart their life.'

June realised where this was going. 'That sounds very interesting, Linda.'

'Well, I've been thinking about that chat we had. I swear it would do you good to have a little clear-out, freshen the house up a bit. I could help if you like? Maybe we could get rid of some of your mum's old ornaments at the next white elephant stall?'

'I'm very happy with the house how it is,' June said, avoiding Linda's eyes.

'Of course you are, love.' Unspoken words hung in the air between them. 'Now, about this not-a-date with Alex Chen. What are you going to wear?'

Chapter Twelve

AT TEN MINUTES TO SEVEN, June left the house and set off towards Alex's family takeaway, trying to ignore the knot in her stomach. What the hell were the two of them going to talk about? They didn't have anything in common: he'd been away to university and was now a solicitor living in the city, only back in Chalcot for a few months, and she was a library assistant who'd never left their small village. Perhaps, after one drink, she could pretend she had a headache and leave.

As she approached the takeaway, June could see Alex waiting for her outside. He'd changed out of his usual scruffy T-shirt into a collared shirt, and June suddenly regretted not making more of an effort with her own appearance.

'Hey, you,' he said, when he saw her, and June was surprised to feel her stomach leap. 'There's a bus at five past. If we hurry, we can catch it.'

As they walked to the bus stop, Alex updated June on his dad's recovery. 'He's meant to be resting in bed, but I caught him trying to do yoga this morning,' he said, as the number 36 pulled up.

They climbed on board and found seats halfway back. It was only when they'd sat down that June noticed Vera from the library was sitting opposite, her face set in a scowl. June averted her eyes and pretended not to have noticed her.

'So, I've got my next book for you.' Alex reached into his back pocket and pulled out a battered copy of Terry Pratchett's *The Colour of Magic*. 'I fell in love with the Discworld series when I was nine or ten. Have you read any of them?'

'No, sorry.'

'Well, you're in for a treat. They're set on this planet that's balanced on four elephants on the back of a giant turtle. And there's a librarian character in the books, who's an orangutan and . . .'

June tried to listen, but she couldn't stop glancing at Vera, who was watching Alex with her mouth pursed in disapproval. What was the woman's problem?

'The books have one of my favourite characters in literature ever, Death, who is hilarious,' Alex said.

The bus pulled up at a stop and June saw Vera haul herself up out of her seat. As she turned to leave, she muttered something that June couldn't make out. She and Alex watched Vera make her way down the aisle and lower herself off the bus. Only when the doors had closed and the bus pulled away did Alex speak again.

'Poor Mrs Cox.'

June looked at him in surprise. 'You know Vera?'

'We lived next door to her when I was a kid.'

June glanced around to check there was no one nearby before she whispered, 'She's an absolute nightmare at the library.'

'Oh, don't say that,' Alex said, frowning.

'She makes my life hell with her complaining. And I'm pretty sure she's racist.'

'You realise that you're probably the only person she talks to all day?'

'But still . . .'

'She's had a difficult life.'

'What do you mean?'

Alex kept his voice low. 'Before my parents divorced, they used to both work long hours at the takeaway, so Vera would often have me over after school. She'd cook me tea and let my friends come round to play.'

'Vera? But she hates kids – she's always moaning about them at the library.'

Alex shrugged. 'I don't know the full story, but I know that Vera and her husband Fred wanted to have children but for whatever reason they couldn't. So, they sort of adopted me as their honorary grandson. Vera spent hours kicking a football with me in her back garden, and she used to make birthday cakes for all the kids on our street.'

'Wow. So, what happened?'

Alex lowered his voice even further and June had to lean in to hear him. 'When I was ten or eleven, Fred left Vera. It was all very sudden: one day he was mowing the lawn and chatting to me about whether Man U were going to win the Champions League, the next day he was gone. Vera was a mess; I remember her crying on Mum. Then Fred sent her this letter, giving her a forwarding address for his post and telling her that he'd moved in with his mistress and their children.'

'What?' June burst out, and several passengers turned to look at her. 'Oh my god!'

'I know, right? It turns out Fred had been having an affair for years and they had two kids together. He'd been leading this whole double life and Vera had no idea.'

'I can't believe it. Poor Vera.'

'After that she stopped letting me go to her house and started moaning to my parents that I made too much noise. She stopped baking and never left home, and she lost all her friends. We moved about a year later when my folks separated, and I've hardly seen her since. I'm not sure she even recognised me.'

June thought of Vera in the library, her face twisted and sour as she watched the activity in the Children's Room. June had always assumed Vera disliked kids, but maybe it was something else that made her so bitter – regret.

'We're here,' Alex said, and June looked out the window to see they were pulling up on Mawley high street.

She followed him off the bus and they crossed the road towards The Chequers. June couldn't remember the last time she'd been in this pub, or any pub for that matter, and she was immediately alarmed by the noise and the number of people. But Alex steered her to a table in a quiet corner and then went to buy them both a drink. While he was gone, June's mind drifted back to Vera. She imagined her at home, baking a birthday cake for one of the local children, and Fred walking in with his suitcase and telling her he was leaving. Vera would have begged him to stay, cried and tried to wrestle the suitcase off him, but Fred would have said—

'Here you go.' Alex placed a large glass of wine on the table. 'Are you all right? You looked a million miles away there.'

'Sorry, I was daydreaming. Thanks for the drink.'

'I remember you daydreaming at school,' Alex said, sitting down opposite her. 'You used to do it in English; you'd stare off into space for ages and then suddenly you'd start scribbling away. Your creative writing was always the best in class.'

'Oh, that's not true,' June said, although she couldn't help but smile. 'But I do like to make up stories in my head, I always have. Sometimes, at the library, I watch people taking out books and try and imagine what their life might be like.'

As soon as the words left June's mouth, she regretted them. She'd never told anyone except her mum, and out loud she realised how silly it made her sound.

'Ooh, let's play it now,' Alex said. 'What about that lady over there?'

'Oh no, we don't have to. It's just a stupid thing I do.'

'No, go on. See that lady in the butterfly dress; what do you think her story is?'

'Really?'

'Yes!'

June turned to study her. The woman must have been in her mid-twenties, wearing a pretty fifties-style tea dress and red lipstick. She was with a man wearing a linen shirt and chinos. June thought for a moment.

'Her name is Hannah. She lives with two friends in a flat full of clothes and laughter. She works in a dull office job, but at the weekend she and her friends dress up and go dancing. She dreams of doing something creative, maybe becoming a painter.'

'And who's the guy? Is he her boyfriend?'

'No, but she wants him to be. They've been seeing each other for a few months but he won't commit to her.'

'Why not?'

'Because he has a long-term girlfriend. She has no idea that he's just stringing her along.'

'Poor Hannah,' Alex said, and he sounded genuinely sad. 'I think the guy is bad news. In fact, do you think he's dangerous? Maybe he's a serial killer and tonight she's his victim.'

June raised her eyebrows. 'I was going for tragic romance and you want a grisly horror.'

Alex laughed out loud and June grinned. She'd never played the game with anyone else before.

'No wonder you were so good at those creative writing assignments. I always got a C because I added zombies and monsters. Do you still write?'

'Not really,' June said, and she took a sip of her wine.

'Oh, that's such a shame. I always thought you were going to be a—'

'Do you have any hobbies, Alex?' June said, before he could finish his sentence.

'Sure, I do have hobbies, June,' he said, and she thought she could see a faint smile on his lips. 'I like to go climbing, and I play football on a local five-a-side team: we're rubbish but the drinking after is fun. I love going to the cinema – there's an amazing independent one near my flat in London that plays old sixties and seventies horror movies. And on Tuesday nights I go . . .'

June listened with growing amazement. She'd expected him to say one or two things, but how could one person be so busy? It sounded exhausting.

'What about you?' Alex said, when he got to the end of his list.

'I read,' June said. There was a pause as Alex waited for her to carry on. 'And I like walking.'

'Cool. Do you ever go hiking? I used to do a lot with Dad when I was younger.'

'Sure,' June said, and she took a gulp of her wine to cover up the fact that the only walking she did was to and from work.

'Do you like travelling?' Alex said. 'I went backpacking every summer while I was at uni, it was amazing.'

'What was your favourite place?'

'Ooh, the million-dollar question. India was brilliant, and I also loved Vietnam. Have you been?'

June shook her head. The furthest she'd ever been was to Weymouth with her mum.

'You should go, it's amazing. There's such a rich history and the food is . . .'

June nodded as she listened to Alex, but inside she was squirming. This was exactly why she hadn't wanted to come tonight. She had nothing interesting to say, no exciting hobbies or exotic travel to talk about. All she'd done for the past ten years was work in the library and read books. June closed her eyes, wishing she could run out now and spare herself the humiliation of him realising what a pathetic little life she led.

'June?'

She opened her eyes. 'Sorry, what?'

'I said, do you still see many people from school?'

Oh god, this was it. The moment she had to tell Alex that she had no friends, no hobbies and no life. 'Well, the thing is . . .' June stopped as a thought occurred to her. 'Actually, I'm going to Gayle Spencer's hen do in a few weeks.'

'Gayle? No way, how is she?'

'She's good. She got engaged in the Maldives at New Year.'

'Nice,' Alex said. 'I never realised you and her were close at school.'

'We've been friends since primary school.' This wasn't a complete lie, but June could still feel her cheeks colouring.

'Wow, I had no idea. You two always seemed so different,' Alex said, and June cringed at the reminder of what a loser she'd been at school.

'I know, Gayle was a lot cooler than me,' she said, taking a despondent swig of wine.

'Actually, I thought you were the cool one,' Alex said. 'All those girls ever talked about was boys and parties, while you were reading all these amazing, interesting books.'

June was so surprised that she choked on her drink.

'Are you all right?'

'Sorry,' she said, through the coughing.

Alex waited for her to finish. 'This might sound strange, but I always had this image of your life after school, where you'd go to uni and have all these smart, bookish friends, and you'd all have deep, intellectual conversations.' His face had gone quite pink. 'Sorry, that sounds absurd, feel free to laugh at me.'

But June didn't laugh; instead, she felt her stomach fall. What Alex had described was exactly what she used to dream of herself: going to university and finally making close friends, staying up all night talking about books and supporting each other's writing. She went to take another drink and realised her glass was empty.

'Do you want another pint?' she said, standing up and grabbing his glass before he could answer.

June made her way towards the bar. How had Alex so accurately guessed her eighteen-year-old dream? They'd hardly known each other at school; she was amazed he'd even noticed her, let alone understood her so well. She thought back for a moment to that fantasy, the friends and the life she'd imagined for herself, and then pushed it out of her mind.

As she reached the bar, June heard a sudden explosion of laughter behind her, and she glanced round to see where it was coming from. Shit. Brian Spencer, Gayle's dad, was sitting at a table next to the bar with two younger men. Had he heard her just lie about still being friends with his daughter? Brian's mouth was open as he laughed, and June could see the half-chewed food inside. She grimaced and turned away so he wouldn't see her. As she waited to be served, she could hear Brian's voice, full of privilege and self-importance.

'What you have to understand, boys, is the value of a bit of wheel grease.'

'And, in this particular instance, you think that the wheels could be greased?' one of the men said.

'I do. Although I should warn you, it won't be cheap.'

'What can I get you, love?' The barmaid was staring at June impatiently.

'A pint of lager and a white wine, please.'

'Of course, I can't make any promises.' Brian's voice floated back over. 'But I play golf with a couple of the councillors and they trust me. I'm sure they could be incentivised to see the benefits of this idea.'

'I told you, Phil – Brian here could be a good invest-ment.' This guy sounded younger and posher. 'I know this better than most.'

They laughed at this, the deep guffawing laugh that men only seemed to do around other men.

June paid for the drinks and headed back towards the table, careful to keep her face turned away from Brian. As she walked past, she caught a glimpse of one of the men sitting with him, his cheeks flushed with alcohol, his hair so blond he looked like Draco Malfoy from *Harry Potter*.

'And what about Marjorie, won't she mind?'

'Oh, you don't need to worry about that,' Brian said. 'I can handle her.'

Back at the table, June found Alex looking embarrassed. 'Sorry, you must think I'm a complete weirdo for saying all that,' he said.

'Not at all. I'd have loved to have had that life you described, but it just . . . didn't quite work out that way.'

'Why not, if you don't mind me asking?'

June had managed to spill some wine on the table and she traced a pattern in it with her finger. 'I always wanted to go to Cambridge to study English, but Mum got diagnosed with cancer while we were in the sixth form. She still wanted me to go, so I applied and got offered a place, but they let me defer it so I could look after her. And then she died, two years later.'

'Oh, June, I'm so sorry.'

'I know I could have taken up my place after that, it's what Mum would have wanted. But once she was gone, the idea of leaving home felt too . . . terrifying.'

'And you're not tempted to go to university now? There are some great courses for mature students.'

June shook her head. 'No, I don't think that's for me. Besides, I love my life here in Chalcot.'

'Well, I'm glad you're happy here. And you're so lucky to have a job that you love.'

'I honestly can't imagine working anywhere else, which is why all this council stuff is so terrifying.'

'How's the campaign going?'

'I wish I knew. It's been a month now and there still haven't been any public events. I'm trying to eaves-drop at the library, but no one says anything in front of me.'

'What have FOCL been doing all this time?' Alex said, with a frown.

'I've no idea. Although I did pick this up in the village shop the other day . . .'

June reached into her bag and pulled out a crumpled flyer, which she laid on the table. The words 'Save Our Library (please)' were written at the top in large Comic Sans font.

'Jesus, this isn't going to save anything,' Alex said. 'What are they doing on social media?'

'I don't know, I'm not on it.'

Alex took his phone out and typed something in. 'They must be on Twitter, surely?' He scanned the screen. 'A-ha, here they are.'

He passed the phone over to June and she saw there was one tweet.

Friends of Chalcot Library @FOCL
Join us on Saturday 7th August for a protest event at the church hall. A raffle, face-painting, and a performance from Chalcot's very own Colin the Clown. All welcome! #savechalcotlibrary

'Well that's something, I suppose.' June went to hand Alex's phone back and, as she did, she saw a WhatsApp message flash up on his screen.

Ellie
Just got some exciting news – call me ASAP! Xx

June felt her heart drop when she saw the kisses, and then felt stupid: it was none of her business who messaged Alex. He glanced at his phone and smiled, and June took a long drink of wine.

'So, are you sure there's nothing you can do to help FOCL?' he asked, once he'd put his phone away.

'No, I can't risk it. The council would sack me if I do anything in public, it's as simple as that.'

'What if it's not public? What about trying to help them in secret?'

'What do you mean?'

'Well, I know you can't risk the council seeing you being involved, but you could be FOCL's undercover operative?'

June chuckled. 'I'm not sure I'd make a very good secret agent, despite having read *Harriet the Spy* three times as a kid.'

But Alex didn't laugh. 'I know you won't believe me, June, but I think you have much more to offer than you realise.'

'No, I don't,' she mumbled.

'You know, when I was reading *Matilda*, I kept thinking how much you reminded me of her.'

'Matilda?'

'Well, obviously you both love books, but Matilda also had so much integrity and really cared about people. You were always the same at school.' Alex took a swig of his pint before he spoke again. 'I think you need to ask yourself: what would Matilda do?'

That night June slept deeply and didn't wake until after nine on Saturday morning. She lay in bed running over the events of last night: Alex's busy and exciting life, his ridiculous comment about her being cool, the WhatsApp message . . .

She went downstairs and made herself a cup of tea. Alan Bennett lay under the table and lashed out at June's feet every time she walked past, but she was too distracted to tell him off. What about Brian and the snatches of conversation she'd overheard in the pub? Hadn't he said something about 'incentivising councillors', and why had one of the men asked Brian about Marjorie? They must have been talking about the library, surely.

June took a sip of tea and swore as she burnt her tongue. If Brian was up to something dodgy with the library then she should tell someone – but who? She couldn't exactly rock up to the council and make wild accusations when she didn't have a clue what was going on.

June reached for her mobile phone and searched for Twitter, and after several minutes she worked out how to find FOCL's page. She stared at the tweet they'd written about next week's protest and, as she did, an idea began to formulate in her mind. But could she do it? It was risky, she didn't have any evidence, and whoever read the message would probably just think she was a crank.

June put the phone down; she should stay out of this.

And then she remembered Alex's words. *What would Matilda do?*

She took a deep breath, picked up the phone and clicked on sign-up. In a few minutes the account was set up. She composed a short message before she could change her mind.

Matilda @MWormwoo8
@FOCL I have some information that might be of use to you.

June pressed Tweet and threw the phone down on the table as if it were red-hot. She picked up *The Hobbit* and read three sentences before glancing back at her phone. Nothing. She carried on reading, but she hadn't even made it to the end of the page before she checked again. Who would be the person to see her tweet, Chantal or Mrs B? And if they replied to her, what was she going to say?

She needed to do something to distract herself, and if reading wasn't going to work then there was only one other thing for it: cleaning.

June pulled on an old T-shirt and started in the living room. She worked meticulously, starting with the long bookcases and then making her way round the room. She polished each of the snow globes on the shelf above the TV, then moved on to the china ornaments on the mantlepiece: the Charles and Diana commemorative mug she and her mum had found together at a car boot sale, the model of a red bus they'd brought home from a sightseeing trip to London. June was dusting the china girl with a book when she heard her phone ping, and she rushed across the room to look at it. *Friends of Chalcot Library followed you*. June closed her eyes for a moment; she could still back out now, it wasn't too late. Maybe Brian wasn't up to anything dodgy after all? She opened her eyes and started typing a private message.

I think Brian Spencer is plotting against the library.

June pressed send and realised that she'd been holding her breath. A moment later a reply popped up.

Who are you?

> I'm a friend of the library.
> I want to help you.

What do you know about Brian?

> He met with two men and they
> talked about how he could grease
> the wheels and convince county
> councillors about something. They
> referenced Marjorie Spencer so
> I think it's about the library.

Who were the men?

> I don't know.

What do they want to do with the library?

> I don't know. Sorry.

June waited for a response but there wasn't one. From the curt tone she guessed it must be Mrs Bransworth, but what would she do with this information? She might confront Brian outright, but he'd just deny everything. Hopefully FOCL would do some digging and find some concrete evidence for what was going on. June wondered

114

for a moment if Marjorie was involved, but pushed the thought out of her mind. There were many things wrong with her boss, but June's mum had always said that if you cut Marjorie in half it would say 'Chalcot Library' through the middle. Still, maybe June should keep a closer eye on her at work, just in case.

She returned to her cleaning with renewed vigour. It felt good to have finally done something to fight for the library. Alex had been right; June might not be able to publicly join FOCL, but perhaps she could help them behind the scenes after all.

Chapter Thirteen

JUNE HANDED THE COPY of *Gone Girl* to the young woman and watched her walk out the library. She'd never seen her before, and June imagined that the woman had moved to Chalcot because she was on the run. Her parents were a respectable, middle-class couple, with a BMW and annual ski holidays to France, but behind closed doors they were mean and bullying, controlling every aspect of their daughter's life. So, she had faked her own kidnapping, creating a ransom note and leaving false clues so that her parents didn't suspect. But then her dad happened to come to Chalcot for work and spotted her at the library. He waited for her outside and, when she left, he followed her into an alleyway and in a low and threatening voice said—

'I need new book.'

'Hi Leila,' June said, smiling at the patron in front of the desk. 'What did you make of the Hairy Bikers?'

'I think Mary Berry better,' Leila said, shyly. She came into the library at least once a week now, and each time June helped her choose a new recipe book. June had found out that her son, Mahmoud, helped her translate the recipes into Arabic.

'I've put a new book aside for you – would you like to look at it now?'

'Thank you,' Leila said, and she waited while June went to find it.

'Here you go.'

'I have . . . for you . . .' Leila reached into her bag and pulled out a small package wrapped in kitchen paper. June opened it to find a diamond-shaped slice of cake, decorated with crushed pistachios. It smelt delicious.

'Basbousa,' Leila said.

'Oh wow. Thank you so much,' June said, a lump in her throat.

'I try English scone next,' Leila said, as she turned and headed towards a table, a look of concentration on her face. June smiled to herself as she put the cake down next to the keyboard, to enjoy later.

'What's that?' Vera was leaning over the desk, her face scrunched up.

'It's called basbousa.'

She waved her head in the direction of Leila. 'Did she make it?'

In the two weeks since Alex had told her about Vera's past, June had been making extra attempts to engage with Vera and encourage her to join in activities at the library, but, so far, all her efforts had been in vain. Now, she took a deep breath.

'You know, Leila is really keen to learn about English cooking. I heard that you're a good baker, so perhaps you could suggest some recipe books for her?'

'Who told you that?' Vera said, suspicion etched onto her face. 'Well, they're wrong. I haven't baked in years,' she spat, and she turned and headed back towards her chair. She knocked into Jackson on her way past, and the armful of books he was carrying tumbled onto the floor. June hurried over to him.

'Are you OK, Jackson?' she said, bending down to pick them up.

'I'm fine.'

June handed him a tome called *Japan Encyclopaedia*. 'Your gran didn't tell me you're going on holiday.'

'I'm not, I'm just doing a project about Japan. Did you know that it's made up of six thousand eight hundred and fifty-two islands? And the Japanese eat more fish than any other country in the world?'

'I did not know that.'

'Also, Stanley told me that in Japan they have haiku, which are a special kind of poem with only three lines and seventeen syllables.'

'That's fascinating, Jackson.'

'I've written a haiku. Would you like to hear it?'

'I'd love to.'

He stood up straight and started to recite in a monotone voice:

'Libraries are boats
And the books are life jackets.
Without them we'll drown.'

June was so taken aback that she didn't know how to respond. 'Wow, Jackson. That's very . . . powerful.'

'Do you like it? I'm going to perform it at the library protest on Saturday.'

'I'm sure everyone will love it. I'm sorry I won't be there to hear it.'

June really was sad she wouldn't be able to go. Saturday's event at the church hall was all anyone in the library had talked about all week, and June had picked up snippets of information from her eavesdropping. It seemed that Mrs Bransworth had gone all Cersei Lannister and was driving the rest of FOCL mad with her demands for banners, PA systems and 'a tombola that would rival the one at Favering Summer Fayre'. The one good piece of news was that someone had managed to secure a local news crew to cover the event. The village had talked of nothing else since, and June was delighted that they might finally get some publicity for the library campaign.

Out of the corner of her eye, June saw Marjorie bowling towards her, a determined look in her eye.

'Sorry, Jackson, I'd better get on with my work. Good luck with your haiku.'

'June, a word,' Marjorie said when she reached her. June followed her boss behind the Local History shelf. 'Gayle tells me you still haven't replied to her about the hen do. Why not?'

Oh god. Despite her lie to Alex about being friends with Gayle, the idea of attending was giving June anxiety dreams, and she'd put off sending a reply. 'I'm sorry, Marjorie, I've just been busy.'

'Well, I need you to email now, before Gayle starts to suspect that I've put you up to this.'

'Now?'

'Come on, get your phone out.'

June was aware of Marjorie staring at her screen as she began to type, and prayed she wouldn't get a sudden Twitter notification from FOCL. She hurriedly wrote *Thanks, Gayle, I'd love to come to the hen do. See you on Saturday* and pressed send.

'That wasn't so difficult, was it?' Marjorie said. 'Now, just remember, you're not going there to have fun. You have a job to do.'

At four o'clock, Chantal's mum, Michelle, came into the library. June wanted to ask her about Chantal, who had been ignoring her ever since she'd refused to join FOCL, but Michelle was engrossed in swearing at the computer.

'Those council bastards,' she said, hitting the keyboard as June approached. 'They send me a text telling me a new property has come up, so I drop everything and race here. But by the time I've got onto their website, the sodding house has gone.'

'Not again, Michelle? I'm so sorry.'

'And what am I supposed to do if this place closes down? Do the council expect us all to have computers at home?'

'I was wondering, how's Chantal?'

'God knows. She's in a right grump, has been for ages. I've no idea what's got into her.'

June felt a pang of guilt; she was pretty sure she knew what was wrong with Chantal, and part of it was June's fault.

'Has she told you she wants to drop out of school?' Michelle asked.

'What? That's awful. What about going to university?'

'Says she doesn't want to. She's always been a right little geek, but now she says she wants to get a job instead.'

'Oh no. Would you ask her to come in here and I can have a chat with her?'

'I'll try but I'm not sure it'll do any good. She's going to that protest thing on Saturday – you could talk to her there.'

'I'm afraid I'm at a hen do on Saturday.' It was the truth, but June still felt terrible.

Michelle logged off the computer and got up to leave. 'Was that one of those management consultants I saw here first thing this morning?'

'What do you mean?' June said.

'With Marjorie. I was dropping the twins at nursery, so it was before eight.'

'What did they look like?'

'She was a skinny woman in fancy clothes. Not from round here, I'd say.'

June remembered the Mrs Coulter lookalike she'd seen here weeks ago with Marjorie. 'Did she have long, dark hair?'

'Yeah. She looked a bit snooty.'

'Shit!' June said, and then realised she was talking to a patron. 'Sorry.'

'What is it?'

'I don't know. Nothing, I hope.'

Marjorie was at the other side of the room, helping Mahmoud look something up in the Reference section. June watched her patiently explaining something to the boy. What was she up to? If Mrs Coulter was a management consultant, then why was Marjorie trying to keep her visits secret from June and everyone else? There was something suspicious going on here, June was sure of it.

She went into the toilet, locking the door behind her, and pulled out her mobile. Opening Twitter, she typed a private message to FOCL from Matilda.

Marjorie Spencer has been secretly showing people around the library. I saw her with a woman here weeks ago and I think the same woman was back here this morning before the library opened. Possibly a management consultant?

There was a rattle as someone tried to open the door, so June pressed send. Seconds later she heard a beep outside. June pulled the door open to see Mrs B staring at her phone screen.

'Fuck,' Mrs B said, and she turned and walked back across the library.

June watched as she went to Stanley's chair by the window and showed him her phone. June was dying to hear what they were saying but she didn't want to raise their suspicions by walking too close. She spotted the returns trolley sitting in the middle of the room where she'd abandoned it earlier, so she grabbed it and began to steer it over towards them. But the trolley was in a particularly uncooperative mood today, and as June pushed it right, the thing started veering off towards the left. As she coaxed it nearer to the window, she could hear snatches of the conversation.

'I think we need to pass this information on . . .' Stanley was saying.

'But how do we know we can trust this Matilda?' Mrs B said.

June edged the trolley closer.

'Does it matter who she is? What we need to do is—'

'Ouch!'

June swung round to see Vera bent over in pain.

'What the hell are you doing, you stupid girl? You ran over my foot.'

'I'm so sorry, Vera. Are you OK?'

'No, I'm not. I think you fractured my toe.'

'What's going on here?' Marjorie was pacing towards them.

'June deliberately ran me over with that trolley,' Vera said.

'What were you thinking, June?' Marjorie glared at her as she helped to lower Vera into a chair and elevate her leg.

June bit her lip. 'It was an accident.'

'She's always had it in for me,' Vera said.

'We should call an ambulance,' Marjorie said.

'Quite right. I've a good mind to sue the library – this is gross negligence.'

'For god's sake, stop making such a bloody fuss,' Mrs B said, walking over. 'There's a bus due soon, I'll help you get to Winton Hospital.'

Vera looked up at her with a frown. 'I think we'd better call an ambulance.'

'Don't be soft. The NHS is stretched enough without having to send out ambulances for bruised feet. Come on, stand up and I'll help you.'

Vera opened her mouth to complain but thought better of it. She stood up, hobbling after Mrs B.

'As if we didn't have enough problems already,' Marjorie hissed at June once they'd gone. 'Do you realise what will happen if she makes a formal complaint to the council? They're looking for excuses to shut us down, June. And you could well have handed them one on a plate.'

Chapter Fourteen

ON THE MORNING OF GAYLE'S HEN DO, June was awake at six a.m. in a cold sweat. Why had she told Alex she was going? Now, if she didn't go, he'd realise that she'd been lying and actually had no friends. But if she did go, June would have to see Gayle and all those terrifying girls from school again, plus Marjorie would probably fire her for not stopping the stripper.

'What am I going to do?' she groaned at Alan Bennett, who was lying at the end of the bed. He stared at her with contempt. 'You're right, Alan, of course you are.'

She pulled herself out of bed and opened her wardrobe. Gayle's email had said they had to come dressed as film heroines, so June stared at her clothes for inspiration. Two pairs of black jeans, one black skirt and five identical white blouses, all for work. Several grey cardigans, also for work. Her one black dress that she'd worn to her mum's funeral and some old faded T-shirts and jumpers. How was she going to fashion a fancy dress out of these?

June turned around and scanned her eyes along the bookcase in her room. This was where she kept some of her favourite childhood books, the ones that made her feel most comfortable and safe. One book caught her eye.

'Yes, Alan, Hermione Granger!'

June hurried through into her mum's room and pulled her wardrobe open. A rainbow of different colours greeted her, from a long patchwork coat to a gold sequined dress that her mum had loved. Nothing in this wardrobe was black or grey except for one item, which June rummaged around until she found. Her mum's old university graduation gown – perfect for a Harry Potter themed fancy dress.

Back in her own room, June put the gown on over a white shirt, her old school tie and black skirt, and then stood in front of the mirror. Now there was just her hair. She undid the tight plait that she slept with every night and allowed her hair to fall loose. June couldn't remember the last time she'd looked at her unruly curls like this: every morning she went straight from the plait to a neat bun and vice versa in the evening. But as much as she hated to admit it, her wild mass of hair did look quite like Hermione's in the early films.

At eleven o'clock, June pulled on her shoes, grabbed her bag and stepped outside into the suffocating August heat. She made her way slowly up the hill, keeping to the shady side so she didn't get too sweaty and make her hair even frizzier. Thankfully, Alex had told her he was going to London for the weekend, so there was no risk of him seeing her in this ridiculous outfit.

As June approached the church hall, she could hear the sound of music from inside. That was good; it must mean the FOCL event was underway and busy already. She slowed down as she walked past, keen to get a glimpse inside.

There were only a dozen people in the room, most of whom were FOCL members and their families. Stanley was manning what must have been the tombola, on which June could see a few bottles of wine, some homemade jam and a miserable-looking stuffed elephant, and Chantal was sitting behind the cake stall. To June's surprise, Vera was there too, prowling around the room with no sign of a foot injury. A large hand-painted banner was hanging on the back wall, but the ties had come loose, and all June could make out was 'ave Chalcot Libra'.

Mrs B was standing near to the door, shouting into a walkie-talkie, 'This is Eagle, come in Sparrow. The school choir will be here in ten minutes, I repeat ten minutes. We need more fucking people!'

Was this it? After all the work Mrs B and Stanley had put in, this was one of the saddest scenes June had ever seen. She turned and headed up the road, too embarrassed to watch any more. As she neared the bus stop, she saw there was a grey van parked up, with a woman in a blue suit leaning against it smoking. She looked familiar, and June was trying to work out what books she borrowed when she realised it was the local news journalist, Tessa something-or-other. She was talking to another woman who was fiddling with a fancy-looking camera.

'This is a complete waste of time,' Tessa was saying. 'There's no way we'll get a story out of this.'

'Want me to pack up the kit?' the camerawoman said.

'We might as well film the kids singing but we'll go straight after that.'

The bus pulled up and June jumped on board. As she took a seat, she watched Tessa drop the cigarette on the pavement and grind it out with her foot, a bored expression on her face. This was a disaster. How were they going to save the library when they couldn't even get on the local news?

It was almost twelve o'clock by the time June disembarked on a narrow country lane, and a bus journey spent reading *Rebecca* had done nothing to calm her nerves. She still had a mile-long walk to get to the hotel, and soon June felt sweat streaming off her body under the thick university gown.

Behind her, June heard thumping dance music, and when she turned around she saw a yellow convertible sports car roaring down the lane. There was no pavement, so she had to throw herself out of the way, landing face-first on the overgrown verge. June heard the car slow down, and when she rolled over, it had pulled up next to where she was lying, and the driver was giving her a strange look.

'You all right, love?' he said, turning down the music. He was wearing a white singlet vest that showed off his tanned, muscular physique.

'I'm fine, thanks,' June said, trying to pull herself up in a casual-looking manner.

'I don't suppose you know where Oakford Park hotel is? I'm lost.'

A thought occurred to June, one so ridiculous she felt herself turning even brighter red. No, it was far too dangerous. What if she'd got it wrong? Maybe this man was a serial killer? But if he was who she suspected he was, then this could be the answer to June's prayers.

'Erm, I was wondering . . . are you by any chance a . . . a stripper?' June said, aware her face was scarlet.

The man gave her a look of what she assumed was disapproval, but he'd clearly had so much Botox he couldn't raise his eyebrows. 'I prefer the term exotic dancer,' he said, primly. 'And you are?'

June held her breath for a moment before she replied. 'My name's Matilda. I'm going to Gayle's hen do.'

'Oh, thank god. I've been driving round for the last twenty minutes trying to find this damn hotel.'

'I can show you the way if you like?'

'Great, hop in. I'm Rocky.'

June brushed the grass off herself and climbed into the passenger's seat. 'You need to turn around.'

'You sure? I just came from that way.'

'I promise. I'll direct you.'

He executed a three-point turn and accelerated down the road. June had never been in a convertible before and, as the wind whipped her hair, she began to regret not having tied it up. Rocky started telling her about the routine he was going to do, and how he'd got a new policeman's outfit which had been shipped all the way from America and cost over a hundred quid.

'No one realises how expensive this stuff is, Matilda. They think we cut up a pair of trousers and stick on a bit of Velcro, but this is professional stuff, cutting-edge design.'

June tried to keep her eyes on the road, but she couldn't help glancing over at Rocky every now and then. His skin was the most extraordinary colour she'd ever seen, mahogany mixed with tangerine, and was covered in a layer of what she assumed must be oil. At one point he reached over to get something out of the glove box and June lunged out of the way in case he brushed against her.

'It's up here,' she said, as they crossed Chalcot bridge and drove down The Parade past the library.

'I thought it was a country hotel?'

'There was a last-minute change of venue. Take the left here, please.'

They pulled up outside the church hall. June was relieved to see the news van was still there, although the camerawoman was putting black cases into the back.

'Is this it?' Rocky said. 'The agency told me it was a high-end event. This is a shitty village hall.'

'The thing is, the bride loves the local library, which is being threatened with closure. So, she's combined her hen do with an event to support the library.' June knew it was a ridiculous story and she could see Rocky wasn't buying it either. 'There's a news crew here to film you.'

Rocky's face lit up. 'A TV crew? Why didn't you tell me?' He leapt out of the car and grabbed his bag from the back seat. 'Let's get started.'

'Great. When you get inside ask for Mrs Bransworth and tell her that Matilda sent you.'

'Aren't you coming in?'

'I've got a few other hen do bits to sort out first. Good luck though.'

June got out of the car and walked away before anyone inside the church hall spotted her. When she reached the van, Tessa was on her mobile phone. 'Yeah, complete wash-out. No point even cutting it.'

June gave a small cough. 'Excuse me?'

'No autographs,' Tessa said, not bothering to look up.

'I don't . . . I think you might want to go back in there and start filming again.'

'There's no point, that's not a news story.'

'It's about to get a lot more interesting.'

'What, they're going to make balloon animals?'

'Please, trust me. You're going to want to see what's going on in there.'

Tessa frowned. 'This better not be another waste of my time. Come on, Cleo.' She nodded at the camerawoman, who sighed as she pulled the camera back out of its bag.

June stood at the bus stop as she didn't want to risk getting any closer. She watched Tessa and Cleo step inside. A moment later she heard music starting to blast out from the church hall, the opening bars of some R&B song, followed by a loud, shocked scream. June caught a flash of Rocky as he strolled past the door, wearing nothing but black leather chaps and an American cop's hat, and couldn't help but laugh. If only Alex were here to see this.

'You coming, love?'

She turned around to see the bus had pulled up, the driver staring at her through the open door. June climbed on board and was still chuckling to herself as the bus pulled away.

Chapter Fifteen

BY THE TIME JUNE approached the hotel it was past one o'clock and she was very late. As she hurried in through the front door, she caught sight of her reflection in a mirror and groaned. She had a huge grass stain on her blouse from where she'd thrown herself on the verge, and the ride in Rocky's convertible had wreaked havoc with her hair, which was now a giant halo of frizz. June tried to flatten it, but it was no use; she was going to have to go in looking like this. At least the party was fancy dress so there would be others looking equally ridiculous.

But as soon as June walked into the hotel bar, her heart sank. Twenty or so women were standing around drinking champagne, all wearing the most unbelievably glamorous outfits. There was Becky, who'd come as Audrey Hepburn in *Breakfast at Tiffany's*, and Tara, dressed as Marilyn Monroe from *Some Like it Hot*. In the middle stood Gayle, her blonde hair elaborately piled on top of her head and wearing a huge crinoline gown, a resplendent Marie Antoinette.

'Is that June Jones?' Tara said, and everyone turned to look at her. 'I can't believe *you're* here!'

June hung by the door, wishing she could disappear into thin air.

'Oh my god, you look exactly the same as you did at school,' Gayle said, coming over and kissing her on both cheeks. 'You're even still wearing school uniform!'

'I'm actually dressed as—'

'Where are you living these days?' interrupted Tara.

'Are you single? Married?' Becky said, joining them. 'We need all the gossip.'

June shrank back as they gathered round her. She had a sudden flashback to these same girls laughing at her old-fashioned clothes or the book she was reading.

'Erm, I still live in Chalcot,' June said, her voice betraying her with a wobble.

'And what do you do?' Becky said.

'I work in the library.'

'I can't believe you're still working for my mum,' Gayle said, wrinkling her nose.

'Well, good on you,' Becky said. 'I love libraries, they're so quaint.'

'I haven't been into one in years,' Tara said. 'I don't know why anyone bothers now you can buy books so cheaply on Amazon.'

'What about your love life? Anyone special?' Becky said.

Alex's face flickered into June's mind and she quickly shook her head. He'd told June he was spending the weekend with friends, and ever since she'd been trying not to think about him with the WhatsApp girl, Ellie.

'No, I'm single,' she said, and saw the look of disappointment on the three women's faces. Gayle walked off to talk to some other guests, and there was a moment of awkward silence while June tried to think of something else to say. 'So, what do you both do?'

'I'm a lawyer,' said Tara. 'And Becky's an interior designer.'

'Interior designer slash life coach,' Becky corrected. 'Although I'm on maternity leave at the moment with my son, Monty.'

'Wow,' June said. How did they both have such impressive careers at just twenty-eight?

A woman dressed as Wonder Woman came to join them. 'I've been trying to call the stripper for the past half hour and he's not answering,' she said to Tara. 'Are you sure you gave him the right address?'

'Of course I did.'

'What the hell are we going to do? He's supposed to be performing after lunch.'

'We'll just have to come up with something else,' Tara said. 'Come on, everyone, it's time for food,' she called out to the room, and they all filed through to the conservatory.

A long table had been set up with the most amazing-looking spread. There was a rush as people tried to secure seats near the bride-to-be. June took a place at the far side of the table and found herself between Wonder Woman and someone dressed as Lara Croft.

'How do you know Gayle?' Wonder Woman said as she sat down.

June's knee was jiggling, and she pressed her hand down to stop it. 'We were at school together.'

'And what do you do?'

'I'm a library assistant.'

'Right.' Wonder Woman's eyes glazed over and she turned to talk to Princess Leia on her other side.

June eyed the table. There were platters filled with delicate crust-less sandwiches, exquisite-looking cakes and scones. She hadn't eaten anything since her toast this morning and her stomach let out a loud rumble. She reached for her tiny plate and piled it up with three sandwiches, a scone and a miniature chocolate cake, before realising that the others had all put a single sandwich on theirs. Next to her, Wonder Woman peeled the smoked salmon out of her sandwich, eating it and leaving the bread on the plate. Both she and Lara Croft were still deep in conversation with other people, but June was happy to be ignored. Once she'd finished her plate, she checked her phone. There were three text messages from Marjorie.

How's it going?
Please send an update on the hen do.
WELL???

June put the phone back in her bag and helped herself to some more cake.

'Right, girls,' Tara said, tapping her glass with a spoon. 'Shall we play a little game to break the ice?' She waited for the chatter to die down. 'Most of us know each other well but there are a few unfamiliar faces. So, we thought it would be fun to play "Never Have I Ever", so we can all get to know each other a bit more . . . intimately.'

There was laughter round the table, and June felt her stomach contract. She'd never heard of this game but it sounded ominous.

'I'll kick things off,' Tara said. 'And remember, if you *have* done the thing I say then you drink, and if you *haven't* then you don't. That clear?'

There were murmurs of assent, and most of the women picked up their champagne glasses in anticipation.

'OK, so I'll start with an easy one. Never have I ever been arrested.'

June looked around the table; no one had taken a drink except a woman dressed as a Playboy Bunny.

'Faye, what did you do?' Gayle said, shocked.

'Speeding,' Faye said with a shrug, and everyone laughed.

'My turn,' Becky said. 'Never have I ever joined the Mile-High Club.'

There was more laughter as several women took swigs. June wasn't sure what the Mile-High Club was, but she doubted she was a member.

'Never have I ever cheated on my partner,' Lara Croft said, and there were 'ooohs' as a surprising number took guilty sips.

'Never have I ever visited Australia,' someone else said, and lots of the women took drinks. June clenched her hands in her lap to stop them trembling.

'Never have I ever streaked,' Wonder Woman said, to much laughter.

'Never have I ever been camping.'

June stared at her full glass, willing them all to hurry up and finish.

'Never have I ever been fired from a job.'

'Never have I ever had sex in a public place.'

'Never have I ever been bungee jumping.'

June closed her eyes, her heart pounding. When would this torture end?

'Never have I ever stayed up dancing until six a.m.'

'Never have I ever been pole dancing.'

'Never have I ever had sex.'

'June?'

It took a moment for June to realise that everyone had gone quiet, and when she opened her eyes, they were all staring at her. She sank back in her chair.

'Are you OK, hun?' Gayle said, and June nodded mutely.

'You understand the rules of the game, don't you?' Tara said. 'Because as a joke someone just said never have I ever had sex and you didn't take a drink.'

The tie round June's neck felt tight and she tried to loosen it.

'You're meant to drink when you've done something,' Tara continued. 'Unless you're actually still a virgin?'

One woman laughed at this but everyone else was silent, looking at June with a mixture of sympathy and horror.

'I . . . I need the toilet.' June stood up too quickly and felt a wave of dizziness. She tried to grab hold of the back of her chair but knocked it over and it clattered to the floor, as she turned and ran towards the door.

Chapter Sixteen

JUNE BURST INTO THE toilet and slammed the cubicle door shut behind her. Her breath was coming out in short, ragged bursts and she felt like she was being strangled. She yanked off her tie and tried to loosen her shirt's top button, but her hands were shaking too much and her elbows kept knocking on the walls as she wrestled with the collar. Just as she thought she was going to collapse, the button popped off and June's shirt burst open. She immediately felt the pressure on her throat reduce and she sank down onto the toilet seat and put her head between her knees.

Slowly, June's breathing returned to normal, but with it came the crushing humiliation. How could she have done so little with her life? She'd never streaked or bungee jumped, never been clubbing or danced all night with friends. She'd never visited Australia because she'd never left England. And she'd never even kissed a man, let alone had sex.

Instead, June realised with a shiver, her life's achievements could be summed up in one sad sentence: she'd worked at a library and her mum had died. That was the sum total of her twenty-eight years, the miserable epitaph that would be written on her grave.

There was a bang and June jumped as the toilet door swung open. She hurriedly pulled her knees up to her chest so whoever it was wouldn't see her feet under the cubicle door.

'My god, that was awkward,' said a voice that she recognised as Becky's.

'Well, it's hardly a surprise. She always was a weirdo at school,' said Tara. 'Remember how she followed Gayle round in our first year like a lovesick puppy?'

One of them turned on a tap and there was the sound of gushing water.

'I wonder why Gayle invited her?' Becky said.

'She didn't. Apparently June begged Gayle's mum to get her an invitation.'

'No way, that's so tragic. Can I borrow your lippie?'

'Sure.'

There was silence, and June held her breath.

'I wonder why she didn't just lie and pretend she'd done some of those things,' Becky said, after a moment. 'Do you think she's really a virgin?'

'It wouldn't surprise me.'

'God, imagine being twenty-eight and never having done anything. I wonder if she's got many friends?'

'Well, she didn't have any at school, so I doubt it. Do you want a spray of perfume?'

'Yes, please.'

A strong floral smell filled the air, and June held her nose so she wouldn't sneeze.

'Do you remember her mum got sick when we were doing our A-Levels?' Tara said. 'I heard she died while we were at uni.'

'Did she?'

'I'm sure I heard that. And I don't think June has any other family.'

'Man, that's grim. Shall we get back out there?'

'Yep. Did you see what Alicia's wearing, she looks so . . .'

June heard the door close and the voices fade away. She counted to twenty before she unlocked the cubicle and stepped out. The perfume still hung in the air, sickly sweet and cloying at the back of her throat, and for a moment June thought she might be sick. She stared at her reflection in the mirror: mascara streaked down her cheeks and her hair wild around her head, like some demented clown from a horror movie. There was no way she could go back out there and face those awful women with their pitying smiles and laughter. She had to get out of here, now.

June picked up her phone to call Linda for a lift, before remembering that she'd gone to visit her daughter for the weekend. Sighing, she'd started to put the phone back in her bag when she saw a text message on the screen.

Alex Chen

Hope the hen do is fun - say congrats to Gayle from me! x

At the sight of Alex's name, June felt a flood of relief so strong that, without thinking, she pressed dial and held the phone to her ear.

'Alex, can you talk?' she said when he answered. Her voice came out as a raspy whisper.

'Of course. Are you all right?'

'No. I'm . . .' June felt a sob building and tried to stifle it.

'Are you OK? What happened?' Alex's voice was full of concern.

'The hen . . . it's terrible . . .' was all she managed to get out.

'Where are you now?'

'Hiding in the toilets.'

'You should get out of there. Can someone pick you up?'

June took a deep breath. 'Alex, I'm sorry to ask but I don't have a single person I can call. Please can you—'

'Al, have you seen my black dress anywhere?'

The voice was young, husky and female, and June remembered with a jolt that Alex was in London.

'Sorry, I didn't realise . . .' she mumbled.

'No, that's OK. Hang on one sec . . . Ellie, I'm just . . .' There was a rustling sound as Alex moved the phone away, and June pictured him covering the microphone with his hand. She could make out the odd muffled word.

'Girl from school . . .'

'Lives alone . . .'

'Doesn't have anyone . . .'

June felt each word like a slap across the face.

'Sorry about that,' Alex said when he came back on the line. 'What were you saying?'

June was so mortified that it took a moment for her to find any words. 'Nothing. I'd better go.'

'No, it's fine. Do you want me to—'

'Sorry to bother you. Bye.'

June hung up and looked in the mirror, feeling a wave of revulsion at the pathetic face staring back at her. She wanted to scream in humiliation. Why the hell had she called Alex when he was with his girlfriend? She imagined the two of them laughing about this weird girl from school, who was so tragic she didn't have any friends to ask for help. Or worse still, not laughing but pitying her.

Fighting back hot tears, June threw her phone into her bag and hurried out of the toilets.

June caught a taxi home and spent the rest of the after-noon hiding with the curtains drawn against the bright August sunshine. She tried to read *Great Expectations*, but every time there was a scene with Miss Havisham, she felt a creeping sense of recognition, and eventually cast the book aside. She started cleaning, but each picture and ornament seemed to be mocking her. *How can you still be a virgin at twenty-eight?* the china girl with the book teased, as June dusted her. *What are you so afraid of, Junebug?* her mum asked out of every framed photo. Even Alan Bennett got in on the act. *You're such a loser*, he seemed to say, as June fed him. *You've hidden away in this house rather than get out there and live your life.*

That evening, as June lay slumped on the sofa listlessly watching an old episode of *Four in a Bed*, she heard her phone buzz. She glanced down and saw a message from Alex. At the sight of his name, June felt a stab of pain at the memory of their phone conversation and his words to Ellie. *Girl from school . . . Lives alone . . . Doesn't have anyone . . .* Alex had been the one person who June could call anything near to a friend, but now he knew how sad her life really was.

She picked up the phone and clicked on his message.

Alex Chen

Hey, hope ur ok? Dad told me he just saw the library protest event on the local news - I can't believe those old FOCL fuddy-duddies booked a stripper! Great news for the campaign though x

146

June sat up abruptly. In all her self-pity, she hadn't once thought about the library event this morning. She quickly searched on her phone to find the local news and pressed play. There was a report on some local building development, but June couldn't concentrate on it, willing the story to hurry up.

And then suddenly Tessa was on the screen, standing outside the church hall.

'Six libraries in Dunningshire are threatened with closure by the council. But only one has come up with such a novel way of drawing attention to their cause.'

The news piece cut to inside and there was Rocky, wearing some kind of S&M cowboy outfit, grinding away in the centre of the church hall. There was a small, shocked-looking crowd watching him, and in the middle stood Jackson, his mouth hanging open.

'With just seven weeks to go until the council's consultation ends, organisers in Chalcot have laid on an eye-catching protest,' Tessa was saying.

The piece went to Mrs Bransworth, looking dazed. 'Er, we thought this might help draw attention to our campaign,' she stuttered, as Rocky thrust and gyrated behind her.

Now Stanley was on screen, standing in front of the library. 'We may only be a small library but it's vital to this community. People rely on it for so much more than just books. It will be a travesty if the council shut it down.'

And then the picture was back on Rocky, this time wearing nothing but a tiny thong. As the camera panned around it showed Vera sitting in front of him, rubbing what looked like whipped cream into Rocky's chest, a look of absolute concentration on her face.

The news piece ended, and June sat staring at her phone in stunned silence. It had worked. Rocky's performance had got the library protest on the news. A smile slowly spread across her face, and she laughed out loud, startling Alan Bennett, who'd been sleeping next to her.

'I did it, Alan,' she said, as the cat looked at her in confusion. 'I actually did it.'

June picked up a picture frame from the table next to the sofa. It held a photo of her mum, taken years ago outside Chalcot Library. Beverley was grinning, the clock tower rising above her head as she squinted at the camera. June brushed some dust from the glass.

'I'm sorry I've been so hopeless, Mum,' she whispered. 'I know I've been wasting my life and I've let you down. But I'm going to try to change that now, I promise.'

Chapter Seventeen

WHEN JUNE ARRIVED FOR her shift on Monday afternoon, she found Vera camped out at a table inside the library, telling everyone who'd listen about her exploits with Rocky.

'You know, I thought it might be shaving foam, but it was real whipped cream. I had a taste,' she was telling an excited crowd of ladies from the Knit and Natter group.

'It was the most remarkable sight,' Stanley said, joining June as she started tidying up the noticeboard. 'He had three different outfits: policeman, cowboy and fireman. And he had Velcro on his trousers so he could rip them off easily. Such a prudent idea – I might try it with my suit.'

'Stanley, look at this,' said Chantal, coming over to him with her phone. 'Before the news went out yesterday, we had one hundred and eleven likes on our Facebook page. Now we have almost a thousand.'

'That's wonderful!'

'People keep messaging, asking what we're doing next.'

'We need to ask Mrs Bransworth. She'll have a plan.'

'She's here now,' Chantal said, pointing towards the door.

'Here's the hero of the hour,' said Stanley. 'Three cheers for Mrs Bransworth.'

'Stop it,' Mrs B snapped. 'That stripper had nothing to do with me; I disapprove of sexual exploitation in any form.'

'Well, who organised it then?' Stanley said.

Mrs B lowered her voice, and June had to strain to hear her.

'The stripper told me he'd been redirected to the protest by someone called Matilda.'

As Mrs B said the name, June almost dropped the pile of leaflets she was holding. She quickly turned her back on the group.

'Who the hell is Matilda?' Vera said.

'Matilda is our secret informant,' Stanley said. 'She sends us information via Tweeter.'

'You mean Twitter,' Chantal said.

'Yes. She's our spy and sends us twits. She's the one who told us about Brian Spencer at the pub and Marjorie's secret meetings with the management consultants. And now she's done this for us.'

'Well, I may not approve of her methods, but Matilda has saved our arses once again,' Mrs B said. 'Now, we need to strike while the iron's hot.'

'What about staging something outside County Hall?' Stanley said. 'We could make placards and sing songs.'

'Yes, like in the American civil rights movement,' Mrs B said.

'Don't tell us you were there as well,' Vera muttered under her breath.

The group carried on chatting, but June moved away. A County Hall protest was a good idea, but what the library really needed was more books being taken out. The council had said they'd be basing their decision on issue numbers, and June knew that right now Chalcot's were perilously low. She glanced back at Mrs B, Stanley and Chantal, and then she pulled her phone out and quickly typed a Twitter message from Matilda.

'Get over here, now!'

Marjorie was watching June across the library floor, her eyes narrow. 'What was that stunt you pulled with the stripper?' she whispered, when June joined her.

'I did that for you, Marjorie. It was the only way I could stop him performing at the hen do.'

'But in the process, you put the good name of Chalcot Library in disrepute. I'll be a laughing stock at the next Library Managers' monthly meet-up.' Marjorie fanned herself with a paperback. 'Does anyone know it was you who sent him?'

'No one, I did it anonymously.'

'That's something, at least. If the council found out, then we'd both be out on our ears.'

'You have to admit, it was good publicity for the library campaign though,' June said.

'Hmm . . . So how was Gayle's hen do?'

'It was fine,' June said, praying that Gayle hadn't told her mum what happened.

'Well, I appreciate you helping me out. As a thank you, I'll make sure you're invited to the wedding. Evening only, of course.'

'Oh, there's no need.'

'Don't be silly, I know you want to come.'

'But really—'

'This conversation is over, I have lots to do.' Marjorie turned to walk away, then looked back at June. 'Just remember what I said. The council must never find out you had anything to do with that stripper or FOCL. If they do, I won't be able to protect you.'

For the rest of the week, June did whatever she could to help FOCL secretly. She researched other successful library campaigns around the country and forwarded their details via Matilda. And when Marjorie went to do outreach on Wednesday morning, June plucked up the courage to have a search around her office in case she could discover any information about Mrs Coulter, the management consultant. She didn't find anything, but the adrenalin from her undercover spying made her jumpy for the rest of the day.

On Thursday, June was helping a patron with his online passport application when she heard a familiar voice behind her. She'd been avoiding Alex since their awful phone call, and had skipped her Chinese takeaway on Monday night, so the sudden sound of him nearby made June's skin flush hot. She glanced over her shoulder and saw that he was deep in conversation with Stanley.

'Did she say anything else?' Stanley was saying, in a low voice.

'No, just what I told you already.'

'But what do you think it means? Should I—'

'Excuse me, miss?' The man June was assisting was staring at her. 'What do I need to do now?'

'Sorry,' June said, her whole body burning with shame. Were they talking about her call to Alex on Saturday? It was bad enough that he'd found out how pathetic she was, but now Stanley knew as well. June kept her back turned to them as she helped fill out the man's application, praying that Stanley and Alex wouldn't notice she was there.

But a few minutes later, she felt someone walk behind her.

'Hey, stranger.'

June couldn't bear to turn around and see Alex's pitying face, so she kept her eyes fixed on the computer screen in front of her. 'Hi.'

'How are you?'

'OK.' June typed something on the keyboard, hoping he couldn't see that her hands were shaking.

'You didn't come into the takeaway on Monday, I was worrying about—'

'I'm sorry, I'm just helping a customer here,' June said, before he could finish. She heard a faint sigh behind her, and then a moment later she could sense that Alex was gone.

June finished and headed towards the desk. Stanley was sitting in his chair and June saw him glance at her as she walked past, but he said nothing. As she got back to the desk, Mrs Bransworth came storming in through the front door.

'Those arseholes!' she shouted. 'The cheating, conniving bastards!'

Everyone in the library turned to look at her.

'What's wrong?' Stanley said.

'I just went into the shop to see how many signatures we have on our petition, and Naresh told me that someone has stolen it.'

'No! What about the one in the pub?'

'That's gone too. They said it disappeared from the bar yesterday.'

'My god. We had nearly five hundred signatures supporting the library, all lost.'

'We'll have to start again,' Mrs B said.

'But what if it gets taken again?'

Neither of them spoke for a moment, and June could see them both desperately searching for ideas.

'Maybe we should try one of those online petitions like Chantal suggested?' Stanley said.

'I suppose,' Mrs B said, although she sounded unsure.

'I can't believe someone would stoop so low as to steal a petition.' Stanley was shaking his head. 'Who would do that?'

'Probably the council,' Mrs B said. 'Unless it was someone closer to home . . .'

As she said this, she looked straight at June. For a second their eyes met, and June quickly looked away.

'Don't think I haven't noticed you creeping around eavesdropping on us,' Mrs B shouted across at her, so loudly that everyone in the library went quiet. 'What would your mother say if she knew you were working to get this library closed? You're a disgrace, June, and your mum would be ashamed of you.'

June felt Mrs B's words like a knife in her heart. For a second she wanted to shout that she was Matilda, that she was helping them fight, but instead she turned and rushed towards the back of the library, tears blurring her vision.

Was that really what everybody thought about her, Stanley included? June closed her eyes, willing herself not to cry. It took her a few minutes to compose herself and, by the time she returned to the desk, Mrs B and Stanley had moved over to the computers and out of earshot. June watched them hunched over the keyboard together. By the look of things, they were setting up an online petition, which was all very well but how would anyone in the village find out about it? At least with the paper petition it had been left in prominent places so people could see it, but June knew that lots of the villagers wouldn't know the first thing about an online one. If only there was a way she could spread the word, without anyone knowing it was her.

June looked at Stanley and Mrs B again, and then an idea came to her and she felt a fizz of excitement. Yes, that was exactly what Matilda would do.

A little before midnight, June picked up her rucksack and left the house, making her way back up the hill towards The Parade. The streets were empty at this time of night, but she'd still taken the precaution of wearing dark clothes and an old baseball cap of her mum's, the peak pulled down low over her face.

The library building was dark as she approached, the clock tower silhouetted against the moon. June checked that nobody was around as she unlocked the front door and slipped through. Inside, the library was pitch-black, but June knew this space better than anywhere, and was able to manoeuvre between the tables and shelves without bumping into a thing. When she reached the computers, she switched one on, turning the monitor so its glow couldn't be seen through the window, and began to type.

An hour later, June crept out of the library and re-locked the front door. The rucksack on her back was heavier now, and she pulled it over both shoulders as she crept away from the library towards the village shop. Across the road, a dog walker was strolling in front of the pub, whistling to himself, and June huddled into the shadows until he passed. Then she reached into her rucksack and set to work.

The following morning, June arrived at the library at nine o'clock as usual. She'd had only two hours' sleep, but despite that she hummed to herself as she went through her setting-up routine. At nine fifteen she heard the front door swing open, and Marjorie bustled in.

'Have you seen it out there?' she shrieked, by way of a greeting.

'What's wrong, Marjorie?'

'The Parade has been vandalised!'

'Has it?' June said, with all the fake surprise she could muster. 'I can't have been paying attention on my way in this morning.'

'Well, I don't know how you could have missed it. Every single building has these plastered all over the front.' Marjorie waved a piece of paper at June and then started to read from it. '*If you care about books and education, sign the Chalcot Library petition ... If you believe that every child deserves the best start in life, sign the Chalcot Library petition ... If you want to support those most at need in your local community*, etcetera etcetera. And then there's a link to some online petition thing.'

'Wow. FOCL must have done them,' June said, trying to keep her face neutral.

'There are hundreds of these posters out there – the village looks terrible. I have to call Brian, as chair of the parish council he'll be furious about this mess.'

Marjorie stormed towards the office and June turned to look out of the library front window. The Parade was busy this morning, small groups of people clustering in front of the pub and the bakery to read the posters that had been pasted up overnight. June pulled her phone out and opened up a browser with the new FOCL library petition. Seven hundred and eighty-nine signatures, it said.

She allowed herself a small smile, slipped the phone back in her pocket, and carried on with her work.

Chapter Eighteen

JUNE WATCHED THE MAN, in his mid-twenties and dressed in unseasonably warm clothes, as he slumped in the corner playing on his phone. He had barely looked up from the screen in the past hour, absorbed in whatever game he was playing. His skin was pale, like he didn't go outside much, and June had decided that he was a vampire, hiding out in the library to avoid the blazing sun. Earlier, he'd eaten some roast beef Monster Munch, so clearly he was craving meat. Any minute now he was going to throw his phone aside and walk over towards Vera, who would look up at him in alarm. He would lean forward and open his mouth, and then say—

'This is a public library, not a knocking shop!'

Marjorie was marching two red-faced teenagers out of the toilet. 'I know it's hot outside, but you'll have to find somewhere else to go.' She led them to the front door and then watched as they scurried away, hand in hand.

It was late August, and a heatwave had brought Chalcot to a standstill. The hanging baskets on The Parade had long since wilted, the shop sold out of ice cream within hours of each new delivery, and a hosepipe ban was driving all the gardeners crazy. The coolest building in the village was the library, where the thick stone walls and high ceilings made the temperature almost bearable.

As a result, it was also the busiest building in the village. When June unlocked the doors every morning, she found Stanley joined by a queue of impatient pensioners, who'd barge past her to claim the prime real estate of a window seat. They stayed there all day, fanning themselves with leaflets from the rack, complaining about their swollen ankles and demanding cups of water. And when she wasn't running errands for them, June was in the Children's Room acting as amateur entertainer to dozens of restless little ones, while their parents and carers stared listlessly at their phones.

Marjorie came to join June at the desk. 'Are you still going into Winton this afternoon?'

'I'm not sure I can face it in this heat. Do you need me to do an extra shift here?'

'No. I need three silver cake platters from the catering shop on Winton high street. Can you collect them for me and drop them back here?'

'OK.'

'Gayle has announced that as well as the main wedding cake she also wants cupcakes, so now I have to bake one hundred of those on top of everything else.'

June busied herself with some stock so she wouldn't have to engage in conversation about the wedding. The thought of that hen do still made her whole body ache with humiliation two weeks later.

'By the way, do you know what those so-called Friends of Chalcot Library are up to?' Marjorie said. 'They've been suspiciously quiet since those bloody posters.'

'I have no idea.'

'Well, keep your ear to the ground. I don't want any more nasty surprises.'

At midday, June left the library and caught the bus, disembarking on Winton high street into a sea of shoppers and pedestrians. She hated crowds at the best of times, let alone in this weather, but she put her head down and forced herself to join them. All she needed was to collect Marjorie's cake trays and pop to M&S to buy her usual value pack of plain white high-legged briefs, and then she could catch the bus back.

As she made her way up the high street, June noticed a shop to her left that she'd not spotted before. It had a purple frontage and in the window was a mannequin wearing some black underwear. It was much fancier than the kind of thing June wore and probably twice the price. But, on the plus side, it would save her another ten minutes jostling in the crowds all the way to M&S. June swerved left and headed in.

'Hey, can I help you?' A young woman with facial piercings greeted June as she walked through the door.

'Thanks, but I'm just browsing,' June said. She moved into the shop, but the assistant followed her.

'We've got fifteen per cent off all toys at the moment, so you've come at the perfect time.'

June hadn't realised she was in a toy shop. She looked around her for the first time and her eyes fell on a display holding dozens of boxes containing what looked like lipsticks. She picked one up and almost dropped it on the floor. 'Jesus, is that a—?'

'That's the seven-speed purple python, it's one of our bestsellers.'

June was so surprised that she didn't know where to look.

'We've also got a two-for-one on the vibrating bullet.' The woman offered her a small, spherical object.

'Sorry, I thought this was an underwear shop.'

'We've got lingerie too. Over here.' The assistant led her to a rail behind them, where a selection of lacy underwear was hanging up. With relief, June spotted a pair of plain-looking white knickers and picked them up, only to see that they didn't have a crotch.

'I'm guessing you're new to all of this. The beaded rabbit is a good entry-level toy,' the girl said, handing June a box containing a giant, pink object.

June was desperate to get out of the shop, but she didn't know how to politely escape from this overenthusiastic sales assistant, who was now approaching her with a terrifying-looking silver object.

'I'll just take these, please,' June said, thrusting the crotchless knickers towards her.

'Great choice. There's a matching peep-hole bra and suspenders, if you'd like to get those too?'

'This will be fine, thanks.'

'Would you like a loyalty card? You get—'

'It's OK thanks, I've got to run. Thanks so much for your help.' June grabbed the purple bag and sprinted out of the shop. As she did so, her body collided with someone walking past.

'Well, I never . . .'

June looked up to see Linda grinning at her, her eyebrows raised. 'Good for you, love.'

'I thought it was an underwear shop,' June blurted out.

'Buy anything nice?' Linda was eyeing the bag in her hand. 'Tell me, is it something for you? Or a present for Alex?'

'Stop it!' June shrieked, and Linda threw back her head in laughter.

'Oh, I wish you could see your face now. Come on, I'll buy you a drink while you cool down.' She led June across the road and into a coffee shop. 'You find a table and I'll grab us some teas.'

June found them a spot by the window. She'd never been in here before and it was cavernous, with wooden floors and exposed brickwork. Dozens of people were sitting at small tables, chatting or working on their laptops. It was smart but June preferred the independent cafe up the road, with its mismatched sofas and eccentric proprietor.

'Here, I got us a piece of cake too,' Linda said, putting the tray down on the table.

'Thanks, Linda, you're my saviour once again.'

'I'm glad I bumped into you, I keep meaning to pop round.'

'What's Alan Bennett done now?'

'It's not him. I noticed this in the window of the village shop the other day and thought it might be of interest to you.' Linda rummaged around in her handbag and pulled out a crumpled piece of paper, handing it to June.

Do you have any old books you no longer need? Cherry Tree Retirement Home is in desperate need of second-hand books for our residents. All genres welcome.

'I just thought this could be a great home for some of your mum's old books,' Linda said.

'Thanks,' June said, stuffing the flyer into her bag before Linda could say anything else.

'So, how's it going with Alex? Have you had another date?'

'It wasn't a date. I told you, we're just friends.'

'That's a shame. He's so handsome – don't you fancy him?'

'No,' June said, not looking Linda in the eye. 'Besides, he has a girlfriend.'

'Are you sure? George never mentioned one, and I've grilled him about Alex.'

'He definitely does.' June skewered a piece of carrot cake with vehemence.

'Has Alex told you about her?'

'No, but I heard her on the phone.'

Linda frowned. 'Weird. I wonder why he'd keep her a secret from everyone? Maybe she's really ugly or stupid or something.'

'Linda, you can't say that! I'm sure she's beautiful and smart.' June pictured a tall woman with long, silky hair and a husky voice, wearing a sexy black dress. She imagined her and Alex together on a date, laughing about that stupid girl in Chalcot who had no friends or life. June stuffed a large forkful of cake in her mouth.

'Oh, well, that's a shame. Still, there are plenty more fish in the sea. You know my Martin is single again?'

June could feel Linda's eyes on her; she'd been trying to set June up with her youngest son ever since they were teenagers. June picked up her mug to take a drink so she wouldn't have to reply. But as she went to take a sip, she caught sight of the logo on the side of the cup. At first glance it looked like a red swirl, but when she looked at it closer, she could see it was two intertwined 'C's. June stared at it, trying to place where she'd seen this image before.

'No!' she said, slamming the mug down.

'What? Martin's not that bad, is he?'

'This image – is it for this cafe?'

'Of course, it's the Cuppa Coffee logo.'

'Cuppa Coffee. Oh my god.'

'What's wrong, love? You look like you've seen a ghost.'

June pictured the Mrs Coulter lookalike she'd seen in the library all those weeks ago. 'I've seen this logo before, on the clipboard of a woman at the library.'

'So what?' Linda said.

'She was meeting with Marjorie and I thought she was a management consultant, but what if she wasn't? What if she works for Cuppa Coffee?'

'I'm sorry, love, I'm not following you.'

June looked at Linda, her eyes wide. 'I hope I'm wrong, Linda, but I think Cuppa Coffee might be trying to buy Chalcot Library.'

Chapter Nineteen

WHEN JUNE ARRIVED AT the library an hour later, she expected to find the place in uproar, but it was as calm as ever. There was no sign of Mrs B or Stanley, and when June checked her phone there was still no reply to the message she'd sent from Matilda. Perhaps they'd not seen it yet?

'About time,' Marjorie said, joining June by the door. 'Did you get me those cake trays?'

'I'm so sorry, I forgot.'

'For god's sake, I asked you to do one simple task . . .' Marjorie rolled her eyes. 'I'll go and get them now, so you'll have to close up on your own.'

June watched her march out of the building. Was Marjorie really involved in a plot to close the library? June had spent the whole bus ride back from Winton wondering about this. On the one hand it seemed an absurd idea: Marjorie had worked at the library for thirty years and, however annoying the woman might be, she'd always seemed devoted to the place. But June had seen Marjorie and the Cuppa Coffee woman here together, heard them discussing the building. And she'd overheard Marjorie's husband talking about bribing county councillors about something. What if Brian and Marjorie were working to get the library closed so a Cuppa Coffee could open here instead? June had said all of this in her Twitter messages to FOCL, so why weren't Mrs Bransworth and Stanley here now, kicking up a fuss?

The rest of the afternoon crept by. June tried to focus on her work, but she couldn't concentrate and kept checking her phone. At five o'clock, the last of the visitors left, and June was shutting down the computers when she heard the sound of the front door opening.

'I'm sorry, we're closed,' she called out, but when she turned around, Stanley was standing in the doorway. June was about to blurt out about Cuppa Coffee, before remembering that he still had no idea she was Matilda.

'Don't mind me, you carry on as you are,' Stanley said, and he walked over to his chair and sat down, placing a bag at his feet.

'Um, it's closing time,' June said. 'You need to leave.' Something about the serene expression on Stanley's face was making her nervous.

'I'm afraid I'm not going anywhere, my dear.'

'What do you mean?'

Stanley glanced around the library. 'Is Marjorie here?'

'No, it's just me.'

'Well, in that case, I suppose I'll have to tell you.'

'Tell me what?'

Stanley sat up straight in his chair. 'As of now, I am officially occupying Chalcot Library.'

June did a double take. 'What?'

'FOCL have a whistle-blower who has informed us that Marjorie and Brian are working with a private corporation to get the library closed. So, I've decided to occupy the library until the council finally listens to what we have to say.'

'But I can't let you stay here out of operating hours. Marjorie would kill me.'

'I'll tell her I hid in the toilet when you locked up. That way, you can go home now, and you won't have anything to do with it.'

June didn't know how to respond. Surely she'd be sacked for gross misconduct if she left Stanley in the library? But how was she supposed to get him out? He might have been eighty-two, but he was much bigger than her; she could hardly manhandle him out of the building.

'Please, you can't sleep here. Can you find another way to protest?'

He gave her a small, sad smile. 'I'm sorry, but I can't walk away and let the library be sold out from under our feet.'

June looked at him helplessly. 'But I can't just leave you here.'

'Don't worry, I shall look after this place as if it were my own home.'

'But Marjorie will—'

'Never mind Marjorie,' Stanley interrupted. 'Sometimes we have to break the rules if we care about something, June. And I care a great deal about Chalcot Library.'

June paused, paralysed with indecision. Should she call Marjorie and warn her? But then Marjorie would demand that June got Stanley out, or blame her for this happening. Perhaps the easiest thing was just to leave Stanley here overnight and let Marjorie deal with him in the morning.

Reluctantly, June went to the office to get her bag. When she came back out, he was still sitting in his chair, reading the newspaper.

'Do you really have to do this, Stanley?'

He looked up from the paper. 'I'm afraid so, my dear. But I'll make sure none of this reflects badly on you.'

June walked towards the front door and switched off the lights. She glanced back at Stanley, an elderly man in a tweed suit. A sudden image flashed into her mind of her mum standing at that very same table, helping a patron with something. Her mum looked up from what she was doing and stared straight at June, unsmiling.

What are you so afraid of, Junebug?

June faltered, her hand on the doorknob.

Imagine being twenty-eight and never having done anything.

She closed her eyes, hearing the blood pumping in her ears.

Your mother would be ashamed of you.

June opened her eyes and let go of the door handle.

What would Matilda do?

She swung round to face Stanley. 'I'll stay with you,' she blurted out, before she could stop herself.

He looked up at June in surprise. 'What?'

'I'll join you, Stanley; I'll stay here too.'

'That's very kind, but there's really no need. I'm perfectly fine on my own.'

'But one person isn't really a protest, is it? If you want the council to listen, then you need more people.'

'I appreciate your offer, but what would Marjorie say if she found you here? You don't want to risk your job for a silly old man like me.'

June felt as if she was standing on the edge of a precipice, peering down from a dizzying height, and for a moment she wondered if she should take a step back and run to the safety of home before it was too late. She swallowed before she spoke again. 'Stanley, there's something I need to tell you.'

'Yes?'

'The thing is . . . I'm Matilda.'

He stared at her in astonishment. 'I beg your pardon?'

'I've been sending you the Twitter messages. I'm the one who sent Rocky to the church hall and I put up all the posters round the village. I've been too scared to do anything publicly and risk losing my job, but I'm tired of living in fear.'

'Really? My goodness, I had no idea.' Stanley's face broke into a grin. 'But still, June, there's a difference between helping anonymously and joining me here. Are you sure you really want to do this?'

'Yes, I'm sure,' June said, and as she said the words out loud, she realised that she truly meant them. 'This library is the most important thing in my life, and I want to fight for it. Whatever the consequences.'

'Hurrah!' Stanley said, punching the air. 'Then let the Chalcot Library occupation begin.'

Chapter Twenty

JUNE LOCKED THE DOORS from the inside and turned around to see Stanley pacing the floor.

'Well, this is jolly exciting,' he said. 'I don't suppose you have any food in this place?'

She went into the office and found a packet of salt and vinegar crisps and some stale custard creams, then made two cups of tea and carried them back out. Stanley had set up a couple of lamps on the floor behind the desk, and was sitting in a chair next to them. It looked like a strange kind of campfire.

'It's best no one knows we're here yet. That way we can prepare our surprise attack for tomorrow,' he said.

'You've read too many war novels, Stanley.' June laid their meagre picnic out on the desk and sat down next to him. 'What do you think will happen tomorrow?'

'Well, Marjorie will arrive, and we'll bar her entry,' he said, helping himself to a biscuit. 'I imagine she'll call the council, who will send someone down. And that's when we give them our demands.'

'What demands?'

'That they promise to keep the library open and under council funding.'

'But they'll never agree to that.'

'Then we stay here until they do.'

'And you won't mention my theory about Cuppa Coffee?'

'No. We need evidence before we can go to the police with that.'

At the word 'police', June felt a shiver down her spine. 'Do you think the police will come to arrest us?'

'We're not technically breaking the law as long as we don't damage anything. If they want to get us out, they will need to go through the courts to get an eviction notice, which could take weeks.'

June imagined still being here in several weeks' time, alone with Stanley, eating books to fend off starvation. 'You seem to know a lot about this. Have you occupied somewhere before?'

'A political protest? Goodness, no.' He looked like he was about to say something else, but helped himself to another custard cream.

'So, what do we do in the meantime?'

'Well, we could get to know each other a bit better.' Stanley leaned back in his chair, cradling the mug in his hands. 'I've seen you in this library every day for years, but I know little of your life outside these four walls.'

'I'm afraid there's not much to tell.'

'Nonsense. Let's begin at the beginning. Were you born in Chalcot?'

'No, in Bath, but we moved here when I was four. Mum inherited the house when my grandfather died, and then we came here after she got her job at the library.'

'And what of your father? I don't believe I ever had the pleasure of meeting the fellow.'

'Me neither.'

The sun was getting low in the sky, stretching long shadows against the shelves. June picked at a loose bit of wood on the desk.

'I am sorry to hear that,' Stanley said, after a while. 'May I take the liberty of asking you another question?'

'Of course.'

'Did you ever feel you missed out on not having a father?'

June so rarely thought about the man who had conceived her that the question caught her off guard. 'Not really. I got teased about it a bit at school, but my mum was so brilliant that she did the job of two parents.'

Stanley was staring off into the distance, lost in thought. June looked around the library, trying to work out where they were going to sleep.

'I have a son,' he said.

'I know, I've seen you emailing him.'

He closed his eyes for a moment. 'It's a little more complicated than that. I've not seen Mark for a long time.'

'Well, America is a long way away.'

'No, my dear, you misunderstand me.' Stanley paused. 'I wasn't a very good father. I had some serious problems with alcohol. My wife . . . ex-wife . . . decided that I wasn't good for him.'

June was so stunned that she didn't know what to say. Stanley always seemed so proper; he was the last person she'd ever have imagined having an alcohol problem.

'They left when Mark was thirteen,' Stanley continued. 'Kitty had some family in California and the two of them emigrated out there. It was thirty-two years ago.'

'Have you not seen your son since then?' June tried to hide the shock in her voice.

'I went out there to visit once, the year after they left. And he came over here to see me when he turned eighteen. But I wasn't on very good form back then and I am afraid I rather messed things up.'

'I'm so sorry.' June reached towards him, but he shook his head as if to shake away the sympathy.

'It was my fault entirely. Alcohol and I were not good bedfellows and I made some poor decisions. Kitty did the right thing moving away.'

'But you're not like that anymore. You could be a wonderful father now.'

'That's kind of you to say. And, I'll admit, that's why I've been writing to him. But listening to you talk makes me realise that he's better off without me. Mark is forty-five now, and I hear he's done very well for himself. Why would he want me in his life now?'

'Oh, Stanley, don't say that. Our situations are completely different. My dad doesn't even know I exist; your son knows about you, you've been sending him all those emails. I'm sure—'

June was interrupted by a tremendous hammering sound on the door. They both ducked down to the floor.

'Who's that?' she whispered. 'Do you think it's the police?'

'I'll go and look.' Stanley started to crawl across the library floor.

June cowered behind the desk, her heart knocking against her ribs. The banging continued, louder and more insistent, and she could see a beam of torchlight swinging across the front windows. Whoever it was, they were angry and desperate to get in. Just when June was about to scream, she heard an 'Oh' from Stanley and the sound of the door being unlocked. When June peeked over the desk, she saw an indignant Mrs B marching into the library.

'I was walking past and saw the light on in here. What the fuck are you two doing?'

'We're occupying the library,' Stanley said. 'And June is Matilda; she's been our whistle-blower all along.'

'You're Matilda?' Mrs B looked at June as if she'd gone mad. 'But you've never shown any interest in helping us.'

'I'm sorry. The council said that if any library workers were seen to be involved then we'd be sacked, so I had to help you anonymously.'

'Bloody hell. All along I thought you were a scab, and actually you're one of us.' Mrs B gave June an enthusiastic thump. 'Welcome to the fight, sister.'

'Thank you,' June said, smiling as she rubbed her sore arm.

'We decided it's time to show the council we mean business,' Stanley said, as they all sat down again. 'That's why we're occupying the library.'

'Too bloody right, it's time we stepped this campaign up a gear. And I've not been at an occupation for ages.' Mrs B had a glint in her eye.

'Stanley thinks the council might send in the police,' June said.

'Let them bloody try. I've faced water cannons, tear gas, kettling. A few rural bobbies aren't going to scare me.'

'Were you ever scared at any of your protests?'

Mrs B gave her an indignant look. 'Do you think the Suffragettes were scared when they chained themselves to railings? Or Rosa Parks when they arrested her on the bus?'

'But we're not like them.'

'Why not?'

June felt embarrassed that she had to spell it out. 'Well, obviously the library is vital to us and our community. But they were protesting for huge, universal things, like the vote for women and the end of segregation.'

'And we're fighting for social equality, for literacy and the futures of our children.' Mrs B jabbed a finger at June. 'Did you know that in the past ten years they've closed almost eight hundred libraries in this country? And there'll be more if our bloody government has their way. So, we might be a small village library, but this is much bigger than us. We have to fight for Chalcot as if it's the last library on earth.'

'Hear, hear,' Stanley said, raising his mug.

'So, in answer to your question, June: no. I'm never scared when I'm fighting for something I know is right.'

'I've been terrified,' June said, hugging her knees to her chest.

'What, of being arrested?' Mrs B looked incredulous.

'No, of everything.'

June took a sip of her lukewarm tea. No one spoke, and she inhaled the comforting scent of the building and its stories. For a brief moment she allowed herself to imagine the library closing – the books being taken away, the space becoming a coffee shop like the one she'd been in earlier today – and she was hit by an overwhelming wave of sadness.

'I think some of my happiest memories are of me and Mum here together.'

'You must miss her terribly.' Stanley reached out and patted June's knee.

'After she died, the grief was . . . all-consuming. I'd devoted three years of my life to caring for Mum, and with her gone, I felt like I had nothing left. I think the only thing that kept me going was working in this library.'

'Grief can do funny things to you,' Mrs B said. 'I lost someone a long time ago, and for ages after that I lost any desire to fight or protest. I just wanted to curl up and sleep.'

'Were you married, Mrs Bransworth?' Stanley said.

'No, I bloody well wasn't. I've never really seen the point in men. But my partner, she—' Mrs B stopped. June had never seen her lost for words before.

'How did you deal with the grief?'

'I realised that by moping around and feeling sorry for myself, I was doing her a disservice. She loved me because I was angry and noisy and a pain in the arse. And by not living my life, by being scared and hiding away, I was letting her down.'

'So, what did you do?'

'I went to the protests against the poll tax and ended up getting arrested in a riot. I spent three days in prison after that.'

'Goodness,' Stanley said.

'But I felt alive again. For the first time since she died, I felt alive.'

June sank back in her chair. When had she last felt really, truly alive? She cast her mind back over the eight years since her mum died, but all she could picture was being at home, alone with her books. That was hardly living, was it? And then June remembered how she'd felt when she'd watched the news piece about Rocky, that secret thrill at knowing she'd done it herself. Or that night she'd spent creeping round Chalcot, putting up posters.

'We should all get some rest,' Mrs B said, standing up.

June cleared up their mugs and went to rummage through the lost property box. She found an abandoned coat and brought it back out.

'In case you get cold,' she said, handing it to Stanley.

'Thank you, my dear. It's going to be a long day tomorrow, try to get some sleep.'

June watched him push some chairs together to create a makeshift bed, while Mrs B fashioned a mattress out of her Afghan coat over by the Audiobook shelf. She was amazed by the ease with which they made themselves at home.

June lay down in the corner by Fiction A–E and closed her eyes, but she wasn't tired. She was acutely aware of the sounds coming from Mrs B and Stanley, the snuffles and breathing of other human beings. This was, she realised, the first night she'd spent in the same room as another person since her mum died. June adjusted her position, but her mind was racing, and after a few minutes she got up and collected a pile of picture books from the returns trolley. She carried them through to the Children's Room, where she began sorting through the shelves.

Ahlberg, A., Alborough, J., Antony, S. The Children's Room had been redecorated years ago, but June could still remember what it had been like when she was a child. Where the mural now was there used to be a picture of Winnie the Pooh, and the miniature sofa by the window had replaced a table and chairs.

Campbell, R., Carle, E., Child, L. June could picture her mum sitting in here, reading stories to the assembled children. And it was here that June had read a book herself for the first time, sounding the words out loud while her mum listened, grinning.

Dahl, R. Donaldson, J. Years later, when June's mum was in the final stages of her cancer and living in the hospice, she'd insisted they go to the library one last time. It had been a terrible palaver involving an ambulance and all sorts of equipment, but when they got here June wheeled her mum into the Children's Room and they sat watching Marjorie conduct Rhyme Time, her mum singing along with the kids.

Hargreaves, R., Hill, E., Hughes, S. This last memory brought tears to June's eyes, and she curled up on the floor and allowed them to fall in the darkness. Every inch of this room was steeped with memories, her mum's DNA woven into the story rug and well-thumbed books. If the library was lost, June's mum would be lost again too; and that was something June could never let happen.

Chapter Twenty-One

AT SOME POINT JUNE must have fallen asleep, because when she opened her eyes she was lying on the floor, the coat she'd given to Stanley laid over her. The sun was already up, throwing long shafts of light across the books in the Children's Room. June stood up, stretching, and walked back into the main room.

'What the hell?'

Every spare bit of wall space had been covered in posters saying 'KEEP YOUR HANDS OFF OUR LIBRARY' and 'SAVE CHALCOT LIBRARY'.

'We've done a bit of interior decorating,' Mrs Bransworth said, as she stuck another poster up over a framed picture of the Queen.

'How many are there?' June asked.

'Forty-five, to be exact. I did them all by myself on the computer,' Stanley said, proudly.

Mrs Bransworth jumped down from the chair she was standing on. 'What time does the dragon get here?'

'Around nine fifteen,' June replied.

'Right, we have two hours to get everything ready.'

'Ready for what?'

'We're not going to sit around drinking tea all day. This is a war and we have to plan our attack.'

The next few hours were a whirlwind of activity. Stanley typed up and printed out a hundred flyers about the protest, stating why they were occupying the library and what their aims were. June rearranged the tables to maximise space, and hand-drew several A3 signs, which they hung up in the front windows for passers-by to see. After so long sitting on the sidelines, watching, it felt wonderful to be finally working alongside Mrs B and Stanley as part of the team.

Mrs B was pacing around the front door. 'Oi, June. I need something large and heavy that can't be moved easily.'

June looked around and spotted the ancient returns trolley, and together the two of them manoeuvred it to the front. Mrs B explained it was so they could barricade themselves in if things got nasty.

'What do you mean, if things get nasty? Mrs Bransworth?'

Mrs B shrugged and told her to track down 'that skinny woman from the news' to see if she'd cover the occupation.

By ten past nine they had everything in place and were standing behind the locked door, waiting for Marjorie to arrive.

'Are you sure you want her to see you here?' Stanley said to June. 'You could still hide, and we'll tell her you left last night.'

June took a deep breath before she answered. 'No, I don't want to hide anymore.'

'Very well,' he said, and gave her arm a squeeze.

'What will we say when she gets here?' June said.

'We tell her that she can't enter the premises until the council agree to keep the library open.'

'Have you ever seen Marjorie in a bad mood? There's no way she'll put up with that.'

'You've not seen me in a bad mood either,' Mrs B said, giving June a wink.

A moment later they saw Marjorie crossing the road towards the library, a murderous look in her eyes.

'What the hell is going on here?' she bellowed as she approached. 'June?'

'This is a political protest,' Mrs B shouted through the door. 'This library is now occupied and will remain so until the council agrees to our demands.'

'What nonsense! Let me in.'

They didn't move.

'June, open the door!'

June pulled the door open a fraction. 'I'm sorry, Marjorie. I can't sit back and watch in silence any longer.'

'You know what this means, don't you?' Marjorie said. 'I won't be able to protect you from the council.'

June nodded. She felt sick.

'We want to speak to a representative of the council and hand over our demands,' Stanley said. 'Until that happens, you may not come in. Thank you.'

'Oh, for goodness' sake, I don't have time for this. Do you have any idea how busy I am?'

'We're here for as long as it takes,' Mrs B said. 'Down with library cuts! Down with the council!'

Marjorie glared at them. 'Very well, I'll call them. But don't you dare mess anything up in my library.'

She turned and stomped back across the road. June shut the door, her hands shaking.

'Stage One complete,' said Stanley with satisfaction. 'Let's have a cup of tea, shall we?'

Over the next few hours, as people turned up to use the library, June, Stanley and Mrs B gave them flyers and explained what they were doing. Some looked confused and walked away, but most offered their support. By midday, there were around thirty people inside, all chatting excitedly. Someone brought some sandwiches from the bakery, and June was sitting down to eat one when she heard a shout from Mrs B.

'The council are here!'

Everyone crowded round the window.

'Look, it's Richard Donnelly and that Sarah woman,' Stanley said. 'And Brian Spencer's here too. I wonder where Marjorie is?'

Over everyone's heads, June could see the group reach the other side of the locked door. Richard had his arms crossed.

'All right, you've pulled your little stunt and we're here. Now open up and we can talk,' he shouted through the window.

'Not until you've agreed to our demands,' Stanley said, opening the door a crack and passing a handful of leaflets through.

Mrs B read the words out loud. 'We, the Friends of Chalcot Library, make the following demands. One, that the council promises to keep the library open and fully funded. Two, that the future safety of the library is guaranteed. Three, that the building will not be sold off, and especially not to a multinational company or chain. We don't want big corporations in this village, we want to protect local, independent businesses. Four—'

'Hang on, hang on,' Richard said. 'There seems to be some kind of misunderstanding here.'

'Do you deny that the council are considering selling off the building?' Mrs B said.

'I think you've all got a bit carried away. The consultation is still ongoing; no decisions have been made about the future of the library.'

'Answer my question. Are you in talks with any companies to sell them the library building?'

'I have no idea what you're talking about,' Richard said. June had to give it to him – either he knew nothing about Cuppa Coffee, or he was an excellent poker player. Brian, on the other hand, was the colour of a beetroot.

'Look, we're all on the same side here,' Sarah said, stepping forwards. 'This is painful for all of us, but we have to face up to reality. Our budget has been slashed and we need to ensure that all of our public services are providing value for money.'

'Of course the library is good value for money,' Stanley said. 'Look at all the people who use it and the facilities it provides.'

'But what would you rather we made cuts to?' Sarah said. 'The library service or, say, the local hospital? Or our schools? We need to make the savings somewhere.'

There were a few mutters from the crowd in the library.

'That's a ridiculous question,' Mrs B shouted, banging her fist against the glass. 'This is the bloody Tories. You shouldn't be having to make cuts in the first place.'

'Let's all calm down, shall we?' Sarah raised her hands in a placatory manner. 'There's no need to get so heated. Why don't you let us in, and we can have a little chat?'

'We're not letting you in until you agree to these demands,' Stanley said.

'This is getting us nowhere,' Richard said to Sarah through gritted teeth. 'We'll have to go with Plan B.'

'Yes, bugger off,' Mrs B shouted. 'And don't come back until you can prove to us the library will be safe.'

The group all turned to leave, but Sarah stopped.

'Wait, you, there at the back. What's your name?' she said, pointing through the window.

'Me, madam? My name is Stanley Phelps.'

'No, not you. The woman behind you.'

Everyone turned around and June realised that Sarah was looking at her.

'She's no one,' Mrs B said.

'You're a library worker, aren't you?' Sarah asked.

June didn't say anything, but she saw Sarah and Richard exchange a glance.

'Let's get out of here,' Richard said.

Inside the library, the crowd dispersed from the window and resumed their conversations. June's legs were trembling and she sank down onto a chair.

'Did you see the look on Brian Spencer's face when I mentioned the council selling off the building?' Mrs B said. 'He looked like he was having a seizure.'

'What do you think the council's Plan B is?' Stanley said.

'I imagine they'll try to get a court order to have us evicted.'

'What do we do until then?'

'We could make ourselves useful?' Mrs B said. 'I can't remember the last time this place had a lick of paint.'

'I can go to the shop now and buy some supplies,' June said, keen to get out of the library for some fresh air.

'No, you need to have something to eat first,' Stanley said. 'It looks like it might be a long old slog. You'll need your energy.'

By the middle of the afternoon, the library was busier than June had ever seen it. Word had got out about the protest and more people had turned up, filling every corner of the room. All the chairs were taken, and people stood around chatting, children running between their legs. Mrs Bransworth was debating the merits of socialism with a group of students by the Periodicals rack and Stanley was sitting in the Children's Room reading *The Twits* to some of the little ones. Chantal was there with several of her friends and Jackson was reciting his haiku to anyone who'd listen. Even Vera was there, acting as unofficial security on the front door. June looked round the room and felt a rush of affection for them all.

'June, there's someone here to see you,' Vera shouted. When June got to the door, she saw the journalist Tessa and her camerawoman scanning the room.

'Any strippers?' Tessa said.

191

'Rocky preferred the term exotic dancer,' Vera said. 'I told June we should have invited him.'

'Did people really sleep here last night?' Tessa said.

'Yep.' June pointed out Stanley and Mrs Bransworth.

'Those two? Cleo, get some shots over there.' Tessa signalled towards Stanley reading with the kids. 'I think we can make a nice little story out of this.'

June spotted Leila approaching the library with her son, Mahmoud, who was carrying a cardboard box.

'Sorry, it's a bit chaotic in here today,' June said, when they walked in. 'We're having a protest against the council wanting to shut the library.'

'We heard,' Mahmoud said.

Leila nudged him and he handed the box over to June. She lifted off the lid and saw it contained several cakes, each beautifully decorated.

'Victoria sponge . . . chocolate . . . coffee,' Leila said. 'Delia Smith.'

'Oh, Leila, you didn't have to.'

'Is that cake?' Vera was peering over June's shoulder into the box.

June unloaded the cakes onto the table and soon there was a crowd of older ladies cooing over the delicate icing flowers and helping themselves to generous slices. Tessa nodded and Cleo turned her camera to film them.

'Oh, this sponge is delicious,' said one of the women.

Vera picked up a bit of chocolate cake and sniffed it.

'Go on,' the women said.

Vera put a small piece in her mouth and chewed it, her face scrunched up.

'Thank you, Leila,' June said. 'It's so kind of you to bring the cake.'

'I . . . I think . . .' Leila frowned and looked at Mahmoud, then began speaking in Arabic. Her son translated.

'Mum says she'd be sad if the library closes. She likes coming here for the cookery books, but also because she likes to see all the different people here. The children singing. It reminds her of home.'

June felt a lump in her throat for the second time in twenty-four hours. 'Please tell your mum we're fighting to save the library. I promise, we're doing everything we can.'

Chapter Twenty-Two

BY SIX O'CLOCK MOST people had begun to drift off, making their excuses for why they couldn't stay overnight. June thought of her own home, with its comfortable bed and a microwave lasagne-for-one waiting in the freezer. Then she spotted Stanley sitting in his chair, looking exhausted.

'Why don't you go home tonight and get some rest?' June said to him.

'Thank you, but I'm not leaving this place until the council assure us it's safe.'

'Mum, can I stay?' Chantal asked Michelle, who was trying to coax her three-year-old twins into the buggy.

'If the others don't mind. But don't you dare cause any bother.'

When the last visitor had gone, June locked the front door.

'Well, this is the motliest crew of protesters I've ever seen,' Mrs B said, looking from Stanley to June and Chantal.

They began tidying up the mess from the day. Once the library was looking a little clearer, June pulled out her phone and typed a message to Linda, asking her to feed Alan Bennett. A minute later, a reply popped up.

SPENDING THE NIGHT WITH ALEX?!! MAKE SURE U
TAKE CLEAN KNICKERS WITH U – MAYBE THE
SLUTTY ONES U GOT FROM THAT SHOP??

June thrust her phone away. She spotted Chantal over in
the corner, searching through the food leftovers.

'I'm glad you're here,' June said, when she joined her.
'I've been wanting to talk to you about something.'

Chantal continued rummaging through the bags without
looking at June.

'Your mum mentioned you might not go back to school
in September.'

Chantal found a packet of crisps at the bottom and
pulled it out, sending everything flying.

'I just wanted to say, please don't let what's going on
with the library get in the way of your school work. You're
such a bright girl and you shouldn't give up on university.'

Chantal finally turned to June. 'You don't get it, do
you?'

'Get what?'

'This is just some job for you. And if the library closes,
all you'll have to do is find a new job somewhere else,
right?'

'That's not true. My mum—'

'Don't you live on your own, down on Willowmead?'

June nodded.

'Well, imagine if you lived in a house with six other
people. A house so small that you don't even have your

own bed, let alone a bedroom. Then imagine trying to revise for your exams like that. That's why I need this place, June, because without it, I'll never get my A-Levels and I'll be stuck in this shitty village forever.'

June started to reply but stopped herself. What could she possibly say to make Chantal feel better? The teenager was right; if the library closed there would be lots of people like her whose lives would suffer, and June had been so absorbed with her own problems that she'd barely stopped to think about any of them. She looked away from Chantal towards Stanley, who was sitting in front of one of the computers. He was always the first to arrive at the library and the last to leave. Where would he go all day if it closed?

As if sensing she was thinking about him, Stanley looked up and signalled to June. 'Come on, the local news is on.'

The four of them huddled round the computer to watch the first two items, but there was no mention of the library occupation.

'Maybe we won't be featured this time,' Stanley said.

'Vera was right,' Mrs B said. 'We should have got Rocky along.'

Just then Tessa appeared on screen, standing outside the library. 'First, there was a stripper. Now, the sleepy village of Chalcot has gone one step further in its attempt to save its library.'

'Look, Mrs Bransworth, it's you,' Stanley said, as they watched images of Mrs B in the crowded library.

'Pensioners from the village have occupied the library in protest at the council's threat to close it down,' Tessa said over the shots.

'Pensioners!' Mrs B shrieked. 'Who's she calling a bloody pensioner?'

'I turned up this morning and all this was going on,' an elderly lady was saying to Tessa. 'Usually on a Wednesday I come for the Knit and Natter group, but today it's a bit more exciting.'

Now Stanley appeared in front of them. 'Older people like me need the library. I don't have a personal computer at home – I didn't even know how to turn one on until June here taught me. If the library closes, how will I go surfing?'

'Go surfing?' Chantal said. 'Don't you mean surfing the internet?'

'That's not everything I said,' Stanley said.

'We started occupying the library last night.' Mrs B was being interviewed. 'I've been protesting for more than forty years. I was at Greenham Common in the eighties and I went to Wales for the miners.'

Tessa was on the screen again. 'OAPs like these hope that their protest will convince Dunningshire Council to protect the village library. And in the meantime, there's plenty of tea and cake for everyone.'

It cut to shots of Vera and the older ladies eating Leila's cake. 'This sponge is delicious,' one of them said, licking her lips. Then the news cut back to the studio.

June turned the monitor off and everyone stood in silence, staring at the blank screen.

'I can't believe she called me a fucking OAP,' Mrs B said.

'I said so many eloquent things,' Stanley said. 'Why did they only use that surfing line?'

Chantal was frowning. 'It looked really lame.'

'Look, let's all calm down, please,' June said. 'I know that piece seemed a bit skewed but at least we got our protest on the news.'

There was a knock on the door.

'If it's that Tessa woman, tell her to piss off,' Mrs B growled.

Stanley went to see who it was. A moment later he reappeared, followed by Alex, who was carrying two large carrier bags. June's heart momentarily lifted at the sight of him, and then fell when she remembered their embarrassing phone call and Ellie.

'Hi all. I've brought your food,' Alex said, putting the bags down on a table.

'Did anyone order Chinese?' Mrs B asked, and they all shook their heads.

'Well, it's yours,' Alex said.

'Is it free?'

'Someone paid for it earlier.'

'Well, hurry up then, I'm starving.'

They gathered round the table as Alex began unloading the cartons, the food a welcome distraction from the news.

'Here, I brought you this,' he said, handing June a large dish of chicken in black bean sauce.

'Thank you.' She took the box without looking him in the eye.

June opened the lid but felt too self-conscious to start eating. For eight years, she'd eaten this dish alone at home with a book – had eaten almost every meal alone at home with a book. It felt strange to be having it here, in the library, with four other people chatting around her. June looked across the table. Mrs B and Stanley were having an animated conversation about the news piece, and Alex was telling Chantal a story about his time at university that was making her laugh. They all looked so at ease together, reaching across each other to grab spring rolls and prawn crackers as they talked. June took a mouthful of her food. When was the last time she'd had a meal with a group of people, other than at that hideous hen do? She scanned her mind back but realised with a start that she couldn't remember. Had it really been before her mum died? How was that possible?

'You guys, Facebook has gone crazy.' Chantal was looking at her phone. 'And we've had another six hundred signatures on the online petition.'

'That's marvellous.' Stanley grabbed his glass of water and lifted it in the air. 'To the Friends of Chalcot Library!'

'To the Friends of Chalcot Library,' they all replied, and June laughed as she raised her glass and joined in the toast.

Half an hour later, June was so full of food she could barely move. Mrs B and Chantal were clearing up the table, and Stanley and Alex were deep in conversation, their heads close together. June stretched out in her chair, enjoying the satisfied warmth of a good meal.

After a while, Alex stood up. 'I'd better get back to the takeaway – my aunt will kill me for being gone so long.'

'June, why don't you walk out with him?' Stanley said.

'Thanks, but I'm fine here.' June didn't want to spoil this pleasant feeling by having an awkward conversation with Alex.

'You should get some fresh air,' Stanley said. 'You've not left the library all day.'

'Quite right. You need to keep healthy during an occupation,' Mrs B added, appearing at her shoulder.

June opened her mouth to resist, but realised they were all staring at her.

'Fine,' she said, pulling herself up and following Alex outside. She was conscious of the fact she was still wearing yesterday's clothes, and her hair was escaping from its bun, loose curls falling round her face.

'So, I've got a bone to pick with you,' Alex said, as they set off down The Parade.

'What have I done?' June said, alarmed at the tone of his voice. Was this about her calling him while he was with his girlfriend?

'Why didn't you warn me about *Charlotte's Web*? I almost burst into tears in front of a customer when I finished it.'

June smiled, relieved. 'Oh. Well, just because a book is meant for children doesn't mean it can't pack an emotional punch.'

'But still, why did the writer have to kill Charlotte? I'll never hurt a spider again.'

June laughed and felt some of the tension release from her shoulders.

'Also, I've not known what to read for the past few weeks without your recommendations,' Alex said. 'Where have you been?'

'Sorry, I've just been busy.'

They chatted about books as they made their way down The Parade. After more than twenty-four hours inside the library walls, it felt wonderful to be outside, breathing in the cool evening air and discussing something other than the protest. As they turned down the hill towards the Golden Dragon, June was aware of their steps getting shorter and slower.

'I think *The Handmaid's Tale* might be a good choice for you next,' she said, as they edged towards the takeaway. 'In a way it's like science fiction because—'

'I'm sorry I couldn't help you at the hen do,' Alex interrupted. 'I know you've been angry with me for not being there, and I feel terrible about it.'

'I haven't been angry with you.'

'Well, you've definitely been avoiding me.'

June thought of Ellie's voice and swallowed. 'I just felt bad for disturbing you when you were with your . . . someone.'

'Don't be crazy, I wanted to help you. You sounded so upset.'

She picked up her pace. 'It was nothing.'

'What happened?'

June was about to dismiss him again, but she stopped herself. Alex had already heard her at her lowest; why shouldn't she give him the full, miserable picture?

'OK, fine. The girls played this stupid game at the hen do and I was totally humiliated.'

'What game?'

'It's called "Never Have I Ever".'

'Oh god, I remember that from uni. A guaranteed way to get everyone wasted.'

'Not for me, because I hadn't done any of the things they said. Not one of them.'

'Don't beat yourself up about that,' Alex said. 'Those girls were always super privileged, so you shouldn't feel bad because you've never driven a Ferrari while wearing Jimmy Choos and drinking Dom Pérignon.' He laughed but June didn't join in.

'It wasn't just stuff like that. There were some really ordinary things that I'd never done, like going out dancing all night or camping.'

'Well, I hate camping too.'

They'd reached the takeaway, and June stopped. 'I haven't done anything with my life, Alex. Ever since Mum died, I've just shut myself away at home, hiding in the same old books so I didn't have to go out and face the real world.'

'You've been grieving, June.'

'But I let myself become so isolated, even before she died.' June turned to look at Alex. 'You know I told you I was friends with Gayle? Well, that was a lie – I was only at the hen do because Marjorie made her invite me. I don't have any real friends.'

'Come on, I'm your friend. And what about Stanley?'

'Stanley's kind to me but only because he feels sorry for me.'

'I know that isn't true.'

'One of the women at the hen do said my life was *tragic*, and she was right.' June swallowed. 'My mum would be so disappointed in me.'

They were silent for a moment, and June watched people moving around inside the takeaway. Why was she telling Alex all of this?

'You know that's not true, don't you?' he said. 'You may not have hundreds of friends or been camping, but you've done lots that your mum would be proud of.'

June gave a small, bitter laugh. 'That's rubbish. She wanted me to follow my dreams and be a writer.'

'But what about everything you've done for the library?'

'What about it? The place I love more than anywhere has been threatened, and until yesterday I'd done nothing except hide in the background, too scared to put my head above the parapet. If my mum was here, she'd have been—'

'June, you need to stop comparing yourself to your mum,' Alex said, cutting her short. 'You're your own person with your own qualities. Yeah, maybe you're shy and prefer to keep to the back rather than shout from the front. But you're also smart and kind and loyal, and I for one think you're pretty amazing.'

Alex stopped talking and looked a little stunned at what he'd just said. The takeaway door opened, and a couple walked out. As they did, a small, grey-haired woman behind the counter caught sight of them. 'Alex, where've you been? I need you in here!'

'Coming, Auntie,' he called back, as the door slammed shut. He looked at June. 'I'm sorry, I have to go in.'

'That's OK.' There was a pause and June stared at her feet. 'I'm sorry I've been avoiding you, Alex. I just felt humiliated after that phone call.'

'Well, I'm sorry I wasn't around to help you. I really wish I could have been there for you.'

'Alex!' came the voice from inside, louder.

He looked at June and shrugged helplessly. 'Goodnight.'

'Goodnight, Alex.'

June watched him walk into the takeaway and the door swing shut behind him. She looked down the hill, towards her road and the comforts of home: her bed, the books, solitude.

And then June turned and made her way back up the hill, towards the people waiting for her at the library.

Chapter Twenty-Three

JUNE WAS REPAIRING SOME damaged books when Alex walked in through the library front door. When she saw him she smiled, her heart beating faster. Alex kept his eyes locked on hers as he walked towards her, never breaking gaze. When he reached June he didn't say anything, just reached out and took her hand, pulling her up to standing in one deft movement. He leaned towards her, across the issue desk, so that his face was just centimetres from June's. She held her breath, not daring to move as Alex stroked her cheek and whispered—

'Wake up, lazy bones.'

June opened her eyes and sat up, dazed. There was Stanley, sitting in his chair reading the newspaper. There was Chantal, eating a chocolate croissant. And there was Mrs B, thrusting a mug of tea towards her.

'This isn't the time for a bloody lie-in – we have work to do.'

June took the mug and walked over to Stanley, hoping no one could see how flushed her cheeks were from that dream.

'Good morning, my dear.' He gave her a smile, but June noticed he looked pale.

'Are you OK?'

'I'm fine, just a small headache. I didn't sleep well last night.'

'Why don't you go home today and get some rest?'

'Oh, I'll be as right as rain once I've had this coffee. Besides, I wouldn't want to miss the drama here.' He indicated Mrs B, who was stabbing the air with her finger.

'I think we should make a formal complaint to Ofcom,' Mrs B shouted. 'That news report was blatantly ageist.'

'And they didn't use any footage of me and my friends,' Chantal said. 'It's like we weren't even there.'

'Exactly. This is why I've never paid my licence fee, they're all right-wing b—'

'There's someone at the door,' June said, pointing outside towards a man wearing combat trousers and an exhausted expression. He had a camera slung over his shoulder.

'He looks like one of those bottom-feeder journalists,' Mrs B said. 'Go and tell him to piss off.'

'He'll just want to humiliate us again,' Stanley said.

June ran a hand through her hair and walked to the door. 'Can I help you?'

'Is this the library with the pensioners' protest?' the man asked.

'Well, you see, it's not exactly a pensioners' protest.'

'That's what everyone's calling it.'

'Everyone?'

'It's gone viral. It was trending on Twitter last night.'

'What?'

'Here.' He pulled out his phone and showed it to her. The words #oapprotest were everywhere on the screen. 'People have gone mad for it – your old dears are famous now. Especially that guy who talked about surfing.'

'But we thought the news made us all look a bit, well, silly?'

'Nah, people love a feel-good story. And I'm not the only one to think so.' He signalled over his shoulder to where several other men and women were crossing the road towards the library. 'Can I come in and do some interviews before this lot get in?'

'Hang on a minute.' June shut the door and returned to the group.

Mrs B was mid-rant when June arrived. 'I hope you told him to put his camera where the sun don't shine.'

'Not quite.' June explained what the man had told her.

'I'm sorry, but what does viral mean?' Stanley said. 'It sounds rather unpleasant.'

'But they completely misrepresented us,' Chantal said.

'Look, if we're going to stand any chance of saving the library, we need to get as much attention as possible,' June said. 'And if that means playing up to this "pensioner protest" thing to get in the papers, I think we should do it.' She turned to Stanley. 'You were the one who started this occupation. What do you think?'

He sighed. 'Reluctantly, I agree with you. We'd be fools to miss this opportunity.'

'But I've never been called an OAP in all my life,' Mrs B muttered. June looked at her and she frowned. 'Fine. If it's for the good of the library, I suppose I can handle it one more time.'

'There's just one problem,' Chantal said. 'If they only want to see pensioners, it's going to seem like a pretty small protest.'

June looked from Stanley to Mrs B. 'I could put out calls to the Knit and Natter group to see if some of them could come?'

Mrs B shook her head. 'That's still not going to be enough. We need to fill this library if it's going to make a news story.'

At that moment, the library door creaked open. They all looked towards it hopefully, but the only person to walk in was Vera, scowling. 'There's a minibus just turned up,' she said. 'They've parked in the disabled spot, can you believe it?'

'It must be more journalists,' June said, looking outside as the driver's door of the minibus opened and a silver-haired woman wearing a Barbour jacket and tartan skirt climbed down.

'Do you reckon she's from Saga?' Stanley said.

A stream of women were coming out of the minibus, helping each other disembark. June went out to meet them. 'Can I help you?'

'Mary Cooper-Marks.' The Barbour lady stepped forward and gave June a firm handshake. 'We saw you on the news last night.'

'I'm sorry, who are you?'

'We're from the Dornley Women's Institute. Our library got closed down a few years ago. Bloody tragedy. So when we saw your protest, we thought we'd come along and lend a hand.'

The women had finished filing off the bus now. There must have been at least fifteen of them and the majority looked well past retirement age.

'You've come to help us?' Stanley asked.

'Is that all right?' one of the WI ladies said. 'We all quite fancied the idea of joining a pensioners' protest. Much nicer than the rowdy ones you normally see on the news.'

'This is amazing,' June said. 'You're all amazing. Thank you!'

'Look, love, can we come in or not?' one of the journalists said. 'I need to get back to London by lunchtime.'

'Yes, of course you can. Please come in, all of you.'

June spent the morning running around the library, helping the journalists and fetching cups of tea for the protesters. Some of the sprightlier WI ladies were marching around the shelves waving homemade placards and chanting, 'Save Chalcot Library.' Others were sitting in small groups talking with locals about the library. June noticed that Mrs B and Mary Cooper-Marks spent much of the morning huddled in a corner together, deep in conversation. At ten o'clock another minibus turned up, this one full of residents from Cherry Tree Retirement Home, who had seen the news piece too.

'I used to come here with my children fifty years ago,' said an elderly gentleman, helping himself to one of the sandwiches that Chantal and Stanley were busy making. 'It's a crying shame to see places like this get shut down.'

'We get a mobile library in our village now,' said one of the WI women. 'The librarian is a sweet lad but it's just not the same.'

'I miss seeing the children playing in the library,' said her friend.

'Shall we have a singalong?' asked a lady in a wheelchair, who June had been told was ninety-four. 'Does anyone know any Vera Lynn?'

As the protesters burst into song, June saw Leila walking through the front door. She headed over to her.

'Thanks so much for the cakes yesterday,' June said. 'They were a huge success.'

'Can I take a new book?'

'Of course.'

They walked over to the cookery section and began scanning the shelf together.

'What about this Nigella Lawson one?' June said, pulling out *How to Eat*. 'My mum always loved her recipes.'

Leila took the book and studied the cover. Over her shoulder, June saw Vera approaching, a frown on her face.

'Waste of time,' she said in a low voice as she walked past.

June felt a flush of anger. 'What did you say, Vera?'

The old woman paused and spoke more loudly. 'I said, it's a waste of time.' She pointed at Leila holding the recipe book.

'Vera, we do not tolerate any kind of discrimination in this library. I'm afraid I'm going to have to ask you to—'

'You don't want Nigella for baking,' Vera said, cutting June off. 'She's good with savouries but she won't get you anywhere with cakes.' She reached up to a shelf and pulled down an old, battered book. 'This is what you want. A good old-fashioned recipe book, none of this celebrity chef nonsense.'

Leila clearly couldn't understand a word of what Vera was saying and she looked to June for reassurance.

'Also, you used the wrong cocoa powder in the chocolate cake yesterday,' Vera continued, raising her voice to try and make Leila understand. 'You used drinking chocolate, but you want something for baking.' She reached into her bag and pulled out a pot of Bournville cocoa powder, which she thrust at Leila. The woman stepped backwards in alarm. Vera stood for a

moment with her hand stretched out, then put the
Bournville down on the shelf and walked away.

The journalists all left by late morning and things quietened
down. June hadn't had a moment to rest and her eyes
were itchy from lack of sleep, so she stepped outside and
sat down on the bench opposite the library. She and her
mum used to sit in this exact spot when June was a child,
eating jam doughnuts on a Saturday morning. June felt a
familiar pang of longing at the memory and turned to look
into the library window. Mrs B and Mary Cooper-Marks
were standing together by the front door, talking with
intensity. Chantal was reading to a couple of ladies from
the retirement home, the ninety-four-year-old nodding as
she listened. Vera and Leila were sitting together at a table
by the window, bent over a recipe book; Vera was trying
to explain something, waving her hands around with force.
June smiled to herself and closed her eyes, allowing the
sun to warm her face.

'I thought you might like a cup of tea.'

She looked up to see Stanley approaching, holding two
mugs. He handed her one.

'Thanks, Stanley. How's your headache?'

'Oh, it was nothing.'

He sat down next to her and for a few minutes they
remained in silence, enjoying the peace and calm.

'I can't believe we've done this,' June said, after a while. 'Until this week, the most exciting thing to happen to me was winning the reading prize at school.'

'Life could be full of excitement, if you allow yourself to live a little.' Stanley nodded across the road, and June turned to see Alex walking down the pavement on the other side of The Parade. He was staring at his phone screen, his hair falling in his eyes. June looked back and saw that Stanley was watching her with his gap-toothed smile. 'Alex is a fine young man, isn't he?'

June took a sip of her tea.

'I've seen the two of you together in the library, talking about books. He seems to have something of a soft spot for you.'

'Don't be daft.'

'Time is precious, my dear. If you have romantic intentions towards Alex, you should tell him.'

'It's not like that between us – we're just friends. And he has a girlfriend.'

'Really? He's never mentioned anyone to me.'

'He's really private about her for some reason, but I know she exists.'

Stanley frowned. 'June, I apologise if this is too forward, but I would hate for you to end up like me, alone and with a life full of regrets. You have an opportunity here and you should seize it with both hands.'

'You shouldn't have regrets, Stanley. I know you've made some mistakes, but it's not too late to change things with your son. Why don't you fly out to America to see him?'

'I wish it were that simple.' Stanley looked in through the window of the library and exhaled. 'I will never regret what we've done here, though. This has been marvellous.'

'It's been surreal,' June said. 'I can't believe all these strangers came to support us today.'

'Oh, I can.'

'Don't get me wrong, it's brilliant. I just don't understand why the WI ladies would come and protest for a library they've never been to before.'

Stanley looked at her. 'Did I tell you why I got involved with this library campaign?'

June shook her head.

'After Kitty and Mark moved to America, things went downhill for me. I had been drinking heavily before, but, with them gone, I didn't even try to restrain myself. Within twelve months I'd lost my job, my house, everything. I moved around a lot back then, finding somewhere to sleep for a while before being thrown out, like some kind of vagrant. I even lived in a tent for a while.'

'Oh, Stanley, I'm so sorry. That's awful.'

'But here's the thing – wherever I ended up, and however much trouble I was in, there was always a library. A place that was safe and warm and dry, where no one would judge me. Libraries were my only light in some very dark times. And so when the council threatened this place, it felt like a threat to every library I've ever sought sanctuary in – an attack on every librarian who had ever come to my aid. And I think that's why these people are here today. As Mrs Bransworth said, this protest isn't just for Chalcot. It's for all the libraries out there.'

June watched Stanley as he spoke. All these years she'd thought she had no friends, and the whole time he had been there for her every single day: kind and patient and loyal. How had she been so blind? She reached across and put her hand on top of his.

'Thank you, Stanley.'

'Whatever for?'

'For being you. I don't know what I'd have done without you since Mum died.'

He patted her hand. 'That's what friends are for, my dear. Now, let's get back inside before all the Jammie Dodgers get eaten, shall we?'

They got up and walked towards the library. As they did, June saw a smartly dressed man with a briefcase walking across the road towards them.

'I wonder if he's another journalist?' she said.

'I'm afraid the protest has quietened down a bit now,' Stanley said, when they met him at the library door. 'You should have been here a few hours ago.'

'Are you protesters?'

'Yes, we started the occupation,' Stanley said. 'Do come in, sir.'

As they stepped in through the door, the man stopped, reached into his briefcase and pulled out an A4 manila envelope, which he handed to June. 'This is notice that an Interim Possession Order has been served. You all have twenty-four hours to vacate the property or you'll be breaking the law.'

Chapter Twenty-Four

'LOOK AT THIS, WE'RE FAMOUS!'

June woke up, bleary-eyed and sore from a night spent under Marjorie's desk, to find Stanley, Mrs B and Chantal poring over the newspapers. Mrs B handed her a copy of the *Guardian*. On page sixteen was a photo of the library under the headline *Pensioners occupy library as Dunningshire Council threatens six with closure*.

'It's the same in most of these,' Stanley said, indicating the other papers in front of them. 'And Mrs Bransworth has been invited on the radio.'

June glanced at the newspapers. There was a photo of her, Stanley and Mrs B in one of them, grinning at the camera, and another showed the WI ladies with their placards.

'It's not helped though, has it?' Chantal said. 'We're still being evicted today.'

'No, but all this publicity has to be good for us,' June said. 'The council will find it much harder to close the library now we've been all over the news.' She looked to Stanley for agreement, but he wouldn't catch her eye.

The party feel of the last few days was gone, replaced by a sober quiet. They got to work cleaning and tidying the library, making sure it was spotless before the council arrived: Stanley and Chantal were finishing painting over twenty years' worth of graffiti in the toilet, while Mrs B dusted the long-neglected window blinds. Overnight, someone had spilt a small splash of coffee on the carpet and so June got on her hands and knees to scrub the stain. Nobody spoke, lost in their own thoughts.

'They're here,' Mrs B said, a little after midday.

June looked outside to where a police van was pulling up in front of the library. Half a dozen officers climbed down. 'Why are the police here?'

'In case we don't leave peacefully,' Mrs B said, grim-faced. 'They're preparing for a fight.'

'Have they seen us?' Stanley said. 'We're hardly anarchists; I read the *Daily Telegraph*, for goodness' sake.'

'Look who else is here,' June said, as Richard, Sarah, Marjorie and Brian crossed the road and joined the police.

Richard had a conversation with one of the police officers, who handed him a megaphone. He pressed a button and there was a loud squeal, causing everyone outside to put their hands over their ears. The police officer stepped forward and showed him how to work it.

Richard put the megaphone to his mouth and turned to the library. 'Right, you lot, the fun's over. You've had twenty-four hours since we served you the IPO. It's time to get out.'

Inside the library, not one of them moved, all staring through the window at him. June could feel her heart racing. Out of the corner of her eye she could see Tessa and Cleo moving towards the library, Cleo's camera on her shoulder, already filming.

'We're not going anywhere until you promise our library is safe,' Stanley shouted through the glass.

'Really, Stanley?' June whispered. 'They have the eviction order. There's nothing we can do now.'

'This is our last chance to fight.'

'There's no point resisting,' Richard's voice came back at them through the megaphone. 'If you don't leave now, you'll be committing an offence and will be arrested.'

'Chantal, you should go,' Mrs B said. 'Your mum would kill us if you got in trouble.'

She hesitated, then nodded. 'OK. Good luck, guys.'

June unlocked the front door and Chantal walked out, glancing back over her shoulder with an attempt at a smile.

'That's right, out you come, nice and easy.' Richard's expression suggested he was enjoying this power. 'Now, the rest of you have three minutes or I'm sending in the police.'

June looked at Stanley. 'Just because the occupation is ending doesn't mean we have to stop fighting,' she said.

'Now that I'm in this with you, I won't give up. We'll find another way to protest.'

'You know as well as I do that this is over,' Stanley said. 'The council haven't once tried to negotiate with us this week – they haven't shown any interest in hearing what we have to say. All they want is to get us out so they can shut this place down.'

'But surely it must be harder for them to close the library after all of this?'

Stanley shook his head. 'I wish I had your youthful optimism, June.'

'Two minutes,' Richard's voice blared through at them.

'God, that man is a prick,' Mrs B said. 'Stanley, I hate to admit it, but I think June is right. This occupation is over, there's no point in getting yourself arrested for the sake of it. We have to find other ways to keep the fight going.'

'I agree, there's no point in all of us getting arrested,' Stanley said. 'You two should leave now.'

'No one's getting arrested. Come on, let's all get out of here.' Mrs B walked towards the door. 'It's been a great occupation,' she sighed, as she stepped outside.

'One minute,' Richard's voice boomed.

The library felt very empty now. June and Stanley looked at each other.

'You go too, my dear,' he said. 'I'll be fine on my own.'

'I'm not going anywhere without you,' June said. 'We started this together and we'll finish it together.'

'You're more stubborn than you look.' Stanley began walking towards the door, and June felt a rush of relief.

'Thank you,' she said, following him. 'Let's all go home and have a proper rest, and next week we can regroup and plan what to do next.'

He pulled the door open. Outside, June could see Richard, the police officers, the news camera.

'Ladies first,' Stanley said, and June took a deep breath and stepped outside. As she did, she felt a breeze of wind behind her and she turned back around as Stanley pulled the door shut.

'No, Stanley!' she cried, trying to pull it open, but he'd locked it from the inside already and was heaving the returns trolley in front of the door. June looked round to Richard and the police. 'Please don't arrest him. He just cares about the library.'

'I'm sorry, ma'am, but the twenty-four hours is up,' one of the police officers said, giving June an apologetic shrug. 'He's now breaking the law by not complying with the eviction order.'

'But he's an old man.'

The officer took the megaphone off Richard. 'Sir, unless you vacate this property now, we will be forced to enter it and arrest you.'

On the other side of the door, Stanley shook his head.

'Sir, I'm asking you one more time. Open the door and step outside.'

Stanley didn't move.

'For god's sake, get this over and done with before he becomes a martyr,' Sarah muttered, nodding at Cleo, who was filming it all.

Several police officers moved towards the door.

'Everybody stand back,' one of them shouted, and June found herself being pulled backwards by Mrs B.

'Don't damage my library,' Marjorie shouted from somewhere behind them.

The officers positioned themselves by the door. 'Right, I'll unlock it and we all push,' one of them said.

June looked at Stanley through the window. He was standing very tall, his head in the air, staring back at her. He gave her a small nod and she nodded back.

'Right, three, two, one . . . Go!'

There was a sudden surge by the door as the police pushed forwards. June waited for the crash as the doors flew open, but to her amazement the old trolley held its own and was still standing, blocking the door.

'Come on, push harder,' an officer shouted, and there was a grunt as they increased their exertion. The trolley swayed and June willed it to remain upright, but the force was too much. It gave a final, belligerent wobble, then crashed onto its side. The doors swung open and within seconds, the police were inside the library and surrounding Stanley. One of them stepped towards him and pulled Stanley's arms behind his back with what looked like a lot of force. June let out a cry as she lost sight of him in the mass of bodies. For a few moments she could see only the backs of police officers and then Stanley emerged again, an officer holding him on either side, his hands in cuffs.

'Save Chalcot Library!' he shouted as Cleo rushed forwards with her camera. 'This library is a lifeline to hundreds of people.'

'Get him in the van,' one of the officers said.

'Don't let the government destroy our libraries!' Stanley shouted even louder as they bundled him through the crowd.

'Go, Stanley!' Mrs B called, punching the air. 'Down with library cuts!'

The two officers on either side of Stanley half-lifted, half-pushed him into the van, and the back doors slammed shut as it pulled away. June watched it speed down The Parade. Everything had gone very quiet.

'Let's get this library secured,' Richard said, and two men in overalls stepped forwards with a tool kit.

'What will happen to the library now?' June said, but Richard ignored her.

'Bloody hell,' Mrs B said, as the police van disappeared round the corner. 'Yet again Stanley Phelps surprises us all.'

Chapter Twenty-Five

THE NEAREST POLICE STATION was in New Cowley. It was a half-hour bus journey, which June spent imagining Stanley trapped in a small cell, surrounded by hardened criminals. He'd be dragged into an interview room, where a handsome but bad-tempered officer would interrogate him, slamming his fist on the desk and knocking over a cup of water. Stanley would refuse to give up the names or details of his fellow protesters, enraging the officer until he stood up and shouted—

'Next stop is New Cowley town centre.'

June jumped off the bus and hurried across the road to the police station. There was no one in the waiting room, just a few blue plastic chairs and a large hatch in the wall, behind which sat a middle-aged police officer reading a Dan Brown book.

June approached the window. 'Excuse me?'

The officer didn't look up from his page. 'Yes?'

'I'm here to see Stanley Phelps.'

'Your name?'

'June Jones. Can I see him, please?'

He glanced up at her. 'Are you his solicitor?'

'No. I'm his friend.'

'Only solicitors are allowed to see people in custody.'

'Has he got a solicitor?'

'I'm afraid I'm not at liberty to discuss this with you.'

June read his name badge and gave her most charming smile. 'Please, Officer Riley. He's an elderly gentleman and he has no family here. I just want to make sure he's OK.'

Officer Riley stared back at her, unsmiling. 'As I said, only solicitors are allowed to visit a client in custody.' His eyes returned to the dog-eared book.

June stood there for a moment, but when it was clear that he'd finished with her, she took a seat on one of the chairs. Would Stanley have a solicitor? And if he did, would they be good enough to stop him being charged?

A thought occurred to June, and she reached into her pocket for her mobile phone, only to realise she didn't have it on her. In the chaos of the eviction she must have left it in the library. She walked back to the hatch.

'Excuse me?'

Officer Riley raised his eyes grudgingly from the page. 'Yes?'

'Could I please borrow your phone?'

'I'm afraid that's not possible.'

'But don't people get one phone call at times like this?'

'That's people who've been arrested, not members of the public.'

June could tell he wasn't going to budge, but then a door opened behind him and another police officer walked in. He caught sight of June through the hatch. 'Aren't you a librarian at Chalcot Library?'

'I'm the library assistant,' she said.

'I take my kids there sometimes. My daughter loves those Dr Seuss books. I was just there for the eviction.'

'That's why I'm here actually, Officer . . .?'

'Inspector Parks.'

'My friend from the protest has been arrested.'

'Mr Phelps? I've been interviewing him.'

'Is he OK? I'm trying to sort out some help for him. I was asking your nice colleague here if he could find me a phone number and let me use the phone so I could make a quick call.'

'Course we can. Help this young lady, Riley.'

The officer scowled at being bossed around in front of her. 'What number do you want?'

'The Golden Dragon, please, in Chalcot.'

Both police officers looked at June in surprise.

'You want a number for a Chinese takeaway?' Parks said.

'Yes.'

'You're going to order food? Now?'

The two men exchanged glances, and Parks reached for his mobile phone and searched for the number before writing it down and handing the piece of paper to June. She typed the number into the phone on the desk, her hands shaking. They were both still watching her. June heard the ringing on the line and held her breath, praying someone would answer.

'You know, I'm a bit peckish,' Officer Riley said. 'If you're ordering, I wouldn't mind some spring rolls.'

'Shhh,' June said.

'Hello, Golden Dragon.'

'George, it's me, June.'

George let out a grunt. 'Your usual?'

'Not now, thanks. Is Alex there?'

'Sure, you want delivery? Your usual?'

'George, please can I talk to Alex?'

He grunted again and hollered, 'Al!'

'Duck pancakes,' Officer Riley mouthed through the glass.

There was a muffled sound on the line and June heard Alex's voice. 'Hello?'

June wasn't sure she'd ever been so relieved to hear a voice in her life. 'Alex, I need your help.'

'June, is everything all right?'

'Stanley's been arrested.'

'What happened?'

'I don't have time to explain. Please can you come down to New Cowley police station?'

'Of course. I'm on my way.'

June hung up the phone.

'Did you order the food?' Riley said.

'Seriously?'

'Well, if he's coming all this way . . .'

June picked up the phone and dialled the number again.

Half an hour later, Alex ran into the police station, still wearing his apron and carrying a plastic bag. When June saw him, she had an overwhelming urge to rush over and give him a hug, but she hung back.

'Ah, nice one,' Riley said, as Alex handed over the bag. He'd been marginally nicer to June since she'd placed his food order. 'How much do I owe you?'

'Nine pounds twenty,' Alex said. 'Now, can I see Stanley Phelps?'

'Look, lad. I told your friend here, no one can see him except a solicitor. Don't think you can soften me up with a few duck pancakes.'

'I *am* a solicitor,' Alex said.

June saw Riley eye him up and down. 'Is this some kind of joke?'

Alex reached into his pocket, pulled out a business card and handed it over. The officer read it and stood up.

'Right, come this way,' he said, walking round to open the interconnecting door.

'Let me know if I can do anything to help,' June said, and Alex nodded as he went through the door.

The waiting room was empty again. Officer Riley returned to his seat and began to eat. June sat down on a hard plastic chair and tried to ignore the noisy slurps and chewing. There was no clock on the wall and without her phone she had no idea what the time was. The only indicator was her growling stomach as the smell of spring rolls and Peking duck wafted over. Every now and then people came in and out of the waiting room, receiving the same charmless welcome from Officer Riley, but there was no sign of her friends.

'So, why do the council want to shut this library anyway?' Riley said, when he'd finished eating.

'Funding cuts.'

'It's the one in Chalcot, isn't it? Last time I drove past it was looking pretty run-down.'

June thought she might have preferred his unfriendly silence. 'It hasn't had any money spent on it for years. The council keep cutting our budget.'

'Same with us,' he said, raising his eyebrows. 'Our budget was slashed nine years ago. This place is falling apart.'

'Do you think my friend will be here much longer?'

'All depends.'

'On what?'

'Well, let's see. First off, there's refusal to leave the property when told to do so by the court. Then there's resisting arrest.'

'He didn't resist arrest.'

'Apparently there was a tussle in the van.'

June put her head in her hands. 'Oh god.'

'Let's hope that solicitor friend of yours is as good as his spring rolls. Speak of the devil . . .'

The door swung open and Alex walked in.

'What happened . . . ?' June started to say, but the door opened again, and Stanley walked through. He looked grey, his brow furrowed, and this time June couldn't stop herself from running across the room and throwing her arms round him. 'Oh, Stanley, are you all right?'

'Of course I am,' he said, looking embarrassed.

'Let's get outside, shall we?' said Alex.

June turned to say goodbye to Riley, but his head was buried in the book again. She noticed he had a plum sauce stain on his shirt.

'What happened?' she said, when they got out into the car park.

'Not a thing,' Stanley said.

'Really? What about the charges?'

'It turns out Inspector Parks is a fan of the library,' Alex said. 'He agreed to let Stanley off with a warning. Although he asked that you consider dropping his wife's charge for an overdue Michael McIntyre DVD.'

June was so relieved she laughed out loud. 'That's amazing.'

'It was all thanks to young Alex,' Stanley said. 'He was most impressive in there.'

'Parks just likes my dad's cooking. He's a regular at the takeaway,' Alex said.

'Have you been waiting here this whole time?' Stanley asked June. 'You didn't need to.'

Alex walked towards his car. 'I'm afraid I've got to get back to the Golden Dragon, Dad's on his own and he's still meant to be off work. Can I give either of you a lift back to Chalcot?'

'I'll get the bus,' Stanley said. He was leaning on a bollard and June noticed for the first time how tired he looked.

'Why don't we get a lift with Alex?' she said.

'The bus is fine.'

June shrugged. 'I'll get the bus back with Stanley then. Thanks so much for helping, Alex.'

'You're more than welcome.' He gave her a wave, got into his car and drove off.

'You should have gone with him,' Stanley said.

'Don't be silly, I'll come back with you.'

'There's no need – I'm perfectly capable of getting home on my own.' He turned and started walking towards the bus stop.

June rushed to catch up with him. 'I can't believe you did that at the library. You're Mrs Bransworth's new hero,' she said, but he didn't respond. 'Are you all right, Stanley?'

'I'm fine, my dear. Just a little tired.'

The bus pulled up and they got on. Stanley slumped
down in a seat next to the window and closed his eyes.
He'd seemed so buoyant throughout the occupation, but
June could see now the toll it had taken on him. They
didn't talk the whole journey back to Chalcot and, as
they started down the hill towards the village, June
wondered if Stanley had fallen asleep. She didn't know
where he lived and she didn't want him to miss his stop,
but at the same time she didn't want to disturb him. As
she was about to touch his arm to wake him, Stanley's
eyes snapped open and he stood up.

'This is my stop,' he said, leaning forwards to ring
the bell.

'You live out here?' They were still a good mile out of
the village, surrounded by open fields.

The bus slowed down and Stanley stood up to get off.

'Would you like me to come back with you?' June
asked.

'I'm fine, thank you.'

'But you don't look great, why don't I walk you home?'

'I said, I'm fine.' June had never heard Stanley use such
a curt tone. 'Thank you for your concern but I really am
all right. Now go home and we shall regroup at the library
next week.'

He disembarked and June turned in her seat to watch
him as the bus drew away. He took a few steps forwards
and paused to lean on a fence post, before setting off

along a footpath that led into a field. June turned back
to face the front. She'd never known Stanley to be so
abrupt with her, but maybe he was simply tired after the
occupation and being arrested. Besides, he wouldn't appreciate her following him home like some kind of stalker,
and it was really none of her business where he—

'Stop the bus!'

The driver slammed on the brake. 'What's wrong?'

'I'm sorry but I need to check if my friend is OK. Please
can I get off here?'

'I can only let you down at a designated stop.'

'Please, it's an emergency.'

The driver shook her head, but the bus doors swung
open and June jumped down. She hurried back up the
road towards the bus stop. When she got there, she could
see Stanley striding across the field towards some woods
on the far side. June set off after him, but he was walking
fast, and by the time she got to the woods, she was panting.
The footpath carried on along the edge of the field, but
June had seen Stanley head into the trees. What was he
doing all the way out here? June had assumed there was
nothing but farmland around here; she'd had no idea there
were any houses.

The trees closed in around her as she entered the woods,
cutting out the late afternoon light. There wasn't any kind
of path and June found herself tripping over roots and
low branches. Birds shrieked in the canopy above her, and

more than once she had to grab hold of a branch to stop herself from falling over.

'Stanley!'

There was a squawk as some birds flew up in alarm, and her voice echoed through the trees. In the distance, June could make out shafts of sunlight through the gloom so she made her way towards them. At one point her foot slipped on some damp soil and she fell on her side, landing in some stinging nettles and swearing. She limped to the end of the woods and emerged into a clearing, brushing herself down.

The first thing that struck June was how beautiful it was. She was standing on the edge of a small meadow, with long grass and wildflowers soaked in the August sunlight. She could hear water to her left and turned to see a small stream running along the edge of the woods, carrying tiny silver fish in its current. June's eyes followed the stream's path, and that's when she saw it. Parked about thirty metres away, under the shade of a large oak tree, was a small, decrepit caravan. There were tangled vines growing up one side and a washing line strung between the caravan and the tree, on which hung a shirt and one pair of socks, swaying in the breeze.

'Oh my god,' June said, under her breath.

The caravan door opened, and Stanley stepped out, pausing on the front step to take a long stretch. June's instinct was to drop to the ground, but at that moment

Stanley turned to look at her. His expression remained blank, and then he walked back inside.

June's stomach fell. What had she been thinking, following Stanley like some second-rate Nancy Drew? He'd made it very clear he didn't want her to come to his home, and now she could see why. Poor, poor Stanley. She'd started back towards the trees, mortified, when she heard his voice call out after her.

'I suppose you had better come in.'

June headed back towards the caravan. When she got to the door, she hovered outside, unsure, then pushed it open and stepped in. The caravan was dimly lit, and it took a moment for her eyes to adjust to the gloom. To her left was a narrow single bed, neatly made with a sheet and blanket. Against the far wall was what looked like a cooker and a small sink, on the side of which sat a single plate and mug. On the right was a small table covered in papers, at which Stanley was now sitting, watching her survey the caravan.

'Stanley, I—'

'You don't have to say it,' he interrupted. 'The look on your face is the very reason I never invite people to come here.'

June tried to compose her features. 'It's lovely. Very . . . cosy.'

'It does perfectly well for my needs.'

'How long have you lived out here?'

'Twelve years. Before that I was at a spot on the other side of the village, but I got moved on from there.'

'I had no idea, Stanley. Does anyone else know you live here?'

'One or two, but I prefer to keep it private.'

June remembered their conversation about his being homeless in the past; it had never occurred to her that he might still be. She looked around again. Despite its small size, there was hardly anything in the caravan: no pictures or souvenirs, no mementos of a life lived.

'I wish you'd told me.'

'Told you what?'

'Well, you know . . . that you're homeless.'

'I'm not homeless,' he said, and there was a sharp edge in his voice. 'Just because I choose to live here doesn't mean I need your pity.'

'I wasn't pitying you,' June said, although she knew she wasn't convincing either of them. 'It must just be hard living all the way out here.'

'It's not that remote – it's less than a two-mile walk into the village along the river. And soon I'll be getting some damned new neighbours.' He pointed over his shoulder at the trees behind the caravan. 'A new housing development is going up on the other side of this copse. Eighty flats and houses they're building. The developers have been making my life hell.'

'But what do you do for electricity and water?'

'I get fresh water from that stream which I boil up, and I have a gas canister for the cooker and heater. These do me for lights.' He pointed at two small camping lanterns on the table. 'Plus, there's the lovely clean facilities at the library, which I make liberal use of.' He winked at June as he said this, and she found herself smiling in return.

'That's why you're always the first to arrive.'

'Yet another reason why we must protect the library, my dear.'

'But don't the council have a duty to provide you with somewhere to live?'

'What, and be put in some flat on the twentieth floor of a tower block?' Stanley shuddered. 'No, thank you very much, I'd rather live out here.'

'What if something happened to you?'

'I've been looking after myself perfectly well for years. And while this might not be The Savoy, at least I'm free from prying eyes.'

He didn't say it unkindly, but June felt a flush of shame. 'I'm so sorry, Stanley. I shouldn't have followed you. I was worried about you, that's all.'

'I know you were, and I thank you for being such a good friend. But if you don't mind, I'm rather tired, and I'd like to get some rest now.'

'Of course.' June backed towards the door and paused. 'Are you sure you'll be all right?'

'I'll be fine. Although it will be rather quiet after the last few days with you rabble in the library.'

June hesitated. 'You can always come and stay with me for a bit, you know. I have a spare room.'

'Thank you, June, but this is my home.'

Chapter Twenty-Six

JUNE SLEPT DEEPLY THAT NIGHT, the exhaustion of the past few days finally catching up with her. When she woke, she lay with her eyes closed, listening out for the voices of her fellow protesters, before she remembered that the occupation was over, and she was back at home. She sat up, taking in the familiar sights of her childhood bedroom: her favourite books on the bookcase, the quilt that her mum had made for her spread over the bed, her old teddy bear watching from the windowsill. June got up, pulled on her dressing gown and went downstairs. Alan Bennett was sitting by the front door and gave a listless miaow when he saw her.

'Morning. Did you miss me?'

He turned and stalked into the kitchen and June followed. The room was silent apart from the rhythmic ticking of the clock. Had it always been this quiet in the house? June flicked on the old radio in the corner of the kitchen. A pop song blared out, too loud, and she turned it off again. She glanced at the clock: ten a.m. It was a bank holiday weekend, so the library wouldn't be open again until Tuesday morning. That meant seventy-two hours before she'd see anyone again; seventy-two hours of reading and peace and quiet, on her own.

Yet where once a long weekend at home would have filled June with joy, now she felt strangely restless. She went back upstairs, had a shower and got dressed. She ate breakfast, washed up the dishes and dusted the living room. She read *Wolf Hall* for an hour but couldn't concentrate, rereading the same page three times. What would Stanley be doing right now? Would he be alone in his caravan until the library opened again on Tuesday?

June walked into the kitchen and opened the freezer. A microwave lasagne sat on the shelf, waiting for her. She looked at the clock again. Seventy hours until the library opened. Seventy hours until she'd talk to another soul.

June grabbed her keys and headed out of the front door. As she rang the bell next door, she realised she was still wearing her slippers.

'June, what a lovely surprise!' Linda opened the door wearing chandelier earrings, fuchsia lipstick and an apron with the figure of a bikini-clad woman on it.

'Hi. I was wondering if you fancied a . . .' From inside the house, June heard voices. 'Oh, I'm sorry to bother you, Linda. I didn't realise you had guests.'

'It's just the family here for lunch. Come and join us.'

'It's not urgent, I'll come round tomorrow,' she said, backing away. Linda often invited her to join their meals, but June had always declined, not wanting to intrude on family time.

She turned to walk back to her empty home and the microwave meal-for-one. Behind her, she heard a peal of laughter from inside Linda's, and June was reminded of the meals she'd eaten in the library over the past few days, sharing a table and food with others, chatting and laughing. Now that the occupation was over, she would be back to eating every meal alone.

June turned around. 'Actually, Linda, I'd love to join you, if that's OK?'

'Of course it is, love.' Linda looked delighted. 'I'm just carving the beef. Go on through to the living room and say hi to everyone.'

Although Linda's house was the same layout as June's, her living room couldn't have been more different. A huge flat-screen TV filled the wall where June had her bookshelves, and there were no ornaments cluttering up the surfaces, just a few family photos and the odd scented candle. Linda's daughter, Clare, was sitting on the pristine cream sofa with her husband, their three kids sprawled on the floor playing a board game with Linda's son, Martin. Her middle child, Elaine, was there with Jackson, who jumped up as June walked into the room.

'June, you're here!'

'I'm sorry to disturb you all.'

'Don't be silly, it's lovely to see you,' Clare said, standing up and pulling June into a hug. She had a large bump under her T-shirt, which June assumed must be child number four on the way. 'I hope you're staying for lunch. Mum has done far too much, as usual. You'd think there were fifty of us from the amount she cooks.'

No sooner had she said it than Linda marched in through the door, declaring that lunch was served, and June was caught up in the bustle of the family charging towards the dining table. She found herself being steered into a seat between Linda and Jackson.

'Wine?' Linda said, pouring her a glass before she could respond.

In the middle of the table sat the biggest joint of roast beef June had ever seen, surrounded by dishes containing all the accompaniments. People started piling food onto their plates, all the while talking over each other. June's plate was soon overflowing, and she allowed the clamour of conversation to wash over her as she ate. Across the table, Martin and the eldest grandson were swapping rude jokes, and June laughed as she heard snippets of the punchlines. To her right, Linda was having an intense conversation with Clare about the boys' primary school.

'It's shocking,' Clare was saying. 'The school is so under-funded they can't even afford stationery for all the kids. We got a letter at the end of last term asking parents to donate pens and notepads, can you believe it?'

'Outrageous,' Linda said.

'All those MPs with their big salaries and private school educations, and yet state schools don't have enough money to teach kids properly. Honestly, I'm so angry I'm thinking of writing a letter to my MP.'

'You should do a protest like June,' Jackson said. 'She's an expert now.'

'Really?' Clare turned to June, a look of surprise on her face.

'Well, I'm not exactly an expert,' June said.

'Oh yes, she organised an occupation of our library because the council wants to close it,' Linda said. 'They got in the papers and on the TV. Chalcot Library is famous.'

'Wow, that's amazing,' said Martin, who had stopped telling jokes to listen. 'What was the occupation like? Did you sleep there?'

'Yes, for three nights. The council evicted us yesterday.'

'Good on you, girl,' Clare said. 'That takes proper guts.'

June smiled at the compliment.

'What will happen now?' asked Martin. 'Will you carry on protesting?'

'Of course – we have to. The council are doing a consultation, which ends in four weeks' time. We need to make sure the library is as busy as possible so our visitor numbers are high. And we need to keep campaigning, so we don't let the pressure off the council.'

June realised that everyone had stopped talking to listen to her. She was amazed by the vehemence of her own words, and by the admiring looks the family were giving her.

'Listen to you talk, I hardly recognise you,' Linda said, beaming at her.

'To June!' Clare said, and there was a roar of boisterous toasting around the table.

On Tuesday morning, June left the house with butterflies circling in her stomach. For all her bravado on Saturday, she was terrified about what she'd find when she turned up at the library today. Marjorie would be furious with her, of course, and no doubt there would be trouble from the council. But she'd get to see Stanley and the other members of FOCL again, and they could make a plan for the last leg of the campaign. She'd been thinking about it all weekend and had several ideas about how they could keep the momentum going.

June was rounding the corner onto The Parade when she saw Vera standing outside the post office.

'Morning, Vera, how are you?'

'Mustn't grumble. Although my hip is—'

'I'm sorry, I'd love to chat, but I have to get to work.'

'What's going on there today?' Vera said.

'Marjorie's due to host a Techie Tea this morning. Do you want to join?'

'No, I mean now – there's a group of people outside. That man from the council is there.'

'You mean Richard Donnelly?'

'The one who's an oily wan—'

'I've got to go. Sorry, Vera.'

June turned and hurried towards the library. As she approached, she could see Donnelly outside, talking to a man and woman.

'What's going on?' she said, when she reached them.

'Good morning, Miss Jones,' Richard said. 'I was wondering if you'd turn up. Did you receive our email?'

'No, I left my phone here. What's going on?'

'I think we're all done,' Richard said to the other two, who nodded and walked away. He turned to June. 'The council have decided to conduct a full inquiry into the events of last week, including the involvement of a council employee in the occupation and subsequent damage to the library. Until the inquiry is finished, you are to be relieved of all duties at Chalcot Library.'

'What?'

'You're suspended. On full pay, of course, until the council have clarified your role in the matter and decided if any further action needs to be taken.'

'Hang on – what do you mean, damage?'

Richard looked down at his clipboard. 'For a start, there was damage to the paintwork in the main room . . .'

'We only hung those posters up for a few days.'

'Chips to the tables . . .'

'Those tables are at least twenty years old.'

'Stains on the carpet . . .'

Damn, the coffee. 'But I scrubbed that myself.'

'Our surveyors have been around and say that we'll need to replace the whole carpet.'

'That's rubbish, it was one tiny mark.'

'I'm not going to stand here arguing with you, Miss Jones. The council have made their decision, which you would know if you'd bothered to read the email. Until the inquiry is finished, you are not to enter the library for work or personal reasons.'

'This is crazy. There wasn't any damage to the library – we made the place look better. And who will cover me while I'm suspended?'

'We're bringing someone in from Central to assist Marjorie. Unfortunately, the council doesn't have the resources to fully cover you, so the library opening hours will have to be reduced.'

'No! You can't, please. If the library hours are cut then our visitor numbers will go down and that will affect the consultation.'

Richard shrugged. 'The decision is out of my hands, Miss Jones.'

There was something about the way he said her name that made June's skin crawl. 'This is deliberate, isn't it? You want to make it look like the library is failing because you want to close it. Are you in on this Cuppa Coffee deal too?'

'I have no idea what you're talking about,' Richard said. 'And I suggest you stop making such wild accusations.

Your irresponsible behaviour has done enough damage to this library already.' He turned and started walking towards the library.

'My phone is in there,' June called after him. 'Can I at least collect it?'

Richard sighed. 'All right. But wait in the entrance while I find it.'

Inside the library, everything looked exactly as June had left it on Friday, yet something was different. It wasn't the fact the blinds were no longer brown with dust, or the faint smell of fresh paint mixed in with the familiar scents of wood and paper. And it certainly wasn't the tiny coffee stain on the carpet, no bigger than a paperback. No, it was something about the sound of the library; the silence felt different somehow. June might be wrong, but it felt like the stories had stopped whispering to each other.

'Here you go.' Richard walked out of the office and handed June her phone.

She stared at it, unsure what to do next. 'Do you have to do this? Please, can't you keep the library's normal hours until the consultation ends?'

Richard looked at her for a moment. 'What did you think would happen? That you could humiliate the council on the news and we'd just let you get away with it?'

'If you're angry at me then go ahead and sack me. But please, don't punish the whole community because of something I did.'

He let out a dry laugh. 'Perhaps you should have thought about that before you pulled your little stunt? You have no one to blame but yourself for the library hours being cut.'

'Please, Richard. I'm begging you.'

'I suggest you leave the premises now. You're breaking the terms of your suspension and I'll have to call the police.'

June took one last glance around the library. She felt her eyes start to well up, so she turned and ran out the door.

Chapter Twenty-Seven

JUNE SPENT THE REST of the week hiding at home. She couldn't sleep and had no appetite. She tried reading *Sense and Sensibility*, but not even Elinor Dashwood and Edward Ferrars could cheer her up. Richard's words ran through her mind on an agonising loop. *Did you think we'd let you get away with humiliating the council? You have no one to blame but yourself for the library hours being cut.*

June paced the house like a caged animal. If only she'd followed Marjorie's advice and stayed out of the protests, allowed others to fight for the library instead of getting involved. Why had she ever thought she could help, when in fact she'd just made everything worse? And then there were the FOCL members – would they blame June when they found out the library hours had been reduced because of her suspension?

But mostly she thought of Stanley, alone in that small, dark caravan. She now understood why he spent all day in the library, especially in the colder months. How would he survive the next winter without the library? All these thoughts invaded every waking minute and would only stop when June drank so much wine she passed out asleep.

On Friday morning, when she'd run out of alcohol and eaten the last item of food in the freezer, June pulled on a pair of trainers and left the house. As she reached the village green, she saw Stanley sitting on a bench by the pond, engrossed in a book. June didn't want to bother him but, as she walked past, he looked up and waved her over.

'June! Do join me.' He indicated the bench next to him and June sat down. 'Have you read this?' he said, showing her the cover of his book. It was a library copy of *The House at Pooh Corner*. 'It was Mark's favourite when he was small. I must have read it to him dozens of times.'

'It was one of my favourites too,' June said.

He returned to reading, and the silence between them grew until June couldn't bear it any longer. 'Stanley, I'm so sorry.'

'What for?' he asked, his eyes still on the page.

'For everything.'

'I don't follow.'

June took a long breath. Maybe Stanley hadn't worked it out, but she had to be honest with him. 'It's my fault that the library hours have been reduced; the council have done it to punish me for joining the occupation. Now visitor and issue numbers will be down, and they'll have the perfect excuse to close the library.'

When she finished speaking, she looked across to see Stanley watching her with a strange expression. 'Have you been hiding under a rock all week?'

'I've been at home.'

'So, you really have no idea what's been going on?'

June stared at him. 'What are you talking about?'

'Oh, my dear, you've inspired a revolution,' Stanley said, his face breaking into a smile.

'What?'

'I can't believe you don't know. Once word got out that you'd been suspended, the village was up in arms. People started coming into the library furious about it and demanding to know how they could help.'

June felt the colour returning to her cheeks.

'Then I remembered what Matilda – I mean, you – had said about getting people to take out as many library books as possible,' Stanley continued. 'So that's what we've started asking people to do. I wish you could see it; everyone has borrowed the maximum number on their card.' He brandished the book in his hand as evidence of his own borrowing. 'Even people who haven't used the library in years are taking out books. Marjorie can't keep up with the demand and the shelves are half empty.'

June was still too stunned to speak.

'It's all because of you, my dear. People are furious that the council would suspend you after everything you've done for the library and this community.'

'I can't believe it.'

'There's no way the council can claim we're a failing library now. Why, this week Chalcot must be the best-performing library in the whole county!'

'Stanley, this is amazing.'

'We're all going to go to the council meeting on the twenty-fourth, when they'll make their decision. It's our final battle against the giants,' Stanley said with glee. 'You must come too, June dear. We'll need you there.'

'Of course I will.' June allowed herself to smile for the first time in days. 'We can do this, Stanley. I know we can.'

June returned home with her shopping, still grinning at the news. She found her old copy of *The House at Pooh Corner* on her bedroom bookshelf and took it out into the overgrown garden. She was reading the last chapter when she heard her front doorbell ring. June assumed it must be Linda, who'd been finding tenuous excuses to come round and check up on her all week, but when she opened the door she found Alex standing on the step.

'You've not been answering my texts,' he said. 'Are you OK?'

'I'm sorry, I've been holed up here.'

'I've brought you some food,' he said, lifting the bag he was carrying. 'Your usual plus some extras.'

'Thank you. Come in.' As June led him into the kitchen, she was acutely aware of the tired decor and her mum's old ornaments on every surface. 'Sorry, I need to give this place a repaint.'

'Well hello, little fellow.'

June turned around to see Alex bending down to pet Alan Bennett, who was lying in his basket.

'Oh, I wouldn't do that . . .' she started, but it was too late – Alan snarled and lashed out with his paw, connecting with Alex's hand.

'Ouch,' he said, recoiling. 'Bloody hell, your cat is vicious.'

'I'm sorry, Alan's a little antisocial. He adored Mum but he's always hated me.'

'I've never heard of a cat hating someone before.'

'I kept thinking he'd warm to me after Mum died and it was just the two of us. But it's been eight years now and he's still a miserable bugger.'

Alex laughed and began unloading cartons onto the table. 'I've decided it's time you expanded your repertoire. My dad's family come from the Sichuan province, so that's his speciality.' He opened a container. 'This is fish-fragrant aubergine.'

'Fish-fragrant?'

'And these are green beans with pork and chilli, one of my favourites.'

June fetched a plate and sat down as Alex spooned some aubergine onto it. She ate a mouthful. 'Wow, that's delicious.'

'See, what did I tell you?' Alex said, with satisfaction. 'Now try the hot and numbing beef, but only if you can handle spicy food. My dad always says chilli is a natural antidepressant . . .' He paused, looking uncomfortable. 'Not that I'm suggesting you're depressed, but I heard about you getting suspended. Why didn't you call me?'

'Sorry. I've been here all week, thinking everyone must blame me.'

'God no, quite the opposite.'

'Stanley told me about people borrowing books.'

'I've never seen the library so busy. I've taken twelve books out on my card, although without you there to advise me I panicked and took out the most random selection. I even came home with a *Bridgerton* book.'

June chuckled. 'I'm so glad people are doing this. If we have high visitor and issue numbers it'll make it much harder for the council to close us down.'

'I wish it were that simple,' Alex said.

'What do you mean?'

'Well, there's still the whole Cuppa Coffee issue.'

'But how will the council justify closing the library if it's clearly well-used?'

'They could find a way,' Alex said. 'After all, this whole consultation has been about the council trying to save money, not how popular the library is.'

June felt all the positivity of this afternoon fading away. 'I just wish we knew what Brian and Marjorie are up to with Cuppa Coffee.'

'Do you think it's time for you to confront Marjorie about it directly?'

June shook her head. 'There's no way she'd tell me anything – she must hate me after the occupation. Besides, I'm banned from the library and it's not as if I can just turn up at her house.'

'I'd offer to help but I'm not sure what I can do either,' Alex said.

June took another a mouthful of the beans. 'Oh my god, Gayle's wedding!' she said, almost choking on her food.

'You're not going to that, are you?'

'It might be my only chance to talk to Brian and Marjorie.'

Alex looked sceptical. 'They're hardly going to confess everything at their daughter's wedding.'

'No, but Marjorie has told me repeatedly that they've invited the great and the good of Dunningshire. If I go in the evening, once people have had a few drinks, maybe someone will let something slip about Cuppa Coffee?' Even as she said it, June knew it sounded ridiculous.

Alex was watching her with a pained expression. 'Are you sure you want to go, after what happened at the hen do?'

Was she sure? It would be so much easier to carry on hiding at home, never putting herself out there or taking any risks. 'Yes, I'm sure. This feels like my last chance to try and do something to save the library.'

'When is the wedding?'

'A week on Saturday.'

'Well, I'm happy to be your plus one, if you want some moral support?'

June was so surprised by the offer that she stuffed a piece of beef into her mouth. Within seconds the heat exploded on her tongue like a fireball and she let out a gasp, making Alex jump.

'I mean, only if you want me to,' he said. 'As a friend, you know . . .' He was blushing now, but June was too busy necking her glass of water.

'Great, thanks,' she said, trying to stop her tongue hanging out of her mouth in agony.

'I'd better get going.' Alex stood up and headed towards the door. 'Careful of that beef, some bits can be quite spicy. And water won't help, eat some rice instead.'

'Thanks.'

'I'll see you next Saturday.'

'OK, bye.'

June slammed the door shut, ran back into the kitchen and started shovelling rice into her mouth.

Chapter Twenty-Eight

JUNE STOOD IN FRONT OF THE MIRROR, staring at her reflection. She'd bought the dress, which the lady in the shop had described as 'burnt umber', in a panicked shopping trip yesterday. It had a red and gold pattern down the front, and in the changing room June had hoped it looked classy and sophisticated. Now, in the unforgiving light of her bedroom, she realised she looked like a tube of Rolos. She twisted her hair into a French plait and went downstairs. Alan Bennett was sitting in the hallway smirking.

'Do I look that bad? I know these shoes aren't perfect . . .' She looked down at her black heels, which she'd last worn to her mum's funeral.

Alan licked his bottom in response.

In the kitchen, June poured another glass of wine, surprised to see she'd drunk half a bottle already. Why had she said she'd go to this stupid wedding? The thought of seeing all those women from the hen do had kept her awake all night. Plus, they were bound to have worked out by now that it was June who'd diverted the stripper, and they'd be furious about that. This was a terrible idea.

June heard the sound of a car pulling up, so she drained the last of her wine and stepped outside. Alex was standing beside the car, holding the front passenger door open. His usual T-shirt and jeans had been replaced by a smart grey suit and a bright blue tie, his messy hair brushed back. June had never seen him look so stylish, and she felt self-conscious under his gaze as she walked up the path.

'You look lovely,' Alex said, as she reached the car.

June felt herself blush, and she mumbled a thank you as she climbed into the passenger's seat.

They drove in silence, both staring out of the windscreen. June felt light-headed; why was she putting herself through this? She still hadn't worked out what she was going to say to Marjorie and Brian. She wanted to ask Alex his opinion, but every time she glanced over at him, she felt oddly tongue-tied.

They arrived at Marjorie and Brian's house and Alex pulled into a field signposted for parking. The guests who'd been invited for the whole day had parked their cars long ago, and the grass had been churned up into thick mud. As June got out of the car her heels sank into the ground.

'Agh, help!'

'Are you OK?' Alex rushed around to her side of the car.

'I'm sinking,' June said, feeling her shoes slipping under the mud.

'Let me help you.' Alex took her arm gently, but June was stuck fast.

'You're going to need to pull harder,' she said, mortified.

He held her elbow and began to tug. For a moment June wobbled, and then her feet came free with a loud squelch and she tumbled against him. Alex steadied her and then took her hand, helping June through the mud to the road. She tried not to fall over, but she was acutely aware of the tingling heat of his palm against hers. When they reached the road, she expected Alex to let go immediately but he didn't. June felt a flush of pleasure at the contact, then she remembered Ellie and pulled her hand away.

'Look at the state of me,' she said, looking down at her mud-stained shoes and ankles.

'Never fear, I was a Boy Scout, so I'm always prepared.' Alex pulled a white handkerchief out of his pocket with a flourish, and then to June's horror he bent down and began to wipe the mud off her feet.

'Don't be silly, I can do that,' she yelped, but he carried on. It felt strangely intimate to have him cleaning her feet, and June's skin was burning.

'Well, it's not perfect but it's the best I can do,' Alex said, standing up. They both surveyed her brown feet and shoes.

'Thank you,' June said, and her voice sounded strange. 'Shall we go?'

Distant music floated towards them as they approached
the mock-Georgian house. Matching topiary hedges lined
the gravel drive and the front door was guarded by two
pillars.

'No guests inside the house.' A man in a high-vis jacket
came rushing towards them. 'I'm sorry, only VIP guests
are allowed in there. Please go round the side instead.'

They walked round to the back garden, where a giant
blancmange-like marquee had been erected in the middle
of the lawn. A waiter approached them with a tray of
drinks; June took a lethal-looking cocktail and Alex a glass
of water. Guests were milling around them on the grass,
laughing with the noisy exuberance of people who'd been
drinking all day.

'God, look at this,' Alex said, surveying the scene. 'It's
like something out of *The Great Gatsby*, and I don't mean
that in a good way.'

June laughed at the reference and felt another flush of
pleasure at being here with Alex, all dressed up and
drinking cocktails. Then she remembered the reason why
they'd come. 'Shall we go into the marquee and see if
Brian or Marjorie are there?'

Inside the tent, there must have been at least twenty
round tables, each groaning under the weight of huge
vases of pink lilies. Some of the older guests were still
sitting at the tables, shouting their conversations over the
roar of the music. At the far side there was a dance floor

under a giant disco-ball, packed with drunken bodies flailing to 'Come on Eileen'.

June surveyed the room. 'I can't see either of them.'

'Can you recognise anyone from the council?' Alex said.

June was about to say 'No' when she caught sight of a man over on the other side of the marquee, deep in conversation with an older woman. 'Oh my god, it's him.'

'Who?'

June looked again in case she'd made a mistake, but it was definitely him: tall, square-jawed, the white-blond hair. 'It's Draco Malfoy.'

Alex didn't respond and, when June turned to look, he was staring at her with a weird expression. 'O-K. I think you've maybe had enough to drink.'

'What?'

'Seriously, if you're seeing villains from kids' books then you probably need to stick to water tonight.'

'No! Draco is my name for one of the guys I saw with Brian that night you and I were in The Chequers. He was the one who was talking about the council and greasing the wheels.'

'Oh, I see. But why would they invite him to the wedding?'

'I guess they must be trying to impress him.'

'I don't believe we've met.' The woman who'd been dressed as Wonder Woman at Gayle's hen do had stepped between June and Alex, extending her hand to him. 'I'm Isabelle.'

'Hi, I'm Alex.'

'*Enchantée*, Alex. How do you know the happy couple?'

'I'm here with June.'

Isabelle noticed June for the first time. 'Nice to meet you.'

'Actually, we've met before,' June said, surprising herself.

'Really? I don't remember you.'

'We sat next to each other at Gayle's hen do.'

Isabelle paused, obviously trying to place June, and her face split into a grin. 'Oh my god, you're the virgin!'

She let out a burst of laugher and June cringed. She glanced at Alex and saw a look of surprise cross his face, although he quickly hid it.

'God, I'm amazed you came after that,' Isabelle said, still laughing.

June forced herself to smile. 'We were wondering, who's that?' She pointed across the room to where Draco was now standing in the middle of a group of guys, all braying.

'Which one?' Isabelle said.

'The one in the middle, over there. With the white-blond hair.'

'Are you telling me you don't know who he is?' She looked at them both in astonishment. 'That's Rupe.'

'Who?'

'Rupert. You know, the groom? Gayle's new husband?'

It took June a moment to register what Isabelle had said. 'That's Gayle's *husband*?'

Isabelle ignored her and fluttered her eyelashes at Alex. 'Do you fancy a dance?'

'Wait. Do you know what Gayle's husband does for a living?' June said.

Isabelle looked at June in annoyance. 'What a strange question. I think Gayle said he has something to do with property acquisitions.' She turned to Alex again. 'Your glass is empty. Joan, could you be a darling and fetch us a drink? We'll have champers.'

June saw Alex open his mouth to protest, but in her shock she turned and walked towards the drinks table, her brain whirring. If Draco Malfoy was Gayle's husband, did that mean that his pub conversation with Brian was simply an innocent chat between father and son-in-law? Then why the talk of councillors and greasing wheels? June picked up another cocktail and took a long swig as she tried to fit the puzzle pieces together.

'What's that on your shoes?' June jumped as Marjorie stepped in next to her.

'Mud, sorry,' June said, trying to discreetly wipe them on the long tablecloth.

'I can't believe you had the nerve to turn up here after all the fuss you've caused at the library,' Marjorie said, wrinkling her nose. 'Do you have any idea of the headaches you've given me? And on top of all of this . . .' She signalled around her at the marquee.

'It's a beautiful wedding, Marjorie.'

'The decorators completely messed up. We were meant to have blush-pink ribbons on the seat covers and they put on flamingo-pink ones instead. Gayle was so upset she nearly cancelled the whole thing.'

June looked at the tiny bows that Marjorie was pointing at. 'I think it looks lovely.'

Marjorie's eyes were scanning the tent and June noticed she was wringing her hands.

She took another slug of her drink. This was it, her chance. 'Marjorie, there's something I need to ask you.'

'Oh no, what are the caterers doing now?' Marjorie said, as two waiters in white uniforms placed a huge, tiered cheeseboard down on the table next to them. 'That isn't meant to come out until nine. It's only eight thirty.'

'Who does your son-in-law work for?' June said.

'I don't know, some American food and beverage company. Why are they putting the cheese here, it goes on the back table. Why must everyone—'

'Does he have anything to do with Cuppa Coffee?'

'And the grapes are meant to be green, not red. Christ, this is a disaster, I need to speak to the catering manager.' Marjorie started to walk off, but June grabbed her arm. Her boss looked at her in surprise. 'What are you doing?'

'Marjorie . . .' June's voice faltered. 'Are you and Brian involved in a plot to close the library?'

'What on earth are you talking about?'

'I saw Brian in the pub with Rupert. I think they were talking about bribing councillors to let someone buy the building. They mentioned you.'

'That's absolute nonsense. You and your imagination, June.'

'And I saw you showing a woman round the library and she had a clipboard with a Cuppa Coffee logo on it.' June saw Marjorie go pale. 'How could you do it, Marjorie? I thought you loved the library.'

'Of course I love the library,' Marjorie hissed. 'You've always lived in a fantasy land, but this is the most ridiculous thing I've ever heard. That woman I showed round was a management consultant.'

'Then why did she have the Cuppa Coffee logo on her clipboard?'

'I don't know – maybe it was a free gift?'

'And why did she come back to secretly visit you early one morning before the library opened? What are you trying to hide, Marjorie?'

'Look, Brian asked me to keep the management consultant's visit quiet for this very reason, to stop people getting carried away with mad conspiracy theories. Now, if you'll excuse me, it's my daughter's wedding.' She turned to walk away again.

June took a deep breath. 'Are you and Brian receiving money from Rupert's company to help them buy the library building and turn it into a Cuppa Coffee?'

Marjorie spun round, a look of disbelief on her face. 'Now this is outrageous!' Her voice had risen, and several people turned to look.

'What's going on here?' Brian walked over to them. 'People are staring at you, Marjorie.'

'June here is making the most scandalous accusations. She says that you and Rupert are involved in some dodgy scam around selling off the library building. I've a good mind to throw her out but I don't want to make a . . .' Marjorie stopped talking as she saw Brian had turned a dark shade of purple.

'What have you been saying?' he said to June.

'I saw you and Rupert in the pub back in July,' June said. 'I heard your conversation.'

Brian gave a small, forced laugh. 'So what? A man having a pint with his future son-in-law is hardly illegal.'

'There was another man there too, and you told them you had the power to convince people on the council. They discussed giving you money.'

'What's she talking about, Brian?' Marjorie said.

'It was about the library, wasn't it?' June said.

'This is all absolute nonsense,' Brian said.

June was aware that people around them had stopped talking and were listening in, but for once she didn't care.

'And what about that woman you got Marjorie to show around the library? She works for Cuppa Coffee, doesn't she?'

'You told me she was a management consultant,' Marjorie said, taking hold of Brian's arm. From the look on her face, June could tell she wasn't pretending. 'Brian, what on earth is going on?'

'Oh, be quiet, dear,' he said, brushing her off. 'I'm not standing here listening to these lies anymore. June has no proof of anything.'

'Oh my god, the money for the wedding!' Marjorie said, her eyes wide.

'Now, dear—' Brian started, reaching for her, but Marjorie stepped away from him.

'I asked you where that extra money came from to pay for all of this and you wouldn't tell me. Brian, what have you done?'

'For god's sake, woman,' he said. 'You're retiring at Christmas – what difference does it make?'

'All this time you've been telling me to relax, that you were working behind the scenes to save the library. And you've been the one trying to get it closed!'

A large group had now gathered to watch, and Brian lowered his voice to a hiss.

'Look, I can't affect the decision the council makes about the library. But if it does close, and Rupert's company does buy the building, there's no harm in you and I benefiting from that, is there?' He went to put his arm around Marjorie's shoulder, but she lurched backwards.

'Get away from me!' She made no effort to keep her voice down.

'How did you expect me to pay for all of this?' Brian said. 'You told me you wanted this wedding to be the biggest Chalcot has ever seen. Do you have any idea how much all of this costs?'

Marjorie looked like she was fighting back tears. 'I've turned a blind eye over the years. But this . . . my library . . .'

'Mum, Dad, what's going on?' They all turned to see Gayle approaching, wearing a long crystal-encrusted wedding dress. Rupert was following her, his eyes narrowed. 'We can hear you all the way from the gazebo.'

'It's nothing, pumpkin, just a little disagreement,' Brian said.

'Mum?'

'Did you know?' Marjorie said to her.

'Know what?'

'About this deal between Daddy and Rupert. About the library.'

'What are you talking about?' Gayle's confused expression made it clear that she had no idea either.

'We should talk about this later,' said Rupert, taking Gayle's arm and trying to steer her away. 'Right now, I'd like a dance with my new wife.'

'They've been plotting to get the library closed so Rupert's company can open a coffee shop there. All of this' – Marjorie indicated around them – 'has been paid for by dirty money your father got from Cuppa Coffee.'

'What? Dad, is this true?' Gayle said.

'Look, let's all talk about this tomorrow, shall we?' Brian said. 'I think your mother is getting a little worked up, it's been a very exciting day for her.'

Gayle nodded, but she was still frowning.

'Honestly, Marjorie, stop making such a fuss,' Brian said, shaking his head as he started to walk away. 'It's only a little library, you don't need to . . .'

'A little library!' Marjorie roared, with such force that everyone stopped. 'I've worked at that library for thirty years, dedicated my life to it. And you dismiss it like that means nothing. You lying, cheating . . .'

June wanted to turn and walk away but it was like watching a car crash in slow motion. Marjorie started to cast around her wildly. It wasn't clear to June what she was looking for, until she saw Marjorie's eyes fall on the giant cheeseboard on the table behind her. Marjorie reached out and for a moment June thought she was going to grab one of the cheese knives. But instead she lifted up a large wheel of Brie, the biggest June had ever seen, and spinning back round, she slung the cheese with all her might at Brian's head.

'Stop!' June shouted, but it was too late as the white disc flew through the air, spinning two or three times before it hit Brian in the face. He staggered backwards and fell against Gayle, who in turn started to topple over. Rupert reached out to grab her and the three of them collapsed onto the marquee floor. There was a moment of agonising silence.

'We should go,' Alex whispered into June's ear. She stared for a moment longer at the scene in front of her: at Gayle in a heap of ivory silk and lace, Brian's Brie-smeared face, and Marjorie, her whole body shaking with rage.

June opened her mouth to say something, but she felt Alex take her hand, pulling her backwards into the crowd, and she turned and followed him. As June walked away she heard Gayle shout, 'How could you do this to me? On my wedding day!'

Chapter Twenty-Nine

THEY DROVE AWAY FROM the wedding as fast as they could, Alex's car bumping along the country lanes, the headlights startling rabbits in the dark. June's head was spinning from all the alcohol and she felt sick. She'd never meant to create a scene like that. Poor Marjorie – she'd been planning today for years and June had brought the whole thing tumbling down.

'Was that woman your boss?' Alex asked, as they reached the outskirts of Chalcot.

June nodded.

'God, I hadn't realised that was her.'

'What do you mean?' She closed her eyes and leaned her head against the window to try to stop the dizziness. She really shouldn't have drunk so much.

'You remember during the library occupation when I brought you guys a takeaway and no one knew who'd paid for it? Well, it was her.'

'What?' June opened her eyes and looked at Alex. 'Marjorie ordered the food?'

'She came into the takeaway in the afternoon and paid by cash. I didn't recognise her, so I assumed she was a protester.'

'Oh no!' June put her hands up to her face. 'All along I thought she was plotting to destroy the library, and actually she's been secretly supporting us.'

They pulled up outside June's house, and Alex turned the engine off.

'Are you OK? You look really pale,' he said.

'I ruined the whole wedding.'

'It wasn't your fault – Brian is the one to blame.'

'Also, I feel a bit sick.'

A panicked look crossed Alex's face. 'Let me help you out the car.'

He rushed around and opened June's door. She tried to stand on her own, but dizziness washed over her and she allowed Alex to help her to the front door. She dug around in her handbag for the front door key, but she couldn't find it.

'Here, let me.' He took the bag from her, pulled out the key and opened the door. 'Do you want me to come in and get you some water?'

'It's fine, I'll be fine.' June leaned against the door frame so she wouldn't fall over. 'I'm sorry. Forgot to eat.'

'Are you sure you'll be all right?'

He gave June a look of such kindness that she felt her breath catch. What would she have done without Alex tonight? In fact, what would she have done without Alex for the past two months? June remembered Stanley's words during the occupation, something about opportunities and seizing them.

'I should get home,' Alex said. He leaned towards June to give her a goodbye hug and, as he did, she moved forwards as well. Their lips crashed against each other, knocking front teeth. June took hold of his shoulders to steady herself, closed her eyes and waited for the kiss.

But nothing happened.

When she opened her eyes again, Alex was staring at her with a look of complete and utter terror.

'I . . . I'd better go,' he said, backing away.

'Alex—'

'See you soon.'

He was at the car door, yanking it open and jumping in. June heard the engine rev and the car pulled away. She stood on the doorstep and watched him go.

When he reached the corner and disappeared out of sight, June bent over and was sick in the flowerbed.

June opened her eyes and closed them again. She lay in her self-imposed darkness and assessed the damage. Her head was pounding, and her mouth tasted acidic. She reached down and felt the fabric of her dress, which meant she must have passed out fully clothed. Fragments of last night replayed across her mind: Marjorie shouting, Gayle's expression, the ripe Brie flying through the air like a discus.

June let out a moan and buried her head in the pillow. She lay like that until nature's call became too strong and she had to get up.

In the bathroom she stared at herself in the mirror: mascara smeared round her eyes, her skin deathly white. She swallowed two paracetamol and made her way back to the bedroom, passing Alan Bennett on the landing.

'What have I done?' she said to him, but he closed his eyes and pretended to be asleep. June got back into bed and pulled the duvet over her head.

When she woke up again her headache had receded. She reached for her phone to check the time and saw four missed calls from Alex. At the sight of his name, June had a sudden flashback – her drunken attempt at a kiss, his look of horror as he backed away – and felt shame burn through her body. How could she have been so stupid? Stanley had been wrong – of course Alex didn't have a soft spot for her. And he had a girlfriend, for god's sake! June threw her phone on the floor in disgust and closed her eyes, but the image of his shocked face was burnt onto her retina.

June dozed on and off for the rest of the day, waking in blissful ignorance before she remembered and the pain came flooding back. What had happened at the wedding after she'd left? Had Gayle and Rupert spent the rest of their evening in newly wedded bliss? Or had they ended up having a huge argument, with screaming and tears and the guests leaving early, gossiping in hushed voices about it being the worst wedding they'd ever been to? And what about poor Marjorie? All this time June had spent convinced that woman was out to destroy the library, when all along her boss had had no idea what her husband was doing. June put her head under the pillow and willed herself back to sleep.

She was woken by the sound of the doorbell. It was dark, the only light coming from the street lamp outside her bedroom window. Who the hell could it be at this time of night? June rolled over and closed her eyes, but there it was again, the incessant ring. She reached for her phone where she'd discarded it under the bed this morning. There were six missed calls from Alex and one text message. **PLEASE CALL ME ASAP**. With a sinking feeling June got up, pulled on her dressing gown and hurried downstairs. She opened the front door to see Alex standing on the doorstep.

'I'm sorry,' June blurted out before he could speak. 'I shouldn't have tried to kiss you.'

'June—'

'I'm so embarrassed. It was the alcohol, I didn't know what I was doing. I know you don't see me like that.'

'June—'

'Please can we forget it ever happened?'

'June. It's Stanley.'

'What about him?'

'I'm so sorry. Stanley . . . he's dead.'

Chapter Thirty

THEY SAT AT THE KITCHEN table drinking mugs of sugary tea while June listened to what Alex told her. *Found in his caravan by a dog walker. The police think a couple of days.* An image came into her head of Stanley lying alone on that narrow single bed, waiting to be discovered, and she had to put a hand over her mouth to stop a sob escaping.

'Inspector Parks came into the takeaway to tell me,' Alex said. 'They're going to do a post-mortem, but they don't think it was anything suspicious.'

June shivered and pulled her dressing gown around her shoulders. 'I should have seen that he was unwell. I should have been a better friend.'

'There's nothing you could have done.'

'That's not true.' She looked at Alex. 'I knew he was living alone in that caravan, Alex. I found out after the library occupation, but I was so wrapped up in my own problems that I did nothing about it. Perhaps if I'd contacted social services or—'

'June, stop,' Alex interrupted. 'You can't beat yourself up about that. I knew about his living arrangements too.'

'You did?'

June watched him squirm in his seat. 'I've known for a while, but Stanley made me promise not to tell anyone.'

'I don't understand. How did you know?' June asked, but Alex was lost in thought and didn't reply.

They sat in silence for a few minutes.

'We let him down,' June said. 'He should never have been living like that.'

'I think he was happy there. And the library was like his second home.'

Tears started to spill down June's cheeks. 'I have to save the library. Stanley devoted everything to fighting for it. I can't let him down again.'

Alex reached across the table, resting his hand on top of hers. June felt a flush of warmth and let it stay there for a moment, safe and comforting. Then she remembered his panicked getaway last night and pulled away.

'It's late, you should get some rest.' As Alex stood up, his chair let out a loud scraping noise on the floor, and June winced.

'Thanks for coming round to tell me in person, I appreciate it.' She knew she should show him out, but she didn't have the energy.

Alex stopped when he got to the kitchen door. 'I almost forgot.' He reached into his bag and pulled out a book, which he came back and placed on the table. June saw it was *The House at Pooh Corner*. 'Parks gave me this. He said they found it by Stanley's bed. It belongs to the library.'

The following morning, June left the house at ten. There was only one place she wanted to be today, even if it was the one place she wasn't allowed to be.

As she walked towards the library, its old clock tower rising above The Parade, June felt a wave of emotion crashing over her. She remembered approaching the building as a child, holding her mum's hand and feeling such anticipation about what wonderful stories and adventures she'd find inside. She remembered all those days she'd walked this route to work, when the library had been a comfort, a form of security. But today, all she felt was an overwhelming sadness. Never again would she unlock that front door and find Stanley waiting for her, smiling and talking about the weather. Never again would she be able to chat to him as she shelved returns or help him with the crossword.

Chantal was the first person to spot June as she walked into the library. 'Have you heard?' she asked, her eyes red. 'Stanley was in here on Thursday, talking about FOCL and the campaign. He was sitting just there . . .'

June followed Chantal's gaze over to the chair where Stanley always sat. This morning it was empty, although someone had placed a neatly folded copy of the *Telegraph* on the seat.

'I heard they found him in some caravan on the edge of the village, no heating or electricity. Can you believe it?'

'He was very private,' June said, carefully.

'He was like a grandpa to me,' Chantal said, her eyes glistening.

June heard a familiar voice to her left, and she turned to see Marjorie emerging from her office. June braced herself for the onslaught, but when Marjorie looked up, she gave a strained smile.

'I heard about Stanley—' June started.

'Of course, it's only right you should be here,' Marjorie said.

'How did your daughter's wedding go?' Chantal said.

Marjorie's jaw tightened. 'It was lovely, thank you.'

'I've finished this and it's a disgrace. Why anyone reads this shit I do not know.'

They turned around to see Mrs B striding through the door, brandishing a copy of *Hamlet*. She stopped when she saw them all huddled together. 'What's going on? Is there news from the council?'

No one said anything, so June stepped forwards. 'I'm afraid I have some bad news, Mrs Bransworth. Stanley's dead.'

June saw her draw a quick intake of breath.

'Was he here?'

'No.'

'Alone?'

June nodded and Mrs B closed her eyes. When she opened them again, it was with a look of determination. 'You all know what we need to do now.'

'There's still a few weeks of the consultation left,' June said. 'I think we should stage a protest at County Hall, see if we can get loads of young people involved this time. Maybe they could even do a school strike?'

'I'll message all my friends from college,' Chantal said.

'I'm not sure there's much point.' They all looked at Marjorie, who in turn was staring at June. 'You were right, June. Brian finally confessed everything yesterday, although only after I threatened to leave him.'

Mrs B frowned. 'What are you talking about?'

'I'm afraid not everything has been above board,' Marjorie said. 'A coffee chain has set its sights on this building and they've been paying my husband to help them. They've made a ridiculous financial offer for this place. There's no way the council will turn it down.'

'You bastards!' Mrs B shouted. 'You and your damned husband—'

'This has nothing to do with Marjorie,' June interrupted. 'She was as surprised about this as we are.'

'If it's dodgy then can't we go to the police?' Chantal said.

'I'm not sure it will be possible to prove anything,' Marjorie said. 'They've been very careful, there's no email trail or evidence of any conversations. My husband appears to be smarter than he looks.'

'But he confessed to you,' June said.

'He'll deny it,' Marjorie said. 'Not that I care. He can be arrested and thrown into prison. I've had enough of that bloody man and his lies.'

'Marjorie—' June desperately wanted to apologise for what had happened at the wedding, but Marjorie had already turned away.

'We have to report this to the police,' Chantal said. 'We can't let them get away with this.'

'You're right, Chantal, but it won't save the library.' Mrs B shook her head. 'These things take months to investigate, by which time the council will have made their decision about this place. And even if the coffee company loses the building, someone else will buy it instead.'

'So, what, are we just giving up?' Chantal said. 'After everything we've done, are we really walking away?'

'We have to go to the council meeting when they vote on the library,' June said. 'Stanley was the one who suggested it, so we have to go and make them listen. It's our last hope.'

June spent the rest of the morning inside the library. Her access to the network had been blocked, but she busied herself with visitor queries and tidying the shelves. She assisted a woman with her Universal Credit online, and when a young boy with dyslexia came in, June helped him choose some books. It felt good to be back here amongst the shelves and the people, having a purpose again. But every now and then, June would hear someone walk in through the front doors, shuffling their feet or whistling, and she would look up, expecting to see Stanley's smiling face. And then she'd remember and feel the loss all over again.

The library closed at one o'clock, and June found herself alone in the building with Marjorie. While her boss dealt with some paperwork in the office, June sat down at one of the public computers where Stanley had spent so many hours. She opened up a browser and typed in a web address. When it asked for the password she paused. Was it illegal to log in to someone else's email account? Stanley had told her his password many times, so it was hardly hacking. June's fingers hovered over the keyboard and then she typed it in.

The Inbox sat empty, not one single email. She clicked on Sent Items and saw the same. Then June clicked on Drafts and the screen was suddenly filled with dozens if not hundreds of messages. All to the same email address, with subjects like 'Greetings from rainy England' and 'Update on our library battle'. It took June a moment to work out what was going on, and when she did, her heart ached.

Stanley had written all these emails to his son, but never had the courage to send them.

The most recent message had been composed on Thursday, four days ago. It must have been Stanley's last day in the library. June hovered the cursor over it. She wanted to read the words and hear her friend's voice again. How had he been feeling? Was he unwell? Was he happy?

She stared at the mailbox for a moment longer, then scribbled something down and turned off the computer. These weren't her emails to read.

That evening, June considered making pasta pesto for her dinner but at the last minute she headed up to the Golden Dragon. George was standing behind the counter as she walked in.

'Your usual?'

'Hi, George. Please can I have some fish-fragrant aubergine, steamed rice and your green beans with pork and chilli?'

He looked at her in astonishment, raised an eyebrow, then walked into the kitchen. A moment later Alex appeared.

'I saw that order and wondered if it was you. How are you?'

'OK. I went to the library this morning.'

'How was it?'

'Horrible . . . and nice. Do you think we should organise a funeral for Stanley? I'm not sure who else will.'

'I believe Stanley's solicitor is dealing with it.'

'Stanley had a solicitor?' June couldn't hide her surprise.

'I spoke to her and apparently his named next of kin is his sister, so they're trying to trace her before anything's arranged.'

June hated the idea of Stanley's body sitting in a morgue somewhere, all alone. 'He needs a proper send-off.'

They stood in silence.

'June, I need to tell you something,' Alex said.

She studied the Formica counter. Was this going to be about her humiliating attempt at a kiss after the wedding? Or was he about to finally admit that he had a girlfriend? Either way, this was the last thing she wanted to discuss right now.

'I've been wanting to say it for a while, but with everything that's happened, I haven't had a chance,' Alex said.

'Please, you don't have to say anything.'

'But I don't want you to find out from someone else. I—'

'You look well, George,' June said, as she saw Alex's dad walk out of the kitchen carrying her bag. 'How's your hip?'

'Fine, so I don't know why Al is still here,' George said. 'I keep telling him he can go back to London.'

'Dad ...'

'The doctor says my hip is healed. Why are you still hanging round here, getting in my way?' He swiped at his son, although not without affection.

'How much do I owe you?' June said, rummaging in her bag for her purse.

'Nine pounds fifty.'

She handed over a ten-pound note, grabbed her food and ran out of the takeaway before Alex could say another word.

June avoided the takeaway and Alex for the rest of the week. She stayed away from the library, too. On Friday, she received an email from the council, but when she opened it there was just a curt message from some HR person, reminding her of the terms of her suspension. The email said the investigation into the occupation was progressing and they would be in touch with the outcome in due course.

That evening, as she was walking to the village shop to buy her dinner, June heard her name being called from across the street. It was Mrs Bransworth, waving her arms above her head.

'I've been looking for you all week,' she said as she crossed the road towards June, oblivious of the cars screeching to a halt behind her. 'Where the hell have you been?'

'Oh, you know, around.' In truth, June hadn't left the house. She was currently reading *A Little Life*, which was doing nothing for her mood.

'They've set a date for Stanley's funeral. Alex from the Chinese takeaway told me it's taking place on Friday the twenty-fourth at two o'clock, at Winton crematorium.'

'But that's when the council meeting is happening.'

'I know.'

'What are we going to do?'

'I asked Alex if the funeral could be moved but he didn't think it could. Stanley's sister is only coming up for one day, apparently.'

'I can't miss his funeral.'

'Stanley's dead in a box, he doesn't care.'

June winced.

'But you've got to do whatever is right for you,' Mrs B said, and she turned and marched back across the road, drivers gesticulating at her madly.

Chapter Thirty-One

JUNE STOOD IN FRONT OF THE TALL, imposing stone building and looked at the sky. Grey clouds were rolling in, threatening rain, and she'd forgotten her umbrella. She looked around to see if anyone else was coming, but there was no one in sight. So, this was it – she'd have to do this alone. June checked the time; it was one fifty. She tried to ignore the churning in her stomach and walked inside.

June had been in this room once before, eight years ago, and it was exactly as she remembered it. The wooden panelling along the walls, the smell of beeswax polish, the heavy, flat silence. But whereas last time it had been full to bursting, every seat taken and people standing along the walls, today it was deserted. Stanley's coffin stood on the same dais at the front, but whereas June's mum's had been covered in colourful flowers, Stanley's was completely plain. No flowers or photos, no sign of the person inside.

June walked up the central aisle, trying to control her breathing. As she did, she saw a small figure in the front row, so still that she hadn't noticed her at first. The woman had grey hair and was sitting bolt upright, her back to June. This must be Stanley's sister.

'Excuse me?' June's voice echoed round the draughty room.

The woman turned to look at her. She was elderly, well into her eighties, and was wearing an old-fashioned navy woollen suit with a blouse buttoned up to the neck. Her hands, pale and wrinkled, were clasped in her lap.

'I'm June Jones, a friend of Stanley's. I'm so sorry for your loss.'

The woman stared at June with watery grey eyes, then turned back to the front without saying a word. June was unsure what to do, so she took a seat in a row on the other side of the aisle. The two of them sat in silence, the only sound the ticking of a clock at the back of the room, counting out the painful seconds like a metronome. June tried to keep her breathing in time with the clock, in order to fight her overwhelming desire to turn and run out of the room.

'Hi.'

She jumped. Alex was standing in the aisle next to her, dressed in his suit and a black tie.

'You're here.'

'Of course,' he said, sitting down next to her.

Over the next few minutes, several more people drifted into the room; June recognised a woman from the Knit and Natter group, a couple of parents from the Children's Room, and one or two others from the library occupation. Eventually, a man entered through a side door and walked over to Stanley's sister. He was carrying a single sheet of paper.

'Is this everyone?' he said to her. The old lady nodded, and he went to stand at the lectern next to the coffin. 'Ladies and gentlemen, my name is Guy Wilson, I'm the officiant at today's funeral service for Stanley Phelps. Before I begin, a few pieces of housekeeping. First off, please switch all mobile phones to silent. Secondly—'

There was a loud crash at the back of the room.

'Sorry we're late. Bloody traffic.'

June swung round to see Mrs Bransworth marching up the aisle, followed by Chantal, Vera and Jackson.

'I thought you weren't coming?' June whispered to Mrs B, as she took a seat.

'Decided that even though the old bugger won't know I'm here, I wanted to say goodbye.'

'Granny Linda gave us a lift,' Jackson said, sitting down on June's other side. 'She said you'd look after me, June.'

'I wonder if there'll be a buffet afterwards?' Vera said.

The officiant coughed. 'Right, if everyone's here we can begin.'

He said a few words about the service and the fact that Stanley's sister had requested there be no music. He gave a brief speech about Stanley: factual information, his date of birth, where he was born, his parents and sister. He said that Stanley had worked as a chartered accountant for many years and died of a brain haemorrhage. There was no mention of Kitty or Mark, or anything to do with the library. June didn't recognise the man being described.

'Now, seeing as it's a short service, would anyone else like to say a few words about Stanley?' The officiant looked at Stanley's sister, who had sat motionless throughout the ceremony. She gave a tight shake of her head.

'Anyone else?'

He looked out at the small congregation. June thought of all the things she wanted to say about Stanley, about the wonderful man he was and the kind friend he'd been. She wanted to thank him for all that he'd done, not just for the library but for her personally. June could feel Alex's eyes on her, waiting. She glanced over at Stanley's sister, who was staring forwards, stiff as a rod.

'Are you OK?' Alex whispered.

June looked down at her hands and saw they were trembling in her lap. In fact, her entire body was shaking, causing her teeth to chatter. She closed her eyes and willed herself to calm down.

'Oh, for God's sake.'

June opened her eyes to see Mrs Bransworth marching towards the front. She stopped when she got to the lectern and took a deep breath.

'I'm not one for speeches and I hate funerals, so I'll keep it brief. But Stanley deserves more than this pathetic affair.' As she said this, Mrs B looked over at Stanley's sister. June couldn't see her face, but she saw the old woman's shoulders tense.

'I've known Stanley for fifteen-odd years but, to be honest, I never paid him much attention. He always seemed too bourgeois, with his tweed suit and reading that awful Torygraph crap. But it turns out you really can't judge a book by its cover.

'In the last few months, meek little Stanley Phelps proved himself to be a lion. A man who stood up for what he believed in and was willing to be arrested for his convictions. A true comrade who fought with his dying breath to protect something he knew was important, not just for himself but for everyone.'

Mrs B's voice wobbled, and she coughed to clear her throat.

'If we all take one lesson from Stanley's life, it should be that it's never too late to find your voice, to stand up and shout from the top of your lungs about injustice. Because if each one of us had even a little bit of Stanley's courage and humanity, this world of ours would be a damn sight better place.'

She stopped talking and June wanted to burst into applause. But there was a loud, drawn-out creak and she looked over to see Stanley's sister standing up, leaning on her walking stick. Alex jumped up and went to help her, but the woman shook him off without a word. They all watched as she turned and made her way at a snail's pace down the central aisle, not looking at any of them. When she reached the back of the room, she pulled open the door and let it slam shut behind her, the sound echoing round the silent room like a gunshot.

Chapter Thirty-Two

JUNE STAYED IN HER SEAT until everyone had left and then walked up to the coffin. She touched it, feeling the rough wood under her fingertips.

'Goodbye, Stanley,' she whispered. 'I'm sorry I didn't speak up today, but thank you.'

She reached into her bag and pulled out the library copy of *The House at Pooh Corner* which Stanley had been reading. June looked at its aged, faded cover, the plastic protector yellow and cracked, and placed the book on top of the coffin, where the flowers should have been.

Outside, Mrs B, Vera, Chantal, Jackson and Alex were waiting for her in a black cab, the windows steamed up in the driving rain.

'The sister has pegged it,' Mrs B said as June climbed in. 'What a miserable old bat.'

'I hope my funeral lasts longer than that,' Vera said.

'We thought we'd go to The Plough for a drink in his memory,' Alex said, as they drove out of the car park.

June stared out of the rain-streaked window as they reached the roundabout and took the exit back towards Chalcot. So this was it. She'd said goodbye to Stanley and now all she could do was sit and wait for the decision from the council meeting, helpless once again.

Unless . . .

'Stop the taxi!'

'What is it?' Alex said, as everyone turned to look at June.

'This might sound crazy but, if we hurry, do you think we could still make it to the council meeting before they vote?'

'It started half an hour ago, they'll never let us in,' Vera said.

'Maybe not. But we should try, shouldn't we?'

'Seat belts on!' Alex shouted, as the driver slammed on the brakes and executed a three-point turn in the middle of the road. There was a cheer around the vehicle.

'Put your foot down, sod the speed limit,' Mrs B yelled, as they almost jumped a red light.

'You lot run on ahead and I'll catch you up,' Vera said, as they pulled into the council car park.

They piled out of the taxi and raced through the rain towards the building.

'Where's the committee meeting?' June called to the woman on reception as they burst through the doors.

'It's in the main chamber but it's well underway,' the woman replied, but they were already running up the stairs.

As they approached the chamber, June saw a young security guard standing by the door. He looked up in alarm as he saw them charging down the corridor towards him.

'I'm sorry, the meeting started an hour ago,' he said as they reached the door. 'You're too late to go in.'

'Please, we really need to be in there,' June said.

'Those are the rules, I'm afraid.'

'Please, sir?' Jackson said, in his most innocent voice.

The guard shook his head. He couldn't have been much older than eighteen. 'I'm sorry, there's nothing I can do.'

'What about if we slipped you twenty pounds?' Chantal said.

Mrs B stepped forwards to read his name badge. 'Now you listen to me, Sam Tucker. I'm going to report you for obstructing my democratic rights.'

'I'm just doing my job.' He backed away. 'Now please, can you all step away from the door so you don't disturb the meeting.'

They all turned and started walking back along the corridor.

'Well, I guess at least we tried,' Alex said.

'I can't believe we got this close,' Mrs B said, shaking her head.

'Hang on.' June spun back round to the guard. 'Did you say your name was Sam Tucker?'

He nodded and she walked back towards him.

'This is a long shot, but are you any relation of Jim Tucker?'

'He was my grandpa,' Sam said, looking confused.

'Who the hell is Jim Tucker?' Mrs B said.

'Sam, did your grandpa used to take you to Chalcot Library when you were little?' June asked.

Now he looked terrified. 'Yes, why?'

'This might sound weird, but do you remember when he started to read you stories?'

Sam's eyes were wide. 'He learnt to read when I was nine. What is all this about?'

'My name is June, I'm the library assistant at Chalcot. I'm the person who taught your grandpa to read.'

The young man's face lit up. 'You're June Jones?' She nodded and he laughed. 'You're a hero in my family. My grandpa used to talk about you all the time, he thought you were amazing.'

June smiled back. 'Your grandpa worked so hard to learn to read for you and your sister.'

'My mum won't believe it when I tell her I met you! Do you still work there?'

'I do – but here's the thing: Chalcot Library is under threat. Right now, in this chamber, the council are voting to decide whether or not to close it and five other libraries.'

Sam looked appalled. 'They can't do that!'

'That's why we need to get in. We want to try to stop them closing the library.'

'But if I let you in, they'll know it was me. I'll lose my job.'

'Is there another way we can get in? Another entrance?'

He thought for a moment. 'There's a balcony upstairs in the chamber. It's closed at the moment for maintenance work so no one's up there.'

June beamed at him. 'Sam, you're an absolute star. Your grandpa would be proud.'

The boy blushed. 'Go down here, up the stairs and take the door that says "No Entrance". The balcony is the red door on the right.'

They all hurried on down the corridor and up the stairs. When they reached the 'No Entrance' door, Alex stopped. 'We can't all go in, we'll draw attention to ourselves.'

There was a quick discussion amongst the group before it was agreed that June and Mrs Bransworth would go in. The two of them crept down the corridor until they came to the red door.

'Ready?' Mrs B whispered, and June nodded.

She pushed the door open and they snuck in. June could hear voices coming from down below.

'We can debate this all day, but the numbers speak for themselves,' a man was saying in a loud, nasal voice. 'Visits to this library are down fourteen per cent on five years ago, and borrowing is down by twenty-one per cent over the same period, despite the recent spike. I'd argue that it's a perfect candidate for closure.'

June caught Mrs B's eye and could see her own fear reflected back at her. Were they talking about Chalcot?

'But visitor and borrowing numbers are down at all the libraries in the county, even the bigger ones,' a female voice said. 'And, in this instance, the library's cost-per-issue is quite low compared to others. Plus, the response from the local community shows there is huge public support for the library.'

June crawled forwards to the edge of the balcony in case there was any way to look down onto the floor below, but she couldn't see a thing.

'There are other factors we need to consider,' the first man said. 'As the consultants' report highlights, this library would require significant costly refurbishment over the next two years if it's to continue operating.'

'Some of that has already been done for us,' a voice said, and there was a murmur of knowing laughter around the room.

'They're talking about us,' Mrs B whispered, her breath hot on June's ear.

The man continued. 'I propose that rather than keeping this library open and having to pay for the renovations, we close it and consider how better we may be able to use the premises. It could be a valuable asset to the council in these strained financial times.'

'Bloody Cuppa Coffee,' Mrs B said, and June nudged her to keep quiet.

'Thank you, Councillor Pyke. Does anyone else have anything they'd like to add before we take a vote?' an authoritative female voice said. 'Yes, Councillor Donnelly?'

June felt the colour draining from her face. Richard Donnelly.

'Thank you, Madam Chair. I'd like to address the recent events at this library, which as you all know have gained significant local and national publicity.'

June felt something on her hand and looked down to see Mrs B gripping it with her own.

'While all of us here appreciate how passionately local communities feel about this issue, we can't ignore the fact that campaigners in Chalcot engaged in illegal activity with their occupation and criminal damage to the library premises.'

'I was under the impression that no criminal charges were made,' the chairwoman interrupted. 'Was I misinformed?'

'Um, no, that's correct. But there was considerable alteration to the interior of the library,' Richard said.

'The lying shit,' Mrs B said. 'I'll kill him.'

'My concern is that if we vote to keep this library open, it might look as if the council can be bullied, or blackmailed even, by actions such as the protest in Chalcot. And I worry what kind of message that would send out to other local interest groups.'

'Are you saying that we should close Chalcot Library as, what . . . a punishment because they protested?' the female voice from earlier said. June had no idea who it was, but she wanted to high-five her.

'No, Alice, of course not,' Richard said. 'But I do think we should be aware of the optics on this one.'

'Thank you, Councillor Donnelly,' the chairwoman said. 'Now, if everyone has had their say, I think we should take a vote on Chalcot Library.'

June could hear the blood racing in her ears. This was really about to happen; the council were about to vote on the future of her mum's library.

Stanley's library.

Her library.

'Wait!'

June stood up and looked down onto the chamber floor. Dozens of faces turned to stare up at her and June felt a wave of vertigo. 'I need to say something.'

'How did she get up there?' A red-faced man was pointing up at her. 'Send security up there, now.'

'I'm sorry, no unscheduled questions,' the chairwoman said.

'Please. My name is June Jones and I'm the assistant at Chalcot Library.'

'If this is about your suspension, Miss Jones, then we've already decided to reinstate you,' the chairwoman said.

'It's not that.' June felt light-headed. What the hell was she doing? This was the kind of crazy thing her mum would have done, but there was no way June could speak in front of all these people. Her mind was blank, and she stared up at the ceiling above her head, domed and gilded, and closed her eyes. She remembered Mrs Bransworth's words during the occupation. *I'm never scared when I'm fighting for something I know is right.* She thought of her mum standing at the school gates, a one-woman picket line. An image of Stanley floated into June's mind, smiling at her calmly from behind the library door as the police tried to evict him.

She opened her eyes and looked down at the council chamber below.

'Today, I went to the funeral of a friend of mine, Stanley Phelps. If any of you have ever been to Chalcot Library, you'd probably have seen him there. He used to wear a suit every day and he'd read the paper in his favourite chair. He was a quiet man, polite and unobtrusive.'

June saw Richard Donnelly glaring up at her, his eyes bulging. She swallowed.

'When you all threatened to close our library, Stanley became involved in the campaign to save it. He went to every meeting and volunteered to be the group treasurer. And then one day he decided to occupy the library.'

'He was a fighter,' Mrs B shouted from down by June's feet.

'I had the privilege of being Stanley's friend, so I came to understand a bit about why the library was so important to him. You see, despite his smart appearance and friendly manner, Stanley had a difficult past.'

In the distance June could hear raised voices. Sam must be on his way.

'Stanley had done some things he deeply regretted and lost people he loved. But he told me that, however bad things had been, whatever mistakes he made, there had always been somewhere that he could go. A place where no one would judge him, where he would be treated with respect and kindness. He described libraries as a safety net that always caught him.'

'Where the hell are security?' Richard Donnelly said.

'Stanley helped me to understand something invaluable. You see, libraries aren't just about books. They're places where an eight-year-old boy can have his eyes opened up to the wonders of the world, and where a lonely eighty-year-old woman can come for some vital human contact. Where a teenager can find precious quiet space to do her homework and a recently arrived immigrant can find a new community. Libraries are places where everyone, rich or poor, wherever they come from in the world, can feel safe. Where they can access information that will empower them.'

Behind her, June heard a door swing open and the sound of feet walking in.

'A mobile library might still provide books, but it can never be the heart of a community. So please, when you vote on these six libraries, think of all the people out there like Stanley. You may not realise it now, but, without libraries, every single one of us will suffer.'

There was a stunned silence. June felt a hand on her arm and turned to see Sam standing next to her. Behind him were two panting men.

'I'm sorry. You have to leave now,' he said.

June glanced back down at the floor below. Everyone was still staring up at her. Her eyes fell on one dark-haired woman, who discreetly raised her hand in a thumbs up. Then June felt Sam pull on her arm, and she turned and let him lead her away.

Chapter Thirty-Three

'THREE CHEERS FOR STANLEY!'

They were in The Plough, eating the buffet that the landlord had thrown together when they arrived.

'I'm impressed with you making that speech,' Vera said to June, a sherry in one hand and a pork pie in the other. 'I wish I could have seen that Donnelly's face – he must have been livid.'

'I'm not sure it'll make any difference, but I'm glad I said something,' June said. 'I've spent too long being scared of speaking up.'

'You were fantastic,' Mrs B said, slapping June on the back.

'Vera was amazing too,' said Alex.

Vera beamed. 'I told them, I'm eighty years old and eighteen stone, you're not getting past me without a fight. And you know what, that security boy Sam gave me a wink and told those councillor men that he couldn't manhandle a pensioner.'

'Good for you, Vera,' June said.

'Oh, Stanley would have loved to have been there today,' Chantal said, and everyone went quiet.

'Well, he was certainly there in spirit, thanks to June's speech,' Alex said.

Vera was nodding. 'Surely there's no way they can vote to close the library now?'

'We'll find out soon enough,' June said. 'For now, let's focus on celebrating Stanley's life. Do you remember how he used to do the newspaper crossword in pencil and then rub it out so Marjorie wouldn't tell him off?'

Everyone laughed.

'He used to recommend me books to read,' Jackson said.

'He helped me with my revision,' Chantal said. 'He spent hours explaining the Russian Revolution to me.'

'Yeah, but he didn't have a clue how to work a computer,' Mrs B said, with a chuckle. 'Poor June, I must have heard him ask you a hundred times how to log on.'

June smiled, but she thought of all those unsent emails.

'Do you remember that news interview he did during the occupation, when he said he needed to use the library computers for surfing?' Alex pulled out his mobile phone and soon they were all laughing as they watched the clip.

'Look, it's been viewed more than two hundred thousand times,' Chantal said. 'Turns out Stanley was an internet star and we never even knew it.'

More drinks were consumed as everyone carried on sharing their favourite stories about Stanley. After a while, June slipped away and went to sit at a table outside. The rain had stopped, and the sun was fighting through the late September clouds. She felt drained after everything that had happened today. And why wasn't there any news from the council? It was almost two hours since she'd been pulled out of the chamber by an apologetic Sam. Surely the meeting couldn't still be going on.

'Do you mind if I join you?'

June looked up to see Alex standing a few feet away. 'Sure.'

She shuffled along and he sat down on the damp bench next to her.

'Well done for making that speech,' he said.

'I felt such an idiot standing up there with everyone staring at me.'

'But you did it. You put yourself out there and did the one thing that terrified you most.'

They were both quiet for a moment.

'June, there's something I need to tell you.'

She looked over at Alex, his face serious. 'What's wrong?'

'Nothing's wrong. Well, I guess my timing is . . . the timing's terrible.'

'What are you talking about?'

'There's something I've been trying to tell you for a while, and I need to say it now.'

June's heart sank. As if today couldn't get any worse, now this. 'Please, you don't need to explain anything. I understand.'

'I'm not sure you do, June.'

307

'But I do, Alex. I know about Ellie.'

His head swivelled to look at her. 'Ellie? How?'

'I've known for months.'

'Who told you about her? Was it Stanley?'

'No, I saw a message from her on your phone and I know you were together when I called you in London. Why didn't you just tell me you had a girlfriend?'

'Hang on, Ellie is my—'

'Does she know I tried to kiss you?' June asked, cringing. 'I'm so sorry I did that, Alex, it was totally out of order. I was drunk and it was a huge mistake.'

There were a few seconds of silence. 'A mistake?'

'Of course. I don't see you in that way. I mean, you're a friend but I don't fancy you or anything.' June forced a laugh and then wished she hadn't. It didn't sound remotely real.

She looked over to Alex, expecting him to look relieved now it was all out in the open. But instead he was staring at his pint, looking utterly defeated. When he spoke again, he didn't look at her.

'June, the thing I need to tell you is that I'm moving back to London.'

She felt as if someone had given her a karate kick to the chest, knocking all the wind out of her.

'Dad's better now and doesn't need my help at the restaurant, and I need to get back to my job.'

'Of course,' she said, trying to keep her voice level.

'My sabbatical's over and I start work again on Monday, so I'm leaving tomorrow. I'm sorry to just spring this on you, but when I tried to tell you before, you changed the subject.'

'I'm happy for you, Alex. I bet you can't wait to get back to your normal life.'

June couldn't bear to look at him, so she stared across the road towards the library. She'd always known Alex would leave at some point, but she'd never expected the news to hurt like this. She closed her eyes, willing herself not to cry in front of him.

When she opened them again, she saw a figure running past the front of the library, a large handbag swinging from her side.

'Wait, isn't that Marjorie?' June stood up and waved at her. 'Marjorie. Marjorie! She's going into the pub.'

June rushed inside, leaving Alex sitting at the table. She arrived at the group as Marjorie came bursting in. Everyone stopped talking.

'What's the news?' June said.

Marjorie was bent over, panting from the running.

'For Christ's sake, spit it out,' Mrs B said.

Marjorie straightened up. 'The meeting just finished. They've made their decision.'

'And?'

'They're closing all six libraries, including Chalcot.'

June stared. 'What?'

'They're closing it in eight weeks' time. We're getting a mobile library instead, once a fortnight.'

'We lost,' Chantal said.

'After June got taken away, the place was in uproar. They debated Chalcot for another half an hour, but in the end, the vote went twenty-five to twenty-four in favour of closing it.'

'My god,' said Vera.

'That's not all. At the end they said the council will be entering into discussions with private buyers about the Chalcot Library premises, with the aim to sell it off in order to make up some of the budget deficit. It looks like Cuppa Coffee will get the building.'

June felt something inside her crumble. 'It's over.'

They all stared at each other in stunned silence. Jackson was sitting with his head in his hands, and tears were running down Chantal's cheeks.

'I'm just glad Stanley wasn't around to see this,' Mrs B said, quietly.

Chapter Thirty-Four

Two months later

WHEN JUNE ARRIVED AT THE LIBRARY, there was a council van parked outside, two men in overalls leaning against it, their breath misty in the November cold. She walked into the building and found Marjorie shouting into the phone.

'But this is ridiculous, I told you yesterday that we can't manage without them . . . I don't care if they need them in New Cowley, we still have a library to run here.' Marjorie slammed the phone down with force.

'What is it today?' June said.

'The carousels. Can you believe the cheek of it? I told those two clowns, if they touch anything from my library then I'm liable to use violence against them, so help me god.'

'They're only doing their job, Marjorie.'

'But we're open until five o'clock tomorrow. How am I supposed to run a library with half my equipment missing?'

June walked through to the back and hung her coat up. It had been like this all week. On Monday they'd taken the sofa from the Children's Room, and June had hidden in the toilets so no one would see her cry, and on Tuesday they'd carried out several of the racks. On Wednesday they'd come back for the returns trolley, and June and Marjorie had watched from the window as the men tried to load it onto the back of the van. But the trolley had other ideas and kept veering off towards the pub, causing the men to curse in frustration. It had been the first time June had laughed in weeks.

She made two cups of tea and took one out to Marjorie. 'Do you remember I'm going at lunchtime today?'

'Sure.' Marjorie was still glaring out of the window at the van.

June went to switch the computers on. She felt bad leaving Marjorie on her own when there was so much work still to be done, but she had no option. This afternoon, for the first time in her life, June had a job interview. It was for a library assistant role in Kent, and June had been preparing for it all week – a welcome distraction from the pain she felt every time she thought about the library closing tomorrow.

'It's ten o'clock,' Marjorie called across to her. 'Open up, will you?'

June walked to the front door and unlocked it. Jackson had now replaced Stanley as the first to arrive each morning, and as she opened the door she found him standing on the front step, wrapped up in a duffel coat and scarf against the cold.

'Morning,' he said, as he strolled towards the desk.

'Morning, Jackson. Chilly today, isn't it?'

The boy heaved the satchel off his shoulder, and it hit the ground with an audible thud. Opening it up, he counted out twelve books and placed them on the desk. 'I want to return these, please.'

'Of course. Did you enjoy *Catcher in the Rye*? What did you make of Holden Caulfield?'

'It was good, thanks.' Jackson reached into his coat pocket and pulled something out, placing it on top of the books. 'You should have this as well.'

June looked down and saw it was Jackson's library card, the edges creased and battered, so well-used that most of the print had worn off.

'You don't have to give this back – you'll need it for the mobile library.'

'Thanks, but I'm not sure I will.'

'What do you mean?' June tried to keep the panic from her voice. 'You know you can still order books and the mobile library will bring them every fortnight.'

'I'm just not sure I'll really want to use the library bus,' he said with a shrug. 'It won't be the same, will it?'

'No, not exactly the same. But you can still—'

'I'd better go now. We're going to visit my Great-Aunt Pauline; she has osteoporosis. Did you know it weakens bones and means they can break really easily?'

'Is that right?'

'I looked it up here in the encyclopaedia,' he said, and then he turned and walked out of the front door.

June watched him go and bit her lip; she'd promised herself she wouldn't cry again this week, whatever happened.

The morning passed quickly. Now that the library was about to close it seemed everyone in the village wanted to use it, and June was rushed off her feet helping people with their enquiries. At midday, she was re-shelving when she heard her name being hollered across the room. She looked up to see Mrs Bransworth and Chantal bowling towards her.

'There you are!'

'Hi guys,' June said, alarmed at the determined look in their eyes.

'When are you leaving?' Mrs B said.

'At twelve thirty, why?'

Chantal checked her watch. 'That only gives us half an hour, we'd better get going.'

'What are you talking about?'

'What are you wearing to your job interview?' Mrs B asked.

'Er, this.' June indicated her work trousers and white shirt.

'What did I tell you?' Chantal said to Mrs B, rolling her eyes.

June looked between them. 'What's going on?'

314

'You can't go to a job interview looking like that,' Chantal said. 'I'm going to give you a mini makeover while Mrs B gives you some last-minute interview prep.'

'Really?' June hadn't even realised they knew she had an interview today.

'Yes, really,' Mrs B said. 'Now come on, we've got a hell of a lot to do.'

They frogmarched her to the toilets, and for the next twenty minutes June allowed herself to be prodded, poked and squeezed as Chantal attacked her hair and face with a variety of tools. All the while Mrs Bransworth fired fiendish questions at her. By the time they'd finished, June felt exhausted – and she hadn't even had the interview yet. She stood facing the two of them as they surveyed her.

'Not bad at all,' Chantal said.

'We've done a pretty good job, if I say so myself,' Mrs B said, with a satisfied nod. 'Have a look at yourself in the mirror then.'

June turned around to face the toilet mirror and let out a gasp. Her usual plain, sensible outfit been replaced by a bright floral dress, cinched at the waist with a belt. Her hair had been released from its bun and Chantal had somehow tamed the frizz, so that now it hung in lovely loose curls over one shoulder. Her skin was no longer deathly pale, but she had a pink tinge in her cheeks, and her eyes looked like they were sparkling.

'Wow, I look—'

'You look bloody gorgeous,' Mrs B said.

June turned back to them, tears pricking her eyes.

'Don't cry, you'll smudge the mascara!' Chantal said.

'OK,' June smiled. 'But thank you both so much. You've made me into a different person.'

'You're not a different person,' Mrs B said. 'You're the same June that the rest of us have always seen. Now you can just see it for yourself.'

'Mrs Bransworth, are you being sentimental?' June said, laughing.

'No, I was not being sodding sentimental, I was just giving you some . . .'

Chantal looked at June and raised her eyebrows. 'She'll be at it for hours. You'd better go to your interview; good luck!'

Chapter Thirty-Five

'THANKS SO MUCH FOR COMING, June. We'll be in touch.'

The man shook her hand and, as June turned and headed out the front door, she felt a wave of relief. The questions had been a breeze compared to Mrs B's grilling earlier. And although June was probably not experienced enough for working in such a big library, at least she'd got through the interview without completely humiliating herself.

She walked to the station and caught the next train, crowding into a carriage for the long journey back home. As the train moved off, June reached into her bag and pulled out her book, staring at the picture on the front cover. It was a portrait of a pale-skinned Regency-style woman, her brown curly hair pulled back into a bun. She was wearing a white empire-line dress, which was splashed with scarlet blood. On her face, where her mouth and chin should have been, the skin was peeled back to reveal sinister, skeletal teeth. *Pride and Prejudice and Zombies*, the title read.

June had reserved the book from Favering library back in the summer, but it had been out on loan and had never arrived. She'd completely forgotten about it until she opened up the green crate of deliveries yesterday morning and found a copy amongst the pile of books on reserve. June's first instinct had been to put it straight back, but something had stopped her and instead she'd taken it out. Now, she opened the front cover and started to read the opening page. *It is a truth universally acknowledged that a zombie in possession of brains must be in want of more brains* . . .

June had just got to the scene at Netherfield where zombies eat all the servants during Bingley's ball when she arrived back at Winton station. She got off and caught the bus to Chalcot, disembarking on The Parade. But instead of turning left at the post office, she carried on and took the next road instead. June had been taking this longer route home for a while now and had replaced her weekly Chinese takeaway with homemade vegetable rice. She told herself this was because she needed to be healthier, but the truth was she felt a sharp ache in her chest every time she walked past the Golden Dragon. Alex was gone. Stanley was gone. And, as of tomorrow, the library would be gone too. As much as June hated to admit it, all she had left in Chalcot was a house full of memories.

She walked up her front path, unlocked the green door and stepped inside.

'Alan, I'm home,' she called, as she kicked off her shoes and hung up her coat.

June went through to the living room and turned on the light. The room looked exactly the same as it had when she'd left this morning; exactly the same as it had every day for the past eight years. The same old photos on the wall, June and Beverley's faces smiling down from dozens of frames. The same china ornaments on the mantlepiece, the same books on the shelves. June walked over and ran her hand along a row of spines. She came to her mum's old copy of *War and Peace* and pulled it off the shelf, flicking through the pages. There was a bookmark halfway through, left over from her last effort to read it back at the start of the summer. Her mum had loved this book, but as much as June hated to admit it, she was never going to finish it.

A thought occurred to June and she walked back into the kitchen. On the counter she kept a pile of old leaflets and flyers that came through the door, mainly for takeaways that she would never order. She rummaged through the pile until she found what she was looking for, a crumpled piece of pink paper.

Do you have any old books you no longer need? Cherry Tree Retirement Home is in desperate need of second-hand books for our residents. All genres welcome.

June knew the place well; once a fortnight she or Marjorie used to go there to swap library books for the residents.

It was a lovely Edwardian building, with big windows overlooking a well-kept garden. Her mum and Linda always used to joke that when they were old they'd live there together, drinking gin and having their pick of the elderly gentlemen. And some Cherry Tree residents had come to the library occupation: June particularly remembered the ninety-four-year-old who had entertained them all with Vera Lynn songs.

She found an old cardboard box under the sink and carried it through to the living room. June picked up *War and Peace* again, closing her eyes as she lifted it to her nose and inhaled the dusty, smoky scent. She stayed like that for a moment, the book pressed to her skin, and then without looking, she placed it in the empty box.

Once she'd started, June found she worked quickly and methodically, the library assistant in her kicking in. The box was soon full, and she went upstairs and found several others, which were soon overflowing as well. With nothing else to put the books in, June started making tall piles on the floor, ordered into genre.

Next, she turned her attention to the mantlepiece. June picked up the ornament of the girl reading a book, turning it over in her hands. She remembered her mum bringing it home from the white elephant stall when June was seven or eight. *No one else wants her, poor thing*, Beverley had said. *I think she looks a bit like you, Junebug, so let's give her a new life here.*

320

June put the girl to one side, then picked up a china model of a London bus and began wrapping it in a page from an old copy of the *Gazette*. Alan Bennett was sitting on the sofa, watching her with startled curiosity.

'For the next summer fete,' she told him. 'Someone else can give these a home now.'

When June paused to get a glass of water, she was shocked to see that it was past ten and she'd been working for almost four hours. She surveyed the chaos in the living room; piles of books for Cherry Tree House and newspaper parcels for the white elephant stall covered the whole floor. The place had never been such a mess and June suddenly felt exhausted. She hadn't got round to eating dinner, so she went through to the kitchen and made herself a cheese sandwich. As she ate, she absent-mindedly flicked through today's post. There was a flyer from a new Chinese restaurant in Favering, which June put on her leaflets pile, feeling guilty. Underneath it was a copy of the *Gazette*. June was about to put it aside for wrapping purposes when the headline caught her eye: *CUPPA COFFEE PULLS OUT OF LIBRARY DEAL AS POLICE CALLED IN*. Beneath the headline was the name Ryan Mitchell and a tiny photo of his spotty face.

The multinational beverage company behind the Cuppa Coffee chain has pulled out of its deal to buy the Chalcot Library building, as Dunningshire Council faces allegations of corruption surrounding the sale.

As previously reported, an exclusive investigation by this newspaper uncovered bank statements showing Chalcot parish councillor Brian Spencer received payments from Lombart Inc. into his personal account. A council insider, who asked to remain anonymous, told the *Gazette* that the payments Cllr Spencer received were in exchange for bribing county councillors to support the sale. When contacted by the *Gazette*, Cllr Spencer refused to comment.

Last month, Dunningshire Council launched their own internal investigation after being presented with the evidence. Now, sources say police have been called in to help with the inquiry.

A spokesperson for Lombart Inc. said the company's decision to withdraw from the purchase of the Chalcot building is unrelated to the ongoing police investigation.

'We have found a site in Mawley which we believe is better positioned and so have decided to open a Cuppa Coffee branch there instead,' the spokesperson told the *Gazette*.

Dunningshire Council's head of library services, Sarah Thwaite, confirmed that the library is still set for closure and the council are now looking for a new buyer for the Chalcot building.

'Our decision to close Chalcot Library was based entirely on the results of analysis by an independent management consultancy firm, and had nothing whatsoever to do with considerations about the sale of the building to Cuppa Coffee. The library will still be closing on 19th November as planned.'

June threw the paper down. In all the activity of this evening she'd not thought once about the library, but now the reality came crashing back. And while stories like this appeared in the paper every week and gave the village plenty to gossip about, it wouldn't change a thing. Despite everything they'd done, the library was still closing tomorrow.

Yawning, June picked up the last piece of mail, a plain white envelope with her name and address typed on the front. She opened it and pulled out a short, typed letter.

Dear Ms Jones,

I am writing to inform you that you have been named as the sole beneficiary of the residue of the estate under the Will of the late Mr Stanley William Phelps. I enclose a copy of the relevant clause of the Will for your information.

I will be in touch again when the estate process has been completed and I am able to make a distribution to you.

Yours sincerely,

E. Davis

June reread the letter several times, worried her exhausted eyes were deceiving her. What could the 'residue of the estate' be? She'd seen where Stanley lived – he clearly didn't have any possessions except the caravan. And if that was his estate then that was very kind of him, but what on earth was June supposed to do with it?

Chapter Thirty-Six

AT HALF-PAST SIX the next morning, June pulled on her coat, scarf and wellies and left home before the sun was up. She took the long route, avoiding the Chinese takeaway, and turned right onto The Parade. None of the shops were open yet and there was little sign of life, just a few cars carrying dull-eyed commuters.

June slowed her pace as she passed the library. Marjorie would be there in a few hours to unlock the front door for the final time. Soon after, the regulars would start arriving: Vera and Leila to look at recipe books together, families to use the Children's Room and Mrs Bransworth to complain about her latest read. June turned her back on the library and walked down to the bridge, joining the footpath by the river.

After a mile or so, she consulted her phone to check the route, then found the stile, climbed over it and set off across the fields. There was a narrow track, worn by repetitive footprints over the years, and June wondered if it was Stanley's feet that had etched it into the soil. At the far side of the field she crossed a narrow lane and was confronted by a huge metal fence blocking off the fields beyond, the words 'ALEXANDER PROPERTIES' emblazoned on the side. June peered through a gap. It was too early for any work to have started and there was no one about, but through the gloom she could make out diggers and an excavator parked up alongside a Portakabin. What looked like the foundations for some of the new houses were already in place. June walked along the lane, following the large fence for five hundred metres or so, until it ended, and she came to some hedges. She squeezed through a gap and walked along the edge of the building site and into the small copse at the far side.

As she emerged through the trees, June was relieved to see the caravan still there, although it looked even more decrepit than before. As she approached it, she saw brambles climbing up the side and large clumps of stinging nettles had popped up round the wheels. A perfectly formed cobweb hung over the door, glistening in the first light.

Was she really going to go inside? It had seemed like a good idea last night; given the caravan was now her property, she might as well get on with the unpleasant task of clearing it out. But still June hovered at the door. This was where Stanley had died, where his body had lain for almost forty-eight hours before it was discovered. Goodness knows what state the place would be in, having been left unoccupied for two months. For a moment June was tempted to walk away, but she forced herself to turn the door handle. This caravan was the place that her friend had called home, and for some reason he'd wanted her to have it. She braced herself and stepped inside.

The first thing that hit June was the smell. It was worse than she could ever have imagined – a sickly, rotten stench that made her retch. The curtains were drawn, and the caravan was pitch-black, so she pulled her phone out of her pocket and switched on the torch. Holding her breath, she took a step forward and saw the remains of what must have been Stanley's last meal sitting in the sink, now a putrid, semi-liquid mass. June reached into her rucksack and pulled out a pair of rubber gloves and a bin bag that she'd brought with her. She put on the gloves, closed her eyes and put her hand in the sink, scooping up the gloopy mass and the plate it was on, and throwing them into the sack. She also picked up a pan that was sitting next to the sink, covered in a thick layer of mould, and put that in too, before tossing the bag outside.

Next, June pulled back the curtains and opened the two small windows to let some early morning light and fresh air into the caravan. Now she was able to see the space better, it was much as she remembered it. On the left was the narrow single bed, still neatly made, and hanging up next to it was Stanley's suit, the jacket done up and the trousers folded underneath. There was something about seeing these meagre items hung up with so much care that brought a lump to June's throat, and she turned away from the bed. The small table was covered in piles of paper, as it had been the last time June had visited. She recognised the leaflets they'd made up during the occupation, and what looked like some minutes from a Friends of Chalcot Library meeting. June began sifting through them, wondering what she was going to do with it all, when she caught sight of an envelope on the corner of the table. She picked it up and almost dropped it in surprise. Written on the front were five words:

June Jones, c/o Chalcot Library.

With shaking hands, June carried the envelope outside and sat down on the front step of the caravan. She opened it and pulled out a thin sheet of paper, covered in close lines of handwriting. The date at the top was the ninth of September, the day before Stanley died.

My Dearest June,

I hope this letter finds you well. I imagine it may come as a bit of a shock, and for that I sincerely apologise. But please humour an old man, as there are some important things that I must share with you while I still can.

At the start of the summer, I was not in what you young people would call 'a good place'. I pride myself

328

on never letting this show: a childhood spent in English boarding schools gives one an excellent education in hiding one's emotions. But, in truth, the burden of guilt I carry about my past had almost entirely consumed me. Add to that the not inconsiderable stress I have been under from those darned property developers, and all in all, I was having some rather desperate thoughts.

Then our friends at the council announced they wanted to close the library, and everything changed. I have told you at length why I feel so passionately about libraries, not just Chalcot but every one out there. Libraries have quite literally saved my life on more occasions than I care to admit, and finally I felt this was my chance to save one in return. As I write this letter, I do not know what the outcome of our battle will be, and I fear that I will never find out. But whatever happens, I do know that we have fought the very best fight we could.

But it wasn't just the library campaign that changed my life, dear June. It was you. I know you will blush and disagree here, as is your wont. But the friendship you have shown me, the lack of judgement when I told you about my past and the optimism you held for my future, have helped to free me from some of the guilt I have been carrying. I will never forgive myself for the way I treated my wife and son, but you have allowed me to feel some joy – and, dare I say it, hope – and for that I will be eternally grateful.

Now to more recent events. Yesterday, I visited my solicitor in order to sign my Last Will and Testament. I can assure you that this was as much of a surprise to me as it must come to you. I have never had anything of any value to leave; and, if truth be told, I've never had anyone to leave it to. So, you ask, what has changed? Some time ago, I mentioned in passing to dear George Chen that I was coming under pressure from these wretched property developers, who want the land on which my caravan is parked. He suggested I contact his son, Alex, who as you are aware is a qualified solicitor. Alex, in turn, put me in touch with an acquaintance of his, Eleanor Davis, who is versed in adverse possession. I won't bore you with the legal details, but it appears that because I have been living on this land for so long, I had a claim to ownership. It has taken Ms Davis and me over a year to navigate the paperwork and endless red tape, but a few days ago word came through that I am now the registered owner of the plot of land which I call home.

But alas, it appears I do not have long to enjoy it. My fall a couple of months back, and my subsequent trip to the Accident and Emergency department at Winton Hospital, alerted me to the fact of a rather unfortunate mass on my brain. The wonderful doctors of the NHS offered me a number of tests and treatments, but that would have meant protracted periods in hospital and did not seem to offer any long-term solution. So, I have chosen to use what remaining time I have to fight for our beloved library. But the headaches have become much worse in recent days, and now I fear that the sleep of death is approaching fast. This is why I'm writing to you now, for in these final hours it gives me immense satisfaction and a sense of relief to know that I am able to leave something to you, my dearest friend.

I have instructed my solicitor to proceed with the sale of this land to the property developers. I cannot imagine they will pay much for a small piece of scrubland, but I hope that the sale will leave you with a little money. You may do with it as you wish. My only request is that you consider using it to leave Chalcot and see something of the world. I once saw photos of the Klementinum in Prague which has a magnificent frescoed, baroque library hall. Or I'm sure you'd love the Rose Reading Room in the New York Public Library. Whatever you choose to do with the money, I pray that you start to live your life again, my dear June.

Now, I bid you farewell and thank you once again for the kindness you have shown me.

Your friend, Stanley

June looked up from the letter, blinking in the early morning light. She remembered Stanley coming into the library months ago with a small plaster on his head and assurances that it was only a scratch, and he'd complained of headaches a few times. But a brain tumour? Surely he could have had an operation to remove it, or at least chemotherapy to give him longer to live. And why hadn't he told her about it during the many long conversations they'd had together? The thought of his knowing that he was going to die and not telling anyone made June shiver.

She looked out over the meadow, dew sparkling on the long grass. It was so tranquil, with no traffic or disturbance from the outside world, only the sound of birds and the wind in the trees. This peace would be gone soon, when the developer's bulldozers moved in and concreted it over for whatever monstrosity they wanted to build. All trace of Stanley's life here would disappear.

June felt a buzzing in her pocket and pulled out her mobile phone. An unknown number flashed up on the screen. She pressed answer and held the phone to her cheek, still staring out into the meadow.

'Hello, is that June Jones?' a male voice asked.

'Speaking.'

'Sorry to ring so early, I ... damn ... hang on, I spilt coffee on a book. Shit, one sec ...'

June could picture David, the short, harassed-looking man she'd met at the job interview yesterday. Throughout their conversation he'd had a child's sticker caught up in his greying hair, and June had spent the whole time wondering whether she should tell him.

'Right, sorry about that. I just wanted to get this done before things get too hectic here.'

Here it goes. The thanks but no thanks, you're not quite what we're looking for.

'I discussed it with my colleagues yesterday and we all agreed you'd be a fantastic addition to the team. So, I'm delighted to offer you the role of full-time library assistant. Starting as soon as possible, ideally.'

June blinked. 'Really? Wow, that's amazing, thank you so much.'

'Great. We'll email a contract and the details over to you. I look forward to you joining us.'

June ended the call. Behind her she could hear the sound of the diggers starting up, the silence shattered by their mechanical grind. Two miles away, the first visitors would soon arrive at the library for its final day. And in her house, boxes of her mum's belongings were waiting to be taken away. There really was nothing to keep June in Chalcot anymore; but for the first time in her life, that thought didn't completely terrify her.

June stood up, closed the caravan door and made her way back towards the trees. As she walked, she looked at Stanley's letter again. Her eyes scanned down the page and then paused on a line that she'd only glanced over before.

Alex, in turn, put me in touch with an acquaintance of his, Eleanor Davis.

Something clicked in June's mind and she stopped in her tracks. She pulled her phone back out and scrolled through until she found the number she wanted. It was answered on the third ring.

'Hi, it's June. Are you busy? We need to talk.'

Chapter Thirty-Seven

IT WAS GONE THREE by the time June arrived at the library.

'Where the hell have you been?' asked Marjorie, who was standing at the issue desk. Or rather, where the issue desk had once been and where now there was just a chair.

'I'm sorry,' June said. 'Something came up.'

'Can you believe they've taken the computers and desks? They're vultures. Vultures!'

June looked around her. All the tables had been removed and crates were stacked in the corner, waiting to be filled with books. The few patrons in the library were standing in front of the half-empty shelves, looking confused.

'You'd think they'd at least have waited until we shut the doors at five,' Marjorie said, shaking her head.

'Hi June.' Chantal walked over to her. 'I keep thinking I'm going to wake up and this will all be a bad dream.'

'I know, Chantal.'

'Leila and I went over to Winton Library this morning,' Vera said, joining them from the cookery section. 'It's a miserable place, big and impersonal. We wanted to find a cake recipe for Mahmoud's birthday.'

'Oh?'

'He's fifteen next week and Leila has invited me to join them for a family meal. I've said I'll bake him one of those rainbow cakes,' Vera said.

'What complete and utter shit this was.' June looked across to see Mrs Bransworth marching through the door, waving a copy of *Harry Potter and the Philosopher's Stone*. 'It's a load of overprivileged kids and a bit of magic. Absolute crap. Ah, hello June. How was the interview?'

'It went well, thanks. They've offered me the job.'

'That's amazing news,' Chantal said, grinning. 'When do you start?'

'They said as soon as possible.'

'Well, I'm pleased one good thing has come out of this damn library closure,' Mrs B said. 'Stanley would have been happy for you.'

'About Stanley. I have some news.' June felt their eyes on her and swallowed. 'I found a letter from him this morning.'

'A letter from Stanley?' Jackson had appeared from the Children's Room. 'What did it say?'

'Well, it turns out he had a will.'

'What could he have possibly left in a will?' Marjorie said. 'The poor man was homeless.'

'In his letter, Stanley told me that he'd managed to claim rights to the land he was squatting on, and he'd decided to sell the land to the property developers.'

'Why the hell would he do that?' Mrs B said. 'He hated those developers – they made his life a misery.'

'So, that's the other thing. Stanley knew he was going to die.'

'Oh, dear lord,' Vera said, crossing herself. 'That's sent chills down my spine.'

'He had a brain tumour, but he refused all treatment. I think, because he knew he was going to die, he decided to sell his land.'

'The poor old bugger,' Mrs B said, shaking her head. 'But how does all of this involve you?'

June felt her cheeks growing red. 'Well, for some reason, Stanley decided to leave the money to me.'

'Oh, that's wonderful.' Marjorie smiled at June. 'He always had a soft spot for you.'

'What are you going to do with the money?' Vera said.

'If I were you, I'd get the hell out of this village,' Chantal mumbled.

'I could. But there was one other idea I had.'

June's phone bleeped. There was a text message on her screen, just two words. *It's done*.

'What's going on?' Mrs B said.

'It's a message from Alex.'

'For god's sake, we don't care about your love life. You were telling us about Stanley's will.'

'This *is* about Stanley. In his letter, he said that Alex had put him in touch with a solicitor, a woman called

337

Eleanor. I called Alex this morning and he told me she's his flatmate, Ellie, and she's also been dealing with Stanley's will and the sale of his land.'

'Yes, and?' Mrs B said.

'Alex said that Stanley had expected to get ten to twenty thousand pounds for the land. But it turns out the property developers really want it, and they've offered Ellie almost one hundred thousand pounds.'

'For a piece of derelict land? That's insane.'

'Apparently they want to build a luxury leisure complex, and Stanley's plot of land is key to that.'

'So, is all of that money yours?' Marjorie asked.

'There are a few expenses that have to be paid from it, but Alex said I'll end up with most of it.'

Chantal's eyes were wide. 'Just think of all the things you could do with that much money.'

'I've decided there's only one thing I want to do with it.' June looked around her at the library and then at the group standing in front of her. 'I want this building.'

Five shocked faces stared back at her.

'What?' Marjorie said.

'The Cuppa Coffee sale has fallen through and the council are looking for a new deal, so Alex has contacted them about arranging a lease. That's what he just texted me about.'

'But what would you do with it?' Jackson said. 'I mean, you don't wanna live here, do you?'

'No,' June said. 'I want to keep it as a library.'

'Have you gone completely bananas?' Marjorie was staring at her. 'You seem to have forgotten that the council have shut us down. I mean, look at this place.' She gestured at the half-empty room.

'So, I've just been to see Sarah Thwaite and the leader of the council about the library,' June said.

'Are they going to save it?' Vera clasped June's arm. 'Please tell me they've changed their mind.'

'I'm afraid not. Their decision on the library is final – they won't pay for it anymore.'

'Bastards,' Mrs B said.

'But they have agreed to consider an application to reopen it as a community library. The village would have to raise all the funds to run the library ourselves. But if we prove that we can do that, the council will lease us the book stock and all the technology, so we'd stay part of the library service.'

'So, we'd still have a proper library here in Chalcot?' Chantal said. 'That would be—'

'Hold on a minute.' Mrs Bransworth held up her hands to stop them all. 'A community library isn't a proper library. There wouldn't even be a librarian, just volunteers. And, more importantly, we shouldn't have to run the library ourselves. This is what we pay our taxes for and the council should provide it.'

'I know, Mrs B, I completely agree,' June said. 'But the council aren't going to provide it, are they? All they'll give us is the mobile library once a fortnight. So, I know it wouldn't be a proper library like we had before, but at least this way there could still be a space in the village where people can borrow books and have a safe place to go.'

'I'd be happy to help run it,' Marjorie said. 'As of today, I'm officially retired. And I've thrown that snivelling husband of mine out, so now I've got plenty of time on my hands.'

'But I thought you wanted this place shut?' Mrs B said. 'You've never shown any interest in saving the library before.'

Marjorie looked at her feet. 'I was a fool. I was too scared of the council to get involved, and I believed Brian when he told me he was working behind the scenes to save the library. So now is my chance to make up for that.'

'I'll help too,' Vera said. 'Maybe I could sell some cakes to raise money?'

'I could write some more poems for us,' Jackson said.

'And the council will let us do this, will they?' Marjorie asked June.

'You'd need to put forward a bid showing how the library would be run and funded,' June said. 'But Sarah and the council leader said they'd give us a six-month window, during which time they won't accept any other offers on the building.'

'It'll be a hell of a lot of work,' Marjorie said. 'And I'm not having a sub-par library in my village. If we're going to do this, we're going to do it properly.'

'June, are you sure this is what you want to do with the money?' Chantal said. 'Just think of all the things you could do with it.'

'It's not really my money, is it?' June said. 'I think if Stanley had known how much his land was worth, he'd have used it for this. What Stanley wanted more than anything else was to save the library, and now, in a way, he can.'

'I still think it's bullshit,' Mrs B said, frowning. 'But you're right, we owe it to Stanley to try to keep this place open.'

'And what will you do?' Marjorie said, turning to June. 'Will you stay and help us run it?'

June didn't immediately reply. She thought about her job offer at a large, well-resourced library. She thought about her house, full of her mum's belongings in boxes. For a brief second Alex's face flickered into her mind, and June pushed it out.

'Well?' Marjorie said. 'Are you with us or not?'

Chapter Thirty-Eight

Seven months later

JUNE WALKED SLOWLY UP her front path. Through the window she could see the old red curtains, faded from the sunlight. Weeds poked up through the paving stones, and she bent down to pull one up. Her mum had always kept the front garden immaculate, with geraniums planted along the edge of the path, but over the years June had let things slip.

'Can I help you?'

A young woman was standing behind June, a shopping bag in each hand and a small curly-haired boy peering round from behind her legs.

'I'm here to see Linda.'

'She lives next door, at number ten.'

'Thanks.' June paused for a moment. Should she tell her who she was? All the correspondence had happened via solicitors, so June had never met the woman before.

'This is my house.' The boy had stepped out from behind his mum and was staring at June. He must have been about four; the same age as she'd been when she first moved here.

'It's a lovely-looking house,' June said.

'That's my bedroom.' He pointed up at the top front window, to June's old room. 'It has pink walls, my favourite colour.'

'Come on, Danny, we need to go in for lunch,' his mum said, and she gave June a brief nod as she walked up the path towards the front door. But the boy didn't move.

'We have a garden as well,' he said. 'I have a swing.'

'That sounds wonderful. Can I ask you a question, Danny?'

The boy nodded seriously.

'Do you like reading stories?'

'Yes. I can already read by myself and I haven't even started big school yet.'

'Well, can I tell you a secret?' June crouched down to his eye level. 'Up in the loft of your house, at the very back behind the water tank, there's a box of books that used to belong to the little girl who lived in the house.'

Danny's eyes were like saucers. 'Are you joking me?'

'No. She loved reading too, and she left them there for the next little boy or girl who lived here. So, they're yours now.'

'Come on, Danny, hurry up,' his mum called from inside.

'What books are they?' he asked.

'You'll have to wait and see,' June said, and the boy grinned at her. 'Goodbye, Danny, it was nice meeting you.'

'Bye!' He charged past her and into the house. June heard him shouting, 'Mum, there's books for me in the—' and then the door slammed shut and it went quiet again.

Smiling to herself, June crossed the driveway and rang on the doorbell of number ten. She heard the familiar chime, and a moment later the door swung open and there was Linda, resplendent in an emerald-green tracksuit and matching eyeshadow.

'June!' Linda pulled her into an embrace. 'Look at your hair, love, don't you look glamorous?'

June touched her hair, still unused to the sensation. She'd plucked up the courage to have it cut a month ago, and now she had a cropped curly bob, too short to ever tie in a bun again.

'Well, don't be a stranger, come in,' Linda said, and June followed her through into the kitchen. 'How was your birthday?'

'It was fun, thanks. I went out for dinner with Katja and some friends from work.'

'How is that gorgeous flatmate of yours?' Linda had met Katja when she came to stay with June back in March. The two of them had got on like a house on fire and stayed up drinking gin until two in the morning, while Linda regaled Katja with embarrassing stories from June's childhood.

'She's great.'

'And the job?'

'It's good. The library is so busy, there are dozens of different activities every week. I've been more involved with the literacy training and I've set up a cryptic crossword club.'

'Oh, that's fantastic,' Linda said. 'Look who's come to say hello.'

She nodded towards the door, and June turned around to see Alan Bennett sauntering into the kitchen.

'Alan!' June dropped down on the floor and reached out tentatively towards the cat. He paused and for a moment June thought he was going to swipe out at her, but then he put his head down and nudged it against her hand. 'Hey, old friend,' June whispered, and her voice caught in her throat. 'I've missed you too.'

'Little Lord Fauntleroy has made himself right at home,' Linda said. 'I bought him one of those fancy bed things to keep in the lounge, but he likes to sleep on my towels in the airing cupboard. And he loves it when Jackson comes round to play – he lets him stroke him and he's good as gold.'

'He's happy here,' June said, scratching behind Alan's ear. 'I've never seen him so content.'

'Now before I forget, I've got this for you.' Linda took an envelope off the windowsill and handed it to June. 'There's a hundred and twenty-eight pounds from the last car boot sale and what Martin got for your old table and chairs.'

'Thanks so much, Linda.'

'Are you sure you want to give all your mum's ornaments to the white elephant stall? The fete isn't until next weekend, so you can still change your mind.'

'I'm sure; I know this is what Mum would have wanted.'

'Good on you, love.'

Before June moved, she and Linda had spent three days emptying the house. The furniture had gone at several car boot sales, and Cherry Tree House had been delighted with all the books. June had only kept a few boxes for herself. *Matilda* and *The House at Pooh Corner* now sat on the bookshelf in her new bedroom, alongside the china girl with the book.

Linda made them both a sandwich and they took them out into the garden.

'It looks gorgeous out here,' June said, admiring the riot of colourful flowers.

'You should see what they've done with your old garden next door,' Linda said. 'They've cleared all the old weeds and put in a swing set for their little one. I hear him giggling over the fence and it reminds me of when you were small.'

'I met him and his mum briefly,' June said. 'They seem nice.'

'They're a lovely family.'

June took a bite of sandwich and sat back, letting the sunshine warm her skin. She'd been dreading seeing another family living in hers and her mum's old home and had put off coming back to Chalcot for that very reason. But now she was here, it wasn't so bad after all.

'So, you're going to this library thing then?' Linda said.

'Yes, I think so. Although I'm a bit nervous about going in there again – I don't know what to expect.'

June had exchanged emails with Mrs B and Marjorie to begin with, but once the building lease had been sorted, their messages had trickled off and June hadn't wanted to bother them. She hadn't heard anything about the library for months, until last week when she received an invitation to the grand opening this afternoon.

'So, have you got any other gossip then?' Linda said. 'What about that guy from work you mentioned?'

'We went out a couple of times, but I don't think he fancied me.' In truth, it had been June who wasn't interested, her mind on someone else, but she didn't want to admit that to Linda.

'But you're settled in your new place, are you?' Linda asked. 'I've been worrying about you.'

June smiled. 'It's taken me a while to get used to it, but I feel at home there now.'

'Your mum would have been so pleased, love. She always wanted you to spread your wings and leave Chalcot.'

'I know.'

'And you know you always have a home here too,' Linda said, reaching across and taking June's hand. 'Me and Alan Bennett are your family, and don't you ever forget it.'

The first person June spotted as she walked through the library front door was Mrs Bransworth, who was standing behind the desk serving a patron.

'Marian Keyes? Are you sure you want to borrow this?' Mrs B surveyed a book suspiciously. 'I read one of hers once and it was shit.'

'I really like them, actually,' the woman said, snatching the book back.

'Suit yourself.' Mrs B raised her eyebrows and then spotted June. 'Well, well, look who the cat's dragged in.'

'Hello, Mrs B,' June said. 'I can't believe they let you deal with the public.'

Mrs B laughed and gave June a punch on the shoulder. 'It's good to see you again, my friend. What do you think of the old place then?'

June turned to survey the library, bracing herself for a painful rush of nostalgia. But the room was almost unrecognisable from the last time she'd been here. The shelves on the back wall had been replaced by a counter with a coffee machine, and half of the floor space was taken up by small round tables, all occupied with people chatting. Vera was standing behind the counter manning the till and next to her Leila was placing cakes onto a plate. The computers had been moved to the front and Marjorie's office had been turned back into a stockroom, with a shiny new trolley sitting by the door. The Children's Room looked like it had been redecorated too, and she could see Jackson in there wearing a badge that said 'VOLUNTEER CHILDREN'S LIBRARIAN'. But the main thing that caught June's eye was a huge framed photo on the wall above the door. It had been taken during the occupation and it showed Stanley, June and Mrs Bransworth standing outside, a large 'Save Chalcot Library' banner above their heads. Their arms were round each other's shoulders and they were all grinning at the camera. Seeing Stanley brought a lump to June's throat.

'It looks so different,' she said.

'It's been a hell of a battle. We nearly didn't raise enough money, but Marjorie managed to secure us a wealthy sponsor just in time.'

'Is she here?'

'Of course. I can't get rid of the old battleaxe, even if I wanted to.' Mrs B nodded towards the stockroom, and as June got nearer, she could hear her old boss berating an elderly gentleman.

'I know it looks prettier organising books by their colour, Donald, but the Dewey Decimal System has been refined over decades and is a highly efficient classification system. Please try to use it next time.'

'Hi Marjorie,' June said.

'I'm going to kill one of them,' Marjorie muttered, as the volunteer walked away. 'They all think they know best and it's driving me mad. God, I miss you.'

June was pretty sure this was the first time Marjorie had ever paid her a compliment. 'The library looks great.'

Marjorie wrinkled her nose. 'It's not the same – we can't run half the activities we used to – but I'm proud of what we've achieved, especially given how hard it's been to raise the money.'

'And you're still volunteering here?'

'Actually, I'm paid a salary to work part-time. It's all thanks to our donor.'

'What donor?'

'Haven't you met him yet? He's over there.' Marjorie pointed across the room to a man talking to Chantal. He was tall and wearing an expensive-looking suit, his dark hair sprinkled with grey. He looked up and caught June staring at him, then crossed the busy library in long strides.

'Are you June?'

She nodded. There was something vaguely familiar about this man, but she couldn't think where she'd seen him before.

'I'm so happy to meet you,' he said, giving her a warm smile. He had a slight accent, although June couldn't place it. 'They told me you weren't involved with the library anymore, so I thought we'd never get the chance to meet.'

His eyes were blue and intense, and June felt herself blushing under his gaze. He really was very handsome. 'I'm sorry, but who—'

'Could I get everybody's attention?' Mrs Bransworth's voice rang out across the library. She paused, waiting for the room to quieten, and June and the man both turned to listen.

'For those of you who don't know me, I'm the chairperson of the Friends of Chalcot Library. For the past seven months, FOCL have fought tooth and nail to set up this library. Those Dunningshire Council bastards have made life difficult for us at every step of the way, and we nearly gave up several times. So, it's wonderful to be able to welcome you all here today for the grand opening of our community library.'

A small cheer went round the room.

'I'll keep this quick, but there are a few people I need to thank. Firstly, to my fellow members of FOCL. Thank you to Chantal and Jackson, who's brought a much-needed dose of youth to this place, and Vera and Leila for running the cafe. And in particular thanks to Marjorie; you and I may have had our differences over the years, but it's thanks to your expertise and hard work that we're here today.'

June looked across and saw the five of them standing together, grinning.

'I'd also like to thank our solicitor, Ellie Davis, who's worked pro bono to help us with the legal side of things. I hate lawyers, as a rule, but Ellie is one of the good ones.' Mrs B nodded towards a pretty blonde woman, and June felt her stomach drop. So, this was Alex's flatmate. They'd exchanged emails about Stanley's will and the lease, but June had never met her before. She looked lovely.

'Where's June?' Mrs B said.

June raised her hand partially in the air until Mrs Bransworth spotted her.

'Now, anyone who used the old library will remember June, who was so timid she wouldn't say boo to a goose. But what many of you won't know is that June was one of the fiercest defenders of this place, right from the very start. I gave her hell for a long time, but if it wasn't for her we'd be standing in a bloody Cuppa Coffee right now. So, June, I know you've got a new home and life, but you will always be a true Friend of Chalcot Library. Thank you.'

June smiled, too overwhelmed to speak.

'There's one last person I need to thank, and that's our donor, who's committed to help fund the running costs of the library going forwards. He saved our arses when it became clear that our fundraising efforts weren't going to be enough.'

June glanced sideways and saw the handsome man smiling, and suddenly she felt her heart stop. The bright blue eyes. The slightly gappy teeth.

Mrs B cleared her throat. 'Ladies and gentlemen, please join me in saying a huge thank you to our biggest supporter, the son of our much-missed Stanley . . . Mark Phelps.'

Everyone burst into applause, but June was too stunned to move. Stanley's son was here, in Chalcot, helping the library. How was that possible?

The applause died down as Mark stepped to the front. 'Thanks for your kind words, Mrs Bransworth. I'd just like to say something quickly, if that's OK?'

The room hushed and waited for him to speak again. Mark took a moment to compose himself.

'As some of you may know, my father and I had been estranged for many years, which is something I'll always regret.' Mark's voice was quiet, and June strained to hear him. 'When I learnt about Stanley's death last year, the person who wrote to me also included the login details for his email account. I thought this was a bit odd, but when I logged into it, I discovered two hundred and eighteen messages, all addressed to me. None of them had ever been sent.'

'My god, all those hours Stanley spent at the computers . . .' someone said, but Marjorie shushed them.

'His emails were extraordinary: funny, honest, heart-breaking. In many of them he talked about his love of Chalcot Library and the battle to save it from closure. He wrote with such passion about this place and why it was important to him, and it brought back lots of fond memories. You see, even when things were really bad with my dad, he still used to take me to our local library. He loved to read me stories, Winnie the Pooh and Roald Dahl, and he'd do all the voices. I think they were our happiest times together.'

Mark hesitated, and June watched him fighting with his emotions.

'One thing that struck me about his emails was the way he wrote with such affection about one particular person, someone who'd always shown him kindness and compassion, and who'd been a true friend to him long before the library was threatened.'

Mark glanced down at his hands for a moment, anguish written across his face. When he looked up again, his eyes found June.

'June, I'll never forgive myself for not making contact with my dad when he was alive, especially now I know the conditions he was living in. But it gives me huge comfort to know that in the last years of his life, you cared for him and showed him unconditional friendship. He loved you like a daughter.'

June felt tears spring to her eyes, but she didn't try to wipe them away.

'Everything Stanley wrote about you reminded me that libraries aren't made by books, they're made by librarians. And so, while my father may not be here to see it, I want his legacy to be that there'll always be a paid librarian here in Chalcot, someone to help people in the way June helped him.'

He stopped talking and the room erupted into thunderous applause. June joined in with them, smiling at Mark as she did, and so it took a moment for her to realise that the cheers and clapping were for her.

The rest of the afternoon passed in a blur. June talked to Mark and there was wine and laughter as she caught up with the old patrons. She'd spent so long trying not to think about Chalcot Library and Stanley, so it was wonderful to share happy stories and memories without feeling that familiar stab of pain.

'Vera and I are running cafe here,' Leila said, handing June a slice of baklava.

'All the money we raise goes towards the library costs,' Vera said. 'I've never been so busy.' She turned to serve a customer, a smile on her face.

'I'm starting university in September,' Chantal told her. 'Marjorie helped me with my UCAS form. I'm doing a degree in social work.'

'Oh, Chantal, I'm so pleased,' June said, giving her a hug.

'Come on, there's a photographer from the *Gazette* who wants a group shot,' Mrs B said, grabbing June on her way to the door.

Outside, the Friends of Chalcot Library gathered in front of the library, with a crowd of onlookers watching.

'Is that everyone?' The photographer had a camera up to his face.

'I still think we should have invited Rocky,' Vera said.

'OK, everybody say cheese!' the photographer said.

'Down with the Tory government!' Mrs B shouted.

'For goodness' sake, Mrs Bransworth, will you ever give it a rest?' Marjorie said.

'Never. Mary and I are off to a protest up North tomorrow, another council trying to close their libraries.'

'Mary?' June said.

'Mrs B is spending a lot of time with that woman from the Dornley WI,' Vera whispered to June. 'I think she might be one of those les—'

But June didn't hear the rest of what Vera said, because at that moment she spotted a figure standing at the back of the crowd. June hadn't seen Alex since the day of Stanley's funeral, nine months ago, and the sight of him made her stomach somersault. He caught her eye and smiled, and she walked over to join him.

'Hey, stranger,' he said when she reached him. 'How are you? I like your hair.'

'So, I've got a bone to pick with you,' June said.

Alex looked at her in alarm. 'What have I done?'

'I finally read *Pride and Prejudice and Zombies* a while ago, and I have some major reservations about the plot.'

Alex's face broke into a grin. 'What are you talking about? It's an amazing book, much better than Jane Austen's boring original.'

They both laughed, and June felt her heart lift.

'Doesn't this place look great?' Alex said. 'And Ellie just told me Stanley's son is here. This must be so strange for you.'

'This whole thing has been completely surreal.'

'I hear you're not working here anymore?'

'No, I've left Chalcot. I work at a library in Kent now.'

'Wow, that's fantastic,' Alex said, and then he frowned. 'Why didn't you reply to any of my texts?'

'Sorry. I meant to but . . .' June trailed off, unsure what to say. *I was embarrassed because I'd assumed Ellie was your girlfriend and I'd made a complete fool of myself? I thought you wouldn't want to have anything to do with me now you'd gone back to your old life?* She took a deep breath. 'There's something I need to tell you.'

'What?'

'During the occupation, Stanley told me that I should learn to seize opportunities, otherwise I'd end up sad and alone with a life full of regrets.'

Alex raised his eyebrows. 'Woah, that was pretty brutal.'

'I think he knew there was something I wanted, even though I didn't realise I wanted it myself.'

'But still, don't you think telling someone they'll end up sad and alone is a bit full on? I mean, talk about projecting—'

June sighed; this was not how she'd imagined it would go. 'Alex, you're missing the point,' she interrupted. 'He was talking about you.'

She watched his expression go from indignation to surprise. His cheeks flushed and for once he didn't seem to know what to say.

'I tried "seizing the opportunity" once before, after the wedding,' June said, to fill the silence. 'But that was . . . well, you know what happened then. It was a disaster.'

Alex looked mortified. 'I'm sorry, I just wasn't expecting you to kiss me. And you were so drunk, I didn't want to take advantage of you.'

'You don't have to apologise, I was a mess. And I felt so guilty because I thought you had a girlfriend.'

'I tried to tell you that Ellie's just my flatmate.'

'I know that now. I'm sorry.'

'No, I'm the one who's sorry,' Alex said. 'I really wish I could've told you back then what Ellie was doing to help Stanley secure his land, but he'd made us promise we wouldn't tell a soul. I felt terrible keeping it a secret from you.'

'It's fine, I understand. And it's amazing what she did for him.'

'Can I ask you something?' Alex paused, and June could see him weighing something up in his mind. 'After Stanley's funeral, you told me you regretted kissing me and that it was a mistake. Did you mean that?'

Now it was June's turn to cringe. 'I thought you weren't interested in me. I just couldn't face more rejection.'

'Oh. I really thought you meant it.'

'No, quite the opposite. I . . .' June faltered. It was all very well seizing opportunities, but what if she'd still got it wrong? She could completely humiliate herself right here in front of Alex and . . . June stopped herself and looked him in the eye. 'I've been attracted to you ever since you came back to Chalcot, Alex, but for so many reasons I was too scared to say anything. So, I was wondering, would you like to go out with me sometime?'

Alex didn't immediately reply, and June felt heat spread through her body. She wanted to close her eyes and sink into the floor, but she forced herself to keep looking at him. She couldn't read his expression and, when his shoulders moved, she thought for a horrible second he was about to turn and walk away. But then he stepped towards her, and June felt his hands reach for her and then his face was close, and his lips were on hers. Now June did close her eyes as she sank forwards into him. For a moment they were locked together, and June wasn't aware of anything except Alex, his lips, and the sensation of his heart pounding against hers.

'For fuck's sake, would you two get a room?'

June was dragged back down to earth by the sound of Mrs B's voice. She and Alex pulled apart to see everyone grinning at them.

'About time,' Chantal said. 'We've all had bets on when you two would finally get together.'

June felt her cheeks flushing and she glanced across at Alex, who was looking dazed.

'Why is everyone just standing around out here?' Marjorie was marching over towards them. 'We have a busy library to run, for goodness' sake.' She turned to June. 'You see what I mean? Useless, the lot of them.'

'Are you sure we can't tempt you back to Chalcot?' Mrs B asked.

June looked around her. There were hanging baskets up outside the library, their flowers a shock of yellow against the red-brick walls. Next door was the village shop, where she'd bought hundreds of microwave meals over the years. And across the road was the bench where she and her mum used to sit when she was a child, eating their jam doughnuts on a Saturday morning.

'I love Chalcot, but I'm not coming back. I've started a new life now and I'm happy.' June glanced over at Alex, who smiled at her.

'I can't believe you've deserted us for a big fancy library,' Marjorie said, shaking her head.

'Actually, I have some news,' June said.

'Really? What?'

Everyone looked at June and she pulled herself up a little taller. 'I always dreamt of going to university and one day becoming a writer, but when Mum died I let that dream die too. But I've realised it's time to stop living in fear and take some risks. So, I've enrolled in a part-time degree course for mature students, and I've started writing again.'

'Oh, June, that's wonderful,' Alex said. 'Stanley would have been so proud of you, and your mum.'

'Well, make sure you send us a copy of your book when it's written,' Mrs B said. 'I just hope it's better than the rest of the crap we have here. What a load of rubbish – I've a good mind to hand my library card back in protest.'

June looked at Alex and rolled her eyes, laughing.

'Are you busy tonight or do you fancy dinner together?' he said, as they turned and walked down The Parade, away from Chalcot Library.

'Good idea,' June said, taking his hand. 'I've heard about a great place that does an excellent hot and numbing beef.'

'Sounds perfect. Now, June Jones, I need to pick your brain on a book recommendation . . .'

Acknowledgements

When I was a child, I used to go to my local library every week and take out six books. It was there that I first discovered *Matilda*, where I worked my way through the St. Clare's, Nancy Drew and Point Horror series, and where I borrowed my first Jilly Cooper novel. So I have to start by thanking every librarian who ever recommended a book to me, or took the time to ask me what I thought of something I'd just read. Without you, *The Last Library* would not exist.

While writing this book, I spoke to a number of librarians, library campaigners and volunteers who generously shared their stories and experiences with me. Particular thanks to Sylvia Davis, Krystal Vittles, Dawn Finch, David Wolstenholme, Jim Brooks, Mary Palmer and Rashid Iqbal. And thanks to Lotte Pitcher, crossword extraordinaire, and Abigail Palmer-Page, for the invaluable advice on technical issues.

To my incredible agent, Hayley Steed, thank you from the bottom of my heart for first believing in me and June, and for all your support, enthusiasm and endless patience. I am so lucky to have you in my corner. Thanks as well to everyone at the Madeleine Milburn Agency, in particular Liane-Louise Smith, Georgina Simmonds and Sophie Pélissier, the rights dream team.

To my wonderful UK editor, Sarah Bauer, who re-created Chalcot Library in her meeting room the first time we met, and who has blown me away with her passion, vision and baking skills ever since. And thank you to the brilliant team at Bonnier Books who have worked so hard to get

The Last Library out into the world, especially Katie Lumsden, Jess Tackie, Clare Kelly, Jenna Petts, Felice McKeown, Katie Meegan, Alex May, Laura Makela and the whole sales team. Huge thanks as well to Jenny Richards and Anna Morrison for the stunning cover.

In America, a heartfelt thank you to the team at Berkley for falling in love with June and a bunch of eccentric English library patrons. To my fabulous editor, Kerry Donovan, who has been such a wonderful champion of the book, and to Bridget O'Toole, Elisha Katz, Diana Franco, Tara O'Connor, Christine Legon, Dan Walsh and Mary Baker for taking such good care of *The Last Chance Library* across the Atlantic.

To the very first Friends of Chalcot Library, my classmates at the Faber Academy. Thank you for all the encouragement on the dark days and the prosecco-fuelled celebrations on the good ones. Special thanks to Hannah Tovey, Tamzin Cuming, Sophie Binns, Bryan Glick, Ben Ross and Lissa Price for reading various early drafts and giving me such honest feedback. And to Richard Skinner, our teacher, whose 'just keep going' mantra still rings in my ears every time I struggle with a scene.

Finally, a huge, slightly tearful thank you to my parents and brother, for filling my childhood with magic and encouraging me to tell stories at the bottom of the garden. To Bethany, for lifting me up when I need it and ensuring I never take myself too seriously. To Olive and Sid, for always making me laugh and for being (mostly) patient while I struggled to write a book and home school you this past crazy year – I love you both more than you'll ever know. And to Andy, for believing in me when this felt like a pipe dream, for giving me the space and time to give it my best shot, and for never complaining about the piles of books that have overtaken our home. This one's for you.

Dear Reader,

I've always loved libraries. As a young child, I would go to my local library every week to borrow books, and as a student I spent many late nights squirreled away in the university library trying to hit an essay deadline. But it wasn't until my early thirties, and the birth of my first child, that I began to appreciate just how important libraries really are.

Despite living in a bustling city, I found the early months of motherhood quite isolating. I didn't know many other people in the area with babies, and I was too nervous to go to cafés in case my colicky baby started to cry, disturbing paying customers. When I finally plucked up the courage to leave the house with my daughter on our own, the first place I went to was my local library. There was a children's nursery rhyme session on, and I sat surrounded by parents and carers from all walks of life, small children running around the place, and I felt welcome and unjudged.

The more time I spent in the library, the more I began to recognise the same faces that visited regularly. One particular older gentleman came in to read the newspaper. He would often try and start conversations with other people, but most avoided eye contact and ignored him. One day, I watched as a library worker stopped by his table for a chat. I didn't hear what they talked about and the conversation couldn't have lasted more than two minutes. But when she walked away, I saw the man smile, and I realised that that brief moment of kindness from the librarian was possibly the only conversation he would have all day. That was when the idea for *The Last Library* was born: a story about the unlikely friendships that can be made and found, and what a community can achieve when it comes together to fight to save their library from closure.

The characters in my novel visit Chalcot Library for many different reasons. For eccentric Mrs Bransworth it's to escape into books and stories (even though she complains about all of them). For elderly Stanley Phelps it's to use the computers to access email, and for teenager Chantal it's a quiet space to do her homework. But for all of them, the library is also a place where they can feel safe and find human connection. So, I hope that when people read *The Last Library*, they will be reminded of just how important our libraries are: a refuge for some, a lifeline to the world for others, and a place of books and companionship for all of us.

Thank you again for reading *The Last Library*.

Best wishes and happy reading,
Freya

A Final Note

If you'd like to learn more about *The Last Library* and what I'm working on next, then please do sign up to my newsletter at https://freya-sampson.com. I send out the newsletter monthly and in it I share all my latest news and book recommendations, plus there are giveaways and excerpts. The newsletter is also the place I share lots of exclusive updates, so if you want to be the first to know about my future books, or to see my covers before anyone else, you know what to do. Of course, it goes without saying that all your information is entirely confidential.

You can also find me on social media, where I'm @FreyaSampsonAuthor on Instagram and Facebook and @SampsonF on Twitter. I love hearing from readers, so please do reach out to say hello.

Lastly, a gentle request that if you enjoyed *The Last Library*, please consider leaving the book a review on sites like Amazon and Goodreads. Reviews are a huge help to authors, especially debuts like me. Thank you so much!

Reading Group Questions

1. The Chalcot Library sits at the heart of the local community. How is community as a theme looked at in this novel?

2. How does this novel look at grief?

3. Why do you think June clings on to so many things from the past? What role does memory play in this novel?

4. The library in this book is in a small village. How do you think the story would be different if it were set in a local library in a large town or city instead?

5. Although June is twenty-six years old, *The Last Library* explores a lot of big changes in her life. To what extent do you think it is a coming-of-age story?

6. Who was your favourite character apart from June?

7. June, Stanley, Vera and several other characters in the book live fairly solitary lives. How does *The Last Library* look at loneliness, and how does the library help those who feel alone?

8. What other books featuring reading and books have you read?

9. The book's opening line is: 'You can tell a lot about a person from the library books they borrow'. What are your favourite books, and what do you think they say about you?

10. Do you use your local library? Would you like to use it more?

11. June must break the rules to save the library. Have you ever had to bend the rules to work towards a bigger purpose? How did that make you feel?

12. In times of stress, June finds comfort in re-reading favourite books from her childhood, like *Matilda*. What were the books that shaped you as a child?

13. Do you think reading as a child affects your relationships with books in later life?